BY LORENZO CARCATERRA

PAYBACK

PAYBACK

A NOVEL

LORENZO CARCATERRA

BALLANTINE BOOKS

NEW YORK

Copyright © 2020 by Lorenzo Carcaterra

Published in the United States by Ballantine Books,
an imprint of Random House, a division of
Penguin Random House LLC, New York.

BALLANTINE and the HOUSE colophon are registered
trademarks of Penguin Random House LLC.

Hardback ISBN 978-0-399-17759-0
Ebook ISBN 978-0-399-17760-6

Printed in Canada on acid-free paper

246897531

First Edition

Book design by Barbara M. Bachman

GUS CARCATERRA

August 13, 2007—September 28, 2018

———

My best friend. The sweetest, kindest, and most loving dog. Everyone who met you fell in love. I miss you more and more each and every day. You have my heart—always. See you on the other side, my Gussie. I'll bring the treats.

PAYBACK

"Man is not what he thinks he is,
he is what he hides."

—ANDRÉ MALRAUX

1.

POLICE INTERROGATION ROOM

NOVEMBER 2000

"JUST TELL THE TRUTH. THAT'S ALL YOU NEED TO DO. ONCE that's done, then I'll take care of the rest." Detective First Grade Eddie Kenwood walked around the small, windowless room, hands deep inside the pockets of a pair of brown J. Crew slacks, his eyes on the frightened young man slumped against the table, its wooden edges frayed and worn.

"You're only wasting time, Randy," Kenwood said. "Mine and yours. Just tell me what I need to hear and we can both be on our way."

Randy Jenkins rubbed his eyes and gazed up at Detective Kenwood. "I wasn't there. I swear on my mama's grave. I wasn't there."

"Save that my-mama's-grave line of shit for somebody else," Kenwood said. "Gangbanger like you should know better than to play that game with me. I don't buy in to bullshit. Especially not from the likes of you. And especially when I got prints, *your* prints, on a knife I got tucked safe and sound in the evidence room. Now, are you going to fuckin' level with me or not?"

Eddie Kenwood was a highly decorated homicide detective with a long string of arrests attached to his impressive record. He closed his cases at a rapid pace and always delivered a signed-and-sealed confession. Most of the prosecutors working in the homicide division clamored to have one of Kenwood's folders land on their desks, knowing it meant a slam-dunk conviction and a twenty-year sentence, along with a nod of approval from their boss.

Kenwood ridiculed detectives with lower conviction rates, cashing in on the traditional round of free drinks from the other members of the squad whenever he closed another file. He looked and dressed the part of the successful homicide detective—wearing neatly tailored suits or slick-catalog casual slacks and blazers. He was thirty-eight years old and had been on the force for sixteen years. He was tall and slender, ran five miles a day, usually on the streets of his Baldwin, Long Island, neighborhood. He kept his hair trimmed short and had his nails done once a week at a local salon two blocks from his precinct.

He was twice divorced, and both ex-wives had moved out of state once the marriage was over. He had no children and lived alone in a well-furnished two-story attached house on a quiet cul-de-sac. He didn't associate with his neighbors and was a rabid hockey fan, never missing a New York Rangers game, either watching them play from the blue seats at the Garden or, when they were on the road, in his favorite bar. He planned to retire in four years, cash in his pension and full health benefits, and maybe move somewhere where he could count on sunshine every day. He was considered the very model of a professional working at the top of his game.

Randy Jenkins didn't stand a chance locked in a room with Eddie Kenwood.

Jenkins was twenty-six and had a jacket with three prior convictions—two for assault and one for robbery. He had been out less than two months after completing a three-year spin at an upstate prison. He'd put doing time to good use—earning his GED and taking art classes. His mother had died three days after his sixth birthday and he had met his father twice, the last time at his funeral. He was raised by a grandmother who worked two full-time jobs until chronic back pain forced her to spend most days sitting in a La-Z-Boy in a cramped Harlem apartment.

Randy was short and tilted toward chubby. He had a sweet tooth and loved nothing better than a large cup of strawberry ice cream topped with Reese's Pieces. His street friends would tease him about his weight.

"You hear about Randy?" one of them would ask.

"No, what?"

"He's got himself TB."

"Tuberculosis?"

"No, man. Three bellies."

The nickname "TB" stuck, even as Randy put in a solid effort to slim down.

He ran with a tough crowd and hustled for money any way and anywhere he could. He was a mugger, a petty thief, a small-time drug dealer, and a car booster.

What he was not was a murderer.

He knew the victim. But he would never bring harm to her. He stared at her photo, resting faceup in the center of the small table. A woman whose mutilated body had been found less than a block from where Randy lived. A woman who had been seen on more than one occasion in Randy's company.

"Say her name for me," Kenwood said.

"I told you five times already, I know her name," Randy said. "Rachel. Rachel Nieves. I knew her, no lie. But I didn't kill her. And that's no lie, either."

"But you did kill her, Randy," Kenwood said. He was hovering over the younger man, the sleeves of his crisp white shirt folded neatly up his forearms, his face flushed slightly red. "I know it and you know it. You took her into a shooting gallery, that's a fact. There's no denying that. I got two sets of eyeballs that will back me up. The two of you scored some smack, got a nice buzz going, and that's when you made your move."

"I didn't hurt her," Randy said, his voice breaking, sweat streaking the back of his brown T-shirt. "I would never hurt Rachel. She was my friend."

"You carry a blade, don't you, Randy?" Kenwood asked. "Don't say no to me. Understand? Never say no to me. I got the knife, remember? And it's got your prints on it. And your friend Rachel, she got sliced and diced by somebody who knows how to use a blade. To my eyes, that can only be you. Tell me I'm right about that, Randy. You want to get out of this room, don't you? That's easy. All you need to do is tell me the truth. Tell me it was you that killed Rachel Nieves."

Randy shook his head, tears now mingled with sweat, streaming down the sides of his face. The heat in the room was unbearable, and it was hard for Randy to take a deep breath. Kenwood circled the room, and on every second turn he would slap his right hand on the wooden table, kicking up a dust cloud. He would occasionally bend down and glare at Randy, hover over him, their eyes locked. One set determined to get a confession. The other set overcome with fear.

"Time stops in this room, Randy," Kenwood said, taking a break from his pacing, resting his back against a gray wall. "There are no days, no hours, no minutes, no seconds. There's just you and there's me. And there's a murder that needs to be solved. A murder we both know is on you. That's the only way out of this room, Randy. You need to tell me what I already know. What we both know. You need to tell me you killed Rachel Nieves. Then it will be over."

Randy lifted his head and looked across the room at Kenwood. "I didn't hurt her," he said. His voice was barely above a whisper, and both his cheeks twitched in rapid spurts.

"You got it wrong, kid," Kenwood said. He stepped away from the wall and moved menacingly toward Randy. "What you meant to say is you didn't *mean* to hurt her. But you *did* hurt her. Maybe it was the drugs. Maybe it was because she told you she wasn't interested in you anymore. Maybe it was both. You snapped. And you hurt her, Randy. You more than hurt her. You killed her. Look at that picture on the table. Take a good long look at it. That's your work. That's what you did to a young woman you call your friend."

Randy turned away from Kenwood and stared down at the photo of a battered and beaten Rachel Nieves. "She *was* my friend," was all he managed to say.

"That's right," Kenwood said, nodding in agreement. "She *was*. And now she's dead. And she's dead because of you. Because of her friend."

"Can I get some water?" Randy asked. His words more a plea than a demand.

"As much as you want and as cold as you can take it," Kenwood said. "Soon as we wrap up here. Soon as you tell me what it is I need to hear. I'll even throw in a Big Mac and fries. It's all there waiting for you. Believe me, Randy, I want out of this room much as you do. But neither one of us is going anywhere until you open up and start telling me the truth about what you did to Rachel."

Kenwood left the room for a few minutes, as Randy Jenkins sat alone, frightened, shaking his head in disbelief, his mind now reduced to a jumble of rambling thoughts. He knew he wasn't a murderer. He had his head down, drops of sweat running from his head to his face and onto the scarred table. He closed his eyes and tried in vain to fig-ure a way out of the situation he found himself in.

Kenwood came back in and slowly closed the door behind him. He was holding a plastic cup of water and walked over to Jenkins and placed it in the center of the table. He stood and waited as Randy put out a trembling hand and reached for the cup of water. Then, with one swift and violent motion, Kenwood slammed a closed fist on the table, shaking it so hard one of the legs nearly collapsed. The cup of water went sprawling to the floor and Randy Jenkins sat cowering in fear. Kenwood grabbed Randy's face and held it firm in his right hand. "Listen to me," he said in a voice filled with hatred and determination. "There is only one fucking way you're getting out of this room. And that's once you confess to killing Rachel Nieves."

"But I didn't—"

"Confess," Kenwood snarled. "Or die right here, right now, right in this fucking room."

Randy Jenkins lifted his head and stared at Detective Eddie Ken-wood. Their eyes locked, and the look in Kenwood's—red, raw, determined—told Randy what a horrible fate awaited him. It was at that moment Randy Jenkins knew he would never be allowed to leave that room until he admitted to a brutal murder he did not commit.

It could take many more hours, go deep into the night and through the early morning. He would be berated, insulted, beaten, intimidated to the point where he himself would start to believe the confession he would scrawl his name across.

Randy Jenkins knew his time in this suffocating room would be replaced by decades in an even smaller room, with iron bars and a bed cemented into a stone wall. His days would be filled with menial chores and he would never again know a night of restful sleep. He would go in a troubled young man and come out, if he came out at all, as a hardened and ruined old one.

His days as a free man were at an end.

Detective Eddie Kenwood would see to that.

And in that same moment, glancing down at a frightened young man out of options and at a loss for hope or rescue, Eddie Kenwood knew he would walk out of that room with one more signed confession to add to his list.

A confession that would lead to yet another 25-to-life conviction.

Yet one more gold star next to his gold shield.

2.

GREENWICH VILLAGE

AUGUST 2017

I HAD MY LEGS STRETCHED OUT, RESTING MY BACK AGAINST A chain-link fence as I watched my nephew, Chris, shoot baskets from different ends of the cement court. He had grown a bit in the few months he'd been living with me, both in height and in bulk. Chris had been working out in my friend Bruno's gym, around the corner from my brownstone, and the time seemed to have been put to good use.

His world had been turned upside down over the winter. His parents, my brother and his wife, were killed in a car accident on a snowy night in Westchester County, and I gave the fifteen-year-old a choice—come live with me or go through the system for the next three years. I like to think he made the smart move. Not that living with me is a cakewalk, not by any means. I like my routine, am set in my ways, and I don't like change of any kind.

I should mention I'm also an ex-cop, got shot off the job closing in on two years now, along with my best friend and partner, Frank "Pearl" Monroe. The guys on the job call what happened to me and Pearl "cop lotto." Our wounds come with a three-quarter tax-free pension for life along with great health insurance that comes minus a tab. But trust me, as nice as it sounds, it's not worth the damage done to get it. Especially not when it comes to Pearl, sentenced as he is to life in a wheelchair.

It took a while, but I put together a good life for myself, one that works for me. Sure, I miss the job, hunting down a top-tier dealer or a homicidal thug, breaking down a case, putting all the pieces together until they fit. An old cop once told me that putting on that uniform and heading out on a tour was like "being given a front-row ticket to the greatest and most exciting show on earth. There's nothing in the world like it. You piss and moan while you're in the middle of it and you miss it like you would a great lover when it's taken away." Truer words.

Chris walked toward me, basketball cradled under his right arm. He was a handsome kid, long brown hair, eyes alert and always taking everything in, an easy manner to him, at least most of the time. Teenage boys have mood swings that can make your head spin if you make any effort to keep track of them. Luckily, I don't.

He's a crime buff, my nephew. Watches all the shows—both the dramas and the ones on the Discovery Channel—reads the books, sees the movies, studies newspaper and magazine articles like they're the SATs. He even belongs to an online chat group that works toward solving old cases. He's Sherlock Holmes minus the silly hat, the pipe, and the drug habit.

He also doesn't believe his parents' death was an accident. He's convinced they were murdered, set up by the accounting firm where my brother worked. Chris is a whiz with a computer, can find sites and dig up information with speed and accuracy. He did such an impressive job on his theory, piling up facts and details missing from the police, medical, and insurance reports, that it convinced me, against my sounder judgment, to look into the firm and see if they were indeed dirty.

I still catch cases every now and then, usually handed my way by Chief of Detectives Ray Connors. The two of us go back to our early days in uniform, and he's a trusted and valued friend. He doles out a case that's deemed too cold or throws a call my way when the department is stretched too thin, and I work it with Pearl and a team I've assembled in the years since I've been off the job. You'll get to know them all soon enough.

This case, the one dealing with my brother, is the first time I've brought one to the chief's attention. He read through my nephew's reports and gave me the go-ahead to take a deeper look.

"Did you get a chance to read the new file?" Chris asked. His voice was in the middle of the bridge that would take him from boy to man.

I nodded. "Last night. Pretty thorough, as I expected. The accounting firm where your dad worked was no doubt cutting corners and skimming from clients. That part's clear."

"Which part isn't?"

"It's a big leap, Chris, to go from that to pinning them down for killing your father," I said. "Cheating and stealing is one thing. Murder? That's a whole other arena. I'm not saying they're not capable of it. Truth is, everybody is."

"Then what are you saying?" Chris asked.

"I need to see more," I said. "We all do. A stronger piece of evidence would be nice. What you put together in the files you've worked on is enough to rouse my suspicion. The chief's, as well. Makes it worth our while to take a look at the firm. But we're still missing enough evidence to corner them."

"They doctored the brakes on the car," Chris said. "That was in the first file I gave you."

"*Somebody* doctored the brakes," I said. "I doubt any of the accounting partners got under the front end and played with the lining."

Chris shook his head. "Everyone who worked at my dad's firm parked in the same garage," he said. "It's a park-and-lock. Cars are left there all hours of the night. It doesn't take much time to split the lining and play with the electronics system."

"Look," I said, "I'm not saying I don't buy your theory. Truth is, I do. But we have to tie it together, see if one loose end connects to another. If the accounting firm did anything to lead to the death of your mom and dad, we will take them down. That I promise."

Chris nodded, lowered his head, and flipped the basketball from one hand to the other. There are times I forget that, as sharp as he is, he's still a kid. A kid who took a hard blow, losing both his parents and seeing the world he knew and loved left in the rearview mirror.

"I'm sorry about what happened to your mom and dad," I said. "And I'm sorry my brother is dead. And if these bastards are the ones who killed them, then I'm going to make them sorry, very sorry, for what they did."

"Where will you start?"

"I need to see them up close," I said. "Get inside, get a feel for how far they'll go to keep a good thing going. And you can only do that with a face-to-face."

"But they'll know by your last name that you're connected to my dad," Chris said. "They'll never agree to an appointment with his brother. Especially one who used to be a cop."

"I'm the executor of your dad's estate," I said. "I'll be going in to tie up loose ends. See if there's anything they have of your dad's. Vacation days that should be paid out, OT he might be owed. Like that. I won't be there long, just long enough to get a sense of who it is I'm dealing with."

"So you're not going in to ask them to take you on as a client?"

"Not at all," I said. "But that doesn't mean we leave that side of the table empty. We send somebody else for that. Somebody from our little crew that these guys will not only think has money to toss around but that he'll be doing it with cash. The kind of cash he doesn't want too many to know he has. They'll know enough about him to be too nervous to mess with his dough, but they will want his business."

"Why?"

"It opens another potentially lucrative door for them," I said. "If they make one guy with plenty of cash happy, think how giddy they can make his friends. We don't know for sure if these guys have blood on their hands. It looks that way, but we're not nailed-down certain of it. But we do know they're snakes. I'm just going to put a little mongoose in their path and see how deadly the snakes are."

3.

TRAMONTI'S

CARMINE TRAMONTI FLIPPED THROUGH A FEW PAGES OF THE morning edition of the *New York Post* and stopped when he came to the baseball box scores. "Want to see how my Dodgers did last night," he said to me without glancing up.

"The Dodgers?" I said. "You're a Yankee fan. Have been since I've known you."

"Don't get your drawers in a knot," Carmine said. "My interest is strictly a financial one. Got a running bet going with Louie Almonti from the diner that the Dodgers take the National League West. He went and picked the Giants. If I win, means an extra fifteen hundred in my pocket and out of his."

"What if neither one of you is right?" I asked. "What if the D'Backs take it?"

"Then I guess you could say we'll both be shit out of luck," Carmine said.

I smiled and pointed at his empty espresso cup. "You up for another?" I asked. "I need a favor."

Carmine removed his reading glasses and rested them on top of the paper. He folded his hands and looked up at me. "I'm good on the coffee," he said. "Doctor told me to ease up on the caffeine. But it looks to me like you could use a cup."

Carmine signaled to a waitress standing by the bar, lifted his empty cup, and pointed a finger at me. She nodded and headed toward the coffee machines behind the counter. "You remember Lenny Santori?" Carmine asked.

I nodded. "Top-shelf jewelry guy," I said. "He pulled off a few high-end scores before he got nabbed. Met him a few times, seemed like a nice guy as far as jewel thieves go."

"He did his time," Carmine said. "He's living out a well-earned retirement someplace in Maine. Got him and his wife a nice cabin on a lake."

"I bet it's a great cabin," I replied. "High-end jewelry pays well on the open market."

"Anyways, reason I brought up his name is because the young lady bringing you your coffee is his granddaughter, Denise," Carmine said. "She's at NYU. Pre-med."

I looked up as Denise rested a cappuccino in front of me and followed it with a quick smile. She stepped away and turned back toward the bar. "Half the staff in this place has had a relative or two do some prison time," I said. "And the other half is waiting for a family member to make parole."

"What can I say, Tank?" Carmine said. "I only hire the best."

That's my name, by the way. Tank. It's actually Tommy Rizzo, but for as long as I can remember, most everyone, starting with my dad, called me Tank. And the guy across from me is Carmine Tramonti. These days, he's the respected co-owner of a restaurant where the food is tough to beat, the wine list impressive but not wallet-crunching, and the jazz quartets that start to play after nine among the best you'll ever hear. The place is old school in every way you can imagine.

And so is Carmine.

In his younger years, Carmine ran gambling operations for the major crime families in the tri-state area. He branched out into other areas, but his primary earnings came from numbers and sports betting. On a good day, just in the numbers action alone, Carmine brought in close to six figures cut up evenly among the five families minus his 5 percent off the top.

I've known him since I was a kid and, no, to answer your question before you even get to ask it, I never once busted him. For most of my years on the job, I worked homicide and narcotics, two areas Carmine made it his business to steer as far away from as possible. I'm sure he got his knuckles dirty now and then but nothing that warranted my looking his way. Not as far as I was concerned.

When I was a kid, everyone—and I do mean everyone—I knew placed bets with Carmine: the numbers every day, a crumpled dollar bill slipped to one of his runners along with a three-digit number they were convinced would bring home a winner. They bet on horse racing, boxing, football, basketball, baseball, even soccer, whenever there was a game, race, or a match on the board.

My mother bet on a number every day, often one that appeared in one of her dreams. She would give me a dollar and the number as I was heading off to school and tell me to stop by Big Dan's candy store and place the bet. "My father came to me last night in a dream," she told me one morning. "He told me to play the number one hundred and thirteen."

"Your father?" I said, shaking my head. "He told you to bet on a number?"

"That's right," she said. "One hundred and thirteen. He then put an arm around me and held me close to his side."

"I don't get it," I said, heading toward the front door. "Grandpa's been dead for a long time, right?"

"Yes," she said. "What does that have to do with anything?"

"So, he hasn't seen you for the longest time, and when he does show up after all these years, all he does is to tell you to go bet on a number?" I said. "Doesn't make any sense."

"Never mind that," my mother said. "What we talked about doesn't concern you. What does is bringing Big Dan that dollar and that number before he closes the book."

My mother never won on any number she ever bet, regardless of how many different combinations my grandfather passed her way. Come to think of it, I don't know anyone in the neighborhood who did hit on a number. In case you're wondering where the winning numbers come from, they're the last three digits on the day's take from the racetrack. If you want to spot a numbers player, they're the ones who open the tabloids from the back page and go right to the racing stats. One glance and a shake of the head tells you all you need to know.

So if I ever made a move to take down Carmine's numbers operation, I would have had to bring in my mother and half the women in the neighborhood as accessories. Besides, Carmine kept our neighborhood safe round the clock, not only from criminals but from dirty cops as well. He was our angel, his wings a little stained maybe, but an angel nonetheless.

4.

TRAMONTI'S

MOMENTS LATER

I TOOK A LONG, SLOW PULL ON MY CAPPUCCINO, THEN HELD THE cup between my hands and looked over at Carmine. "I'd like you to set up a meeting with an accounting firm," I said. "Make them think you're eager to be a client. A client who prefers to deal only in cash."

Carmine wedged himself in closer to the edge of the table. "This firm got a name?"

"Curtis, Strassman, and Randolph," I said.

"The one your brother Jack worked for," Carmine said.

"The very same."

"What am I looking to get out of them?"

"Same thing I'm going to be looking for when I meet with them," I said. "Get a feel for them, how they come across, how under the table they're willing to go. See if they're more than just money-skimmers. If they're the kind that can and do go deeper than that."

"How much deeper?" Carmine asked.

"Murder," I said, holding Carmine's look.

"So then Chris is not the only one who thinks his mom and dad didn't die in a car accident," Carmine said. "He's got you on board as well."

"He's done the research, and most of the pieces seem to fit," I said.

"And those pieces point to my brother and his wife driving a car meant to kill them."

"Most," Carmine said, "but not all."

"I can come up with some motives the firm had for wanting Jack out of the way," I said. "But I can't prove a single one. I'm working off theory and numbers on a spreadsheet."

"But you know enough to pin these guys as dirty," Carmine said.

I nodded. "They skim their clients," I said. "There's no doubt on that. Chris has dug up enough on these guys that I could have their shop closed on that fact alone. And it's a fair bet they're in heavy on some shady business ventures."

"But that wouldn't be enough, would it?" Carmine asked.

"Not if they killed my brother and his wife," I said. "For that they need to go down a bigger hole than a stretch in a country-club prison."

"How big a hole?" Carmine asked.

He knew the answer to the question. He survived for decades in a dark world that gave no refuge to those who killed a trusted friend or a family member. There was no middle ground on that turf. Carmine just needed to hear me say it.

I pushed back my chair and stood, my eyes still on Carmine. "Six feet deep will do just fine," I said.

5.

THE LIBRARY AT THE NOMAD HOTEL

THE LIBRARY IS A TWO-LEVEL LOUNGE WITH AN ANTIQUE SPIRAL staircase leading the way to the second floor. The staircase was imported from France, while the 3,500 books that line the Library's shelves are neatly organized into seven sections, covering such topics as food, drink, New York, and music. The NoMad Bar supplies the food and drink, both delivered with an expense-account bill.

David Randolph, one of the main partners of the accounting firm of Curtis, Strassman, and Randolph, was sitting with his back to a shelf of books designated MIND AND SPIRIT. Randolph was tall and pencil-thin, dressed in a handmade Ciccarelli gray suit that hung comfortably on his slender body. He was in his mid-fifties and he didn't bother to hide it. His hair was thick but streaked with gray, and his angular face was a road map of nooks and creases. He stretched out his legs and perched his brown Allen Edmonds lace shoes against the side of the nearest wall. He gave off the air of an impatient man, one who was used to having his every whim catered to without question.

Across from him was Samuel Butler, a short and rumpled man in his mid-forties. He had on a Men's Wearhouse suit in desperate need of pressing and smelled of stale cigar smoke. His disheveled appearance seemed deliberate—one of those men who wanted to be seen and quickly dismissed. But Samuel Butler was not a man to be taken lightly, a fact the three partners at the firm were keenly aware of.

"So, Samuel," Randolph said, "since your urgent call pulled me out of a meeting, I assume this is a pressing matter."

"Let's get us a drink first," Butler said. "Then we'll get down to it."

Randolph caught the eye of a hovering waiter and displayed his usual impatience as the young man made his way to their table. "Two Jamesons on the rocks. And a bottle of sparkling water."

"Would you like anything to go with that?" the waiter asked.

"Not for me," Randolph said.

"Maybe later," Butler said. "Let me get a drink inside me first and then we'll see."

"You seem annoyed, Samuel," Randolph said, watching as the waiter left with their order. "It's unlike you."

"I got good reason to be annoyed," Butler said. "More than one, actually."

"Which are?"

"Were you or the other partners aware that Jack Rizzo had a family?" Butler asked.

Randolph nodded. "A son," he said. "A boy, in his teens, if memory serves. Though I don't see why he'd put you in such an agitated state."

"Look," Butler said, leaning hard against the shiny wood table, moving it slightly toward Randolph. "Your crew pays me to get rid of problems that come your way. And I'm goddamn good—no, make that better than good—at it. But I'm only as good as the information you give me. And on Rizzo, you guys fucked up big-time."

Randolph's hands balled into tight fists, and he glared silently across the table at Butler as the waiter rested the drinks in front of them. "If you gentlemen need anything else . . . ," the waiter said.

"We'll find you," Butler said, brushing the young man away.

Randolph moved his drink to the side. "My partners and I are not in the business of fucking up," he said slowly, his cheeks flushed red, the veins in his neck bulging at the edges of the thick, starched white collar. "One of the reasons for that is because we keep people like you on our payroll. People who clean up problems. So, if an error was made on the Rizzo matter, I can only assume it came from your end."

"I didn't know he had a brother," Butler said. "There was nothing in the file and nothing in the research I did. The guy popped up out of the clouds."

"Doesn't seem as if he mattered much to Jack," Randolph said, regaining some of his composure. "Why should he matter to us?"

"Because he's a cop," Butler said. "At least, he used to be. Got shot off the job a few years back. Lives off his three-quarter tax-free police pension plus what extra he earns working as a Tin Badge."

"He's a security guard?"

"Not this guy," Butler said. "On the job he was a hard-charger all the way. Top-shelf adrenaline junkie. Both him and his partner, a black guy named Monroe. They took down some big crews during their years together, working narcotics and homicide mostly. They bumped heads with the best and didn't stop until their man went down or was sent away. Seems like old habits die hard."

"So you're saying they're still active?" Randolph asked.

"The chief of detectives can dig into a discretionary fund and hire off-the-job cops to work a case," Butler said. "It's not sanctioned, and you won't find it written up in any NYPD manual, but it's done nonetheless. The chief can reach out and hand them a case and have them work it until it's solved. They get paid but get no credit for the arrest or the takedown."

"And this cop, Jack's brother, is a problem for us?"

"A potential problem, yes," Butler said. "The boy went to live with him after his parents died in the accident. Cops like this guy tend to ask a lot of questions and aren't happy until they get answers they like. Maybe the kid's been pumping him with information about your firm and how it works."

"There's not much for him to know," Randolph said, taking a long cool sip from his drink. "I doubt Jack told his son much about what was going on here. And if he didn't bother to list a sibling on any of his forms, I would wager he told his brother even less."

"In other words, you're not as concerned about this as I am?"

"I see no cause for concern, Samuel," Randolph said. He was once again relaxed and sat back in his chair, at ease. "Jack is dead, and all he knew or thought he knew is buried with him. And as for the boy, what could he possibly know?"

"And the cop?" Butler asked. "Or I should say the ex-cop?"

"Even if he looks our way, there's nothing for him to see," Randolph said. "It's not like he's going to come barging into my office and start asking questions."

"You're right on that, Randolph," Butler said. "He's not going to barge in. He's going to be invited in and given a cup of coffee by your secretary."

"What are you talking about?" Randolph asked, the edge now back in his voice.

"I asked your office to keep me in the loop in case he called to make an appointment," Butler said. "Which he did. About ten minutes ago. Your secretary texted me the details. He'll be in to see you day after tomorrow, at three forty-five."

Randolph downed the remainder of his drink and wiped at his lips with his left thumb. "What's his name?"

"Tommy Rizzo," Butler said. "But everyone calls him Tank. And if I were you, I wouldn't keep him waiting long."

"I can handle myself, Samuel," Randolph said.

"With those who travel in your circles, no doubt," Butler said. "But don't come off tough with this guy. He'll see right through the act. Keep it simple. Keep it polite."

"What's he looking to see?" Randolph asked.

"Who he's up against, would be my guess," Butler said. "And if he gets even a whiff of something not right, he will take you down."

Samuel Butler finished his drink, pushed his chair back, stood, and walked quietly out of the Library.

6.

THE WINTHROP, WESTCHESTER COUNTY

LATER THAT DAY

I SAT ON A BENCH, STARING OUT AT THE MANICURED GROUNDS of the rehab facility. I waited as Pearl read through the three files Chris had put together, making his case that his parents did not die in a car accident. That their car had been tampered with and they had been sent to their death. Pearl was more than my former partner and best friend. There was no one, and I truly mean no one, who could break down a case file like Pearl. His body might be confined to a wheelchair, but his mind was Steve Jobs sharp, and he could work up a solid plan to crack any case I brought to him.

"The boy's got himself some serious skills," Pearl said. "Back when I was his age, I was lucky if I could finish a damn crossword puzzle. He has put together a very convincing set of facts. Based on what's in these files, that sure as shit wasn't a car accident."

"We need to prove motive," I said, nodding. "It could be Jack caught wind they were double-dealing some clients and putting the skim money in play."

"With no one the wiser," Pearl said. "You do have to ask yourself the why of it. This firm your brother worked for, they were pulling down big numbers just by going at it legal. Well respected by all accounts, a boatload of clients trusting them with their money. Based on the numbers, the three partners had to be taking home high-six figures easy. So why go dirty?"

"Same reason why anyone goes south, Pearl," I said. "Making good money doesn't make you immune to debt, divorce, living beyond even the means found on the big table. Most folks, given the chance, will always spend more than they should, no matter how big the wad of cash they hold."

"We've never gone up against a white-shoe firm," Pearl said. "These folks got means. I'm not saying don't go after them. I'm just pointing out we've never ventured into these waters."

"If we're right—and based on what's in those files, it looks like we are—then white shoes or no, they're just another band of crooks and killers," I said. "They may wear fancy suits and eat in bend-your-wallet restaurants, but they're no different than any gangbanger we hunted down."

"You talk to the chief of detectives about this?" Pearl asked.

"He's aware and has read through the files," I said. "We work this on our own, but he'll be there if we need a helping hand."

"What about the team?"

"Chris is going to be on it," I said. "He's done all the grunt work, and even if I wanted him off the case, there's no way he'd listen. This is about his dad. There's no out for him on this one."

"And the rest of the crew?" Pearl asked.

"I'm not sure yet, Pearl," I said. "I can't offer them cover like I can on the cases Chief Connors hands us."

"So, it's just you, me, and the kid?"

"And Carmine," I said. "He's going to flash a full load of cash in front of them and see if they bite. On paper he's a perfect client. They'll want his money and his contacts."

Pearl cracked a smile. "They take a nickel of Carmine's money, there's going to be some missing persons missing body parts. No doubt about that."

"They won't make a move for his money," I said. "They'll want him to trust them. Bring them more clients with cash in hand. Down the road, it might be a different story."

"So, when's the ball start to roll on this?" Pearl asked.

"Soon as we get you settled," I said.

I stood and stepped behind Pearl's chair and began to wheel him toward the entrance to the physical-therapy wing. "Settled where?" Pearl asked.

"I'm checking you out of here, Pearl," I said. "You've spent more than enough time in rehab, even one as nice as this. Time you had a place you can call home. A place of your own."

"And where would that place be, exactly?" Pearl said.

"The brownstone," I said. "You're moving in with me and Chris. The bottom floor's all yours. Had a couple of guys from Mike Trucco's construction crew make it wheelchair-accessible. Both inside and out."

"And you went and did all this without asking me?" Pearl said. "Or any of the doctors here?"

"I checked with your docs," I said. "Physical therapist will come to the apartment three times a week, soon as the two of you set up a schedule."

Pearl pushed down on the brakes of the wheelchair, bringing it to a sudden halt. He turned and gazed up at me. "Don't go and do this because you feel sorry for me," he said. "I would hate that and, in the long run, so would you."

"I'm doing it because you're my partner and my best friend," I said. "I need you by my side working these cases. And Chris needs you, too. He seems to find it easier to talk to you than me. And, besides, after the way you handled yourself on that last case we worked, you proved that you're a lot more than a smart man in a wheelchair."

"Making me what?" Pearl asked.

"What you always were," I said. "A great cop."

Pearl lowered his head and nodded slowly. "Thank you," he said in a near whisper.

"Don't be so quick with the thanks," I said. "I'm going to need you more than you can imagine. This situation with my brother is going to open some dark doors for me. It's not just another case. Goes deeper than that. I don't know how I'll be when I come out the other end. But I do know I'll need someone to be there if my biggest fears come to pass."

"And be there I will," Pearl said. "Count on it."

"I always have," I said.

7.

THE STRAND BOOKSTORE

THE NEXT MORNING

I WAS ON MY THIRD COFFEE OF THE MORNING, QUIETLY SIPPING from a Starbucks cup, lost in a long, dusty row of books both new and old. There was a time in New York when you could find a dozen bookstores like the Strand strung along Fourth Avenue and Broadway, between Twelfth and Fourteenth Streets. Today, this is the last one standing, the others surrendering to time, gentrification, and online commerce.

If you can't find a book in the Strand, it means that book has yet to be written. The place smells of history, row after row of used and old, crammed so close together as to almost smother, with a rare-book room on the third floor. The staff, a mix of young and old, half hippie, half book nerd, seem transported from another time. They're knowledgeable and direct, much like the great and late store owner himself, Fred Bass.

It is one of my go-to places to drink coffee and think, and I often leave with a tote bag filled with more books than I need. I feel at home here, alone, in a store that is always crowded. It is a great feeling to be invisible in a place packed with books, staff, and customers, practically a city unto itself. And it seemed a good place to sort through my mental checklist.

My life had grown complicated these past few months, more so than at any other time since I've been off the job. Initially, I hated leaving the police department, but I had little choice in the matter.

It took a while for me to adjust to being a civilian, not to get my adrenaline up every time I heard an RMP race down a Manhattan street or spotted what I knew to be two undercovers closing in on their target. But once I got past those minor hurdles and my wounds healed as much as they were going to, I set about building my new life.

And I had made that new life a great one, at least to my way of thinking. I own a brownstone in Greenwich Village left to me mortgage-free by my parents. Until a few weeks ago, I was renting out the top floors and I lived on the first two levels. I work out two hours every day, haunt museums and jazz clubs, and eat most of my meals down the street from where I live—at Carmine's restaurant, Tramonti's.

In addition to the food, wine, and jazz, there's another reason I've made Tramonti's my second home. One other very important reason. Connie, the co-owner.

She's been the love of my life since I was old enough to take notice, but I didn't make a move until I was a few months shy of leaving the job. There were many reasons why I waited as long as I did, but the central factor was this: I cared for her too much to have her be on the other end of a late-night phone call telling her which hospital I was being rushed to or where she could come and ID my body. I never wanted to put anyone through that, let alone someone I cared for as deeply as Connie.

Plus, she was Carmine's daughter, and while I never tangled with her dad while I was on the job, it would have been difficult to sit across from one of the higher-ups in the department and explain that situation. But Connie and me, we fit together. We both love wine, Italian food, and sappy romantic comedies. I give her the space she needs, and she does the same for me. She's drop-to-the-knees gorgeous and doesn't take a back step to anyone. If she's on your side, she's there for life. Unlike most in my profession, I've never been married, which means I've never been divorced and I don't have children. Same holds true for Connie. And I don't play around. I'm an on-the-square one-woman guy. Call it old-fashioned, call it anything you want. It suits me fine.

On the surface, all seemed perfect. Then my brother and his wife died in an accident that more than likely shouldn't have happened. That brought their fifteen-year-old son, my nephew, Chris, into my life. I didn't know much, if anything, about the boy, but he seemed to know a lot about me. He moved in with me and, despite a few bumps in the road, slowly found his place in my tight little world.

While me and Chris butted heads now and then—which, given the circumstances, was to be expected—he had no trouble blending in with my team. And he was a major help in working our last case, bringing down a top-tier Washington Heights drug dealer.

Now he wants me to repay the favor and help him bring down the ones who killed his parents.

So, for the first time in many years, I'm scared. I'm standing here, in the history section of New York's most famous bookstore, and I am afraid of what lies before me. You see, me and my brother, Jack, did not speak for the longest time. We lived separate lives and went through our days as if the other never even existed. And between us we kept a secret, one that deserved to be buried and stay buried. A secret that, if it got out, could forever damage the life I had worked so hard to build for myself. My secret could damage beyond repair the relationships and friendships that were at the very core of my world—my team, Carmine, the delicate balance I had with Chris, the bond that existed between me and Pearl, the enduring love I had for Connie.

And taking on a case involving my brother's potential murder could bring it back out of the dark cave I had long ago sealed it in. I didn't know who I'd be up against, but I knew from what Chris had dug up that they had the means and the funds to unearth the dirt in my background.

I stood in the middle of a crowded bookstore and stared down at my shaking hands, one of them holding a now-empty Starbucks cup.

My shirt was stained with sweat, and my neck and arms were damp to the touch. I lowered my head and closed my eyes, eager to regain my equilibrium, to catch my breath and gather the strength to move away from a row of books and back out onto Twelfth Street.

I have faced up to fear many times in my life. You cannot be a cop and not have felt that grip in the center of your stomach, fighting back the urge to vomit, wondering if you'll ever again be able to take a deep breath, sweat pouring out of your body as if through an open spigot. That is the fear of confronting danger, possibly death. That is the fear a guy in my line of work gets used to over the course of time.

The fear I felt now I had not felt for many years. It was the fear of the unknown becoming known. The fear of betrayal.

The fear that all would know that the Tank Rizzo they admired and respected was someone who had once taken a life.

Not as a cop out working an assignment.

But as a young man with anger in his heart and a weapon in his hand.

The fear that I would be revealed as a killer.

I managed to make my way out of the Strand, using the side entrance leading up to Fourth Avenue, my heart still pounding, my vision blurry, my legs moving as if underwater.

And for the first time since that day so long ago, I had no answer to my dilemma, no solution to my problem.

I was alone and lost, walking down the streets of a crowded city that, for the moment, no longer seemed to be my own.

8.

TOMPKINS SQUARE PARK

LATER THAT DAY

I HELD CONNIE CLOSE TO MY SIDE AS WE WALKED DOWN A PATH closest to 10th Street. "Something wrong, Tank?" Connie asked as we passed a family enjoying an afternoon picnic. "You've been pretty quiet. Not just today, but the past few days."

It was hard to hide much from Connie. She could read a mood better than a seasoned detective. "It can wait," I said. "Let's enjoy the walk."

"You always take long walks in a park when you have something on your mind," Connie said.

"You grow up in a city big as this, a park becomes your backyard," I said. "It's where you play ball, meet friends, sneak in a date, or just sit and read a book."

"I didn't know you snuck dates," Connie said with a smile.

"I threw that in to see if you were paying attention," I said, returning the smile. "Truth is, my dad had a lot to do with my liking parks as much as I do. He loved them. Took my mom for walks any chance he got. And he always made time for me and Jack, too. This one was his favorite."

"Why this one?"

"He had little time for hobbies, working as hard as he did in the Meatpacking District," I said. "His workday began at three in the morning and ended twelve hours later. The money was working-man solid, and his one perk was a ten-pound bag of free beef each Friday.

"'We'll never hurt for food,' my dad used to say. 'Though we'd have a lot more if your mom wasn't so cozy with the nuns in the parish. Total up the roasts, prime ribs, and steaks she gives the sisters and they eat like they live on Park Avenue.'

"I would tell him, 'Mom says they pray for us,' but my dad would shake his head. 'Prayers won't fill your stomach,' he would say. 'But a roast sure as Sunday does.'"

"My mom had a soft spot for nuns, too," Connie said. "Seems like every week me and Dad took platters of baked ziti to their residence. Dad would walk behind me and use the same silly line and I would always laugh."

"What was the line?"

"'This is getting to be a habit with your mom,' he would say, laughing along with me. 'You get it, kid? Nuns? Habit?'"

I smiled. "They had good hearts, all of them. Now, my dad wasn't much on religion, but he loved history. Especially New York City history. He loved to take me and Jack to different parts of the city and fill us in on the hidden history of the places we'd visit. This park fascinated him."

"Why?"

"You know that old parks department building on Avenue B?"

"The one with the fountain in the walkway," Connie said. "It has images of children carved into the sides of the fountain."

"That's the one," I said. "There's an inscription written under the faces of the kids. 'They were earth's purest children, young and fair.'"

"What does it refer to?" Connie asked.

"This used to be Little Germany, this park, this area," I said, gazing out at the crowds milling about, the usual mixed bag of families, street performers, the homeless, and older couples taking a walk on another brutally hot day. "Over a hundred and fifty thousand German Americans lived in these tenements. This was around 1904. Within a year, they had all left. One pretty distinct neighborhood, gone in a flash."

"What happened?"

"From what my dad told us, the heart of the neighborhood was the church—St. Mark's Evangelical Lutheran on East Sixth. In June of that year, they held a picnic for the moms and kids of the area on Locust Grove in Long Island. They leased a ship to get there—the *General Slocum.* But it never made it."

Connie stopped and turned to me. "The fire," she said. "Dad has a good friend who lives in Yorkville. He lost family on that ship."

"A lot of people lost family," I said. "It was a screwup on every level—fire burning through the ship, panic setting in, lifeboats wired to the ship, third-rate life vests. The captain didn't know how to deal with the East River currents."

"How many died?"

"One thousand and twenty-one," I said. "All women and kids. Many crushed by the steamship wheel, the rest died in the fire or drowned. Hundreds of people lined up along the shore, watching it happen, helpless and hopeless."

"Your dad was right," Connie said.

"To have told us?" I said.

"There's that," Connie said. "But more about the hidden history of the city. It's all around us. There's probably a secret behind every building, in every park, every storefront."

I stopped and turned to face Connie. I stroked her tanned face. Her long brown hair had strips of blond along the fringes and covered one of her eyes. I reached for her and brought her closer to me, our cheeks touching, our hands clasped. "Behind every person, too," I whispered. "Just because something's hidden doesn't mean it's not there."

9.

THE BROWNSTONE

A JAZZ QUARTET WAS PLAYING A SOULFUL TUNE IN A CORNER of my small backyard. Two buffet tables were set up, each piled high with food from Tramonti's kitchen. It was a warm and clear night, and the downstairs apartment was filled with friends there to welcome Pearl to his new home. I sipped from a glass of Brunello and glanced across the yard at him. He was in an animated conversation with two members of my team, Bruno Madison and Carl Elliot, and I hadn't seen him this happy since before we both got shot off the job.

Bruno is in his early thirties and works as one of the bartenders at Tramonti's. He's a former heavyweight contender, in solid shape. He is as good with money as he is with his hands and has invested his ring winnings wisely. A few years back, he took over a deli struggling to meet the rising rent and turned it into a boxing club for the neighborhood kids.

Carl is a few years younger and hasn't seen the inside of a gym since high school. He is quick to smile, keeps his thick brown hair long, and has a tattoo of a butterfly on each arm. During the day, Carl plays guitar on street corners and parks, taking in as much as twelve dollars. His take-home grows larger once the sun goes down. Carl's a fence, meaning he moves everything from knockoff designer goods to high-end cars and jewels. When he works on his own, how he goes about his business is none of mine. When he works for me on a case, he wrangles the goods the crew requires in as clean a manner as possible.

I walked over to Pearl and raised my glass to him. "Welcome home," I said.

He nodded, his eyes welled up with tears. "Never thought I would see a day like this," he said. "Figured I would live the rest of my life in one rehab facility or another. Here, I feel like I belong. I feel like I can breathe again. For that alone, I'll never be able to thank you. Never."

"Don't thank me yet, partner," I said, giving him a smile and clinking my glass against his longneck beer. "At least not until you see your rent bill."

"Any word from the chief?" Carl asked. "Been a couple of months since he tossed us a case."

"Those Ferragamo shoes not moving as fast as you'd like them to, Carl?" I said. "Or are you just missing the action?"

"Little bit of both," Carl said. "Besides, fall is just around the corner and singing on street corners in the cold is no fun, let me tell you."

Alexandra Morrasa walked up behind Pearl and gave him a big hug and a huge smile. "There she is," Pearl said, resting his beer against the side of his wheelchair and reaching for Alexandra with both hands. "I swear you get more beautiful by the day. You have to tell me your secret."

"It's Romanian blood," Alexandra said. "We never get old and we never forget. Most especially our friends. And, even more so, our enemies."

"That's a good way to go through life," Pearl said. "And it sure as shit makes me glad you sit on our end of the table."

Alexandra is another member of my little crew of misfits. She has rich curly-brown hair and wears a ring on each finger and a wolf's head pendant around her neck. She has a psychic parlor in Chelsea and another on the Upper West Side. You more than likely have walked past them and never taken notice. Next time, maybe you should. Those parlors—and Alexandra's in particular—are the eyes and ears of the city. If something is said that needs to be heard, she's the first to know about it and pass it our way. Her customers come to her from all walks, some with seven-figure bank accounts, others with wanted posters of their faces pinned to the wall of the nearest post office. It doesn't matter who it is or what their worries are, Alexandra will tell each one what the future has in store for them. They leave with some peace of mind. She gets to pocket a twenty in return for her words of wisdom.

She also has a platoon of street fighters at her disposal, most of them from Romania, now living in the States, and all lethal in the use of a knife during a tussle. They're straight out of another century, similar to the River Pirates and the Hudson Dusters crews that roamed the New York waterfront in the late 1800s. They live on the outskirts of the city or in small apartments nestled close to the river's edge. They make their living off the street and are the most adept pickpockets any street cop could ever confront. They are a secret society living out in the open, impossible to infiltrate and even harder to catch. Their word is sacred, and they always hold up their end of an agreement.

"Never go up against any of those guys with a blade and expect to come out in one piece," Carmine once told me. "They will cut your tongue out before you can call for help and slice off your fingers before you can reach for a weapon or make a fist. They're like those ninjas you see in the movies, only faster and deadlier."

Chris came over and stood next to the group. "You're all set, Pearl," he said to him. "And I left the instructions, in case you need them, on your coffee table. But everything should work."

"What did you two cook up?" I asked.

"All of Pearl's appliances and equipment are now voice-activated," Chris said. "Television, stereo, Wi-Fi, phones. Fingers crossed on the microwave, but everything else is working. All Pearl has to do is talk and the system takes care of the rest."

"Thank you, little man," Pearl said. "You have more than earned those four Yankee tickets."

"I can do the same for your stuff if you want," Chris said to me.

"I'm afraid I'm not as high-tech as my friend Pearl here," I said, giving Chris a wink and a smile. "Besides, I talk in my sleep, and God only knows what I'll turn on in the middle of the night."

I went looking for Connie but stopped short when Pearl wheeled himself next to me. "You got a few minutes for some one-on-one talk?" he asked.

His mood had turned suddenly serious and his upper body seemed to be on edge. "You live here now, Pearl," I said. "Once the party wraps up, this place will turn as quiet as an empty church and we can talk until the sun comes up. But maybe we should keep our voices down. Wouldn't want to say anything that might turn on your toaster."

"I was going to hold off for a few days," Pearl said. "I know you got your brother's situation to look into and that's not going to be a light lift. But some info came my way today that I need to put on the front burner."

"What's this about, Pearl?" I asked. I looked around and made sure no one was close enough to overhear.

Pearl took a deep breath and inched his wheelchair closer to my side. "It's about getting a guy out of prison," he said. "And in order to do so, we have to be ready to go up against one of the dirtiest and most dangerous cops to ever put on a badge."

"Eddie Kenwood," I said, without a second of hesitation.

"Public Enemy number one himself," Pearl said.

10.

THE BROWNSTONE

I WAS IN PEARL'S APARTMENT, THE BLINDS TO THE BACKYARD drawn, the door locked. All the furniture in the place was new and I sat on a soft gray couch, a glass of wine resting on the glass coffee table in the center of the room. Pearl was across from me, gazing down at the yellow police folders scattered on top of the table and across the hardwood floor. "I'm guessing you have been reading about all the cases the DA has had to reopen in the past two, three years. All of them homicides, all of them brought to court with signed confessions."

"Last I counted, there were six," I said. "All young black men with multiple priors on their jackets. All second-tier offenses, none coming close to a murder. And each case was closed out by Detective Eddie Kenwood."

"They were all in their early- to mid-twenties by the time their case got to trial," Pearl said. "And they all got hit with the two-five-to-life sentence."

"DNA cleared them of the murders," I said, gazing down at the folders, "and then the city doled out anywhere from three to six million in tax-free cash to make up for the error of their ways."

"Now, from what I read and hear, the DA is going to look into *all* of Kenwood's closed homicides," Pearl said. "And if my count is on the money, that number totals out to fifty-six."

"And they'll fall on the chief's desk," I said. "He's short on staff as is. Toss that pile on top of the cases they're already working, plus the new ones sure to come in, and he's on a heavy overload."

"Sounds like he could use some helping hands," Pearl said. "Now, I know the way it usually works is he comes to us with a case. Am I right on that score?"

I nodded. "For the most part. Look, for all I know, he already pulled a case from the pile with us in mind. If anyone hates dirty cops more than you and me, it's the chief. He'll find his way to us. Then we'll get our chance to butt heads with Kenwood."

"But that's just it, Tank," Pearl said. "I don't want us to get just any case off the pile. I have a specific one in mind."

I took a sip of wine and stared at Pearl for a few seconds. I had not seen him like this in a long while. He was usually one to keep his emotions in check, but I could tell from his manner that this was more than another case to him. This one was personal.

"Tell me what I need to hear, Pearl," I said. "Tell me which case it is you want us to go after."

"The young man's name is Randy Jenkins," Pearl said. "That is, if you can still be called young after doing seventeen years in prison. He was convicted of first-degree murder. Vic was a woman name of Rachel Nieves."

"He confessed to the murder?"

"Written up by Detective Eddie Kenwood himself," Pearl said. "He was a perfect target for Kenwood. Randy had multiple priors and he knew the victim. They had shared a pipe or two together, maybe more than that. Not sure."

"So, there's a signed confession, drug use, and a possible sexual relationship between doer and the vic," I said. "That's what we're looking at?"

"That's right," Pearl said. "That's what's in the reports, and that's what the jury seen and heard. Didn't take them long to convict. They weren't in the room long enough to order lunch."

"He put up any kind of a defense?"

"There wasn't much family money for a decent lawyer," Pearl said. "There was the usual spiel we've all heard hundreds of times—the confession was coerced, and he would never hurt the victim; he had feelings for her. But it all fell on deaf ears. Kenwood, as you can well imagine, took the stand and did a full Bogart. He had the judge and jury eating out of his hands. Hell, by the time he was done, even Randy's lawyer was convinced the boy was guilty."

"Then why are you convinced he's not?" I asked. "Look, there's no love lost between me and Kenwood. And truth be told, his cases always seemed to have a stench about them. But before I go in and see the chief and ask for this particular case, I need to know we are truly looking to clear an innocent man."

"Randy's street name was TB," Pearl said. "He was a chunky guy with a taste for candy and ice cream. He wasn't a banger, not in a way you and me would define the word. Not even close. But in his neighborhood, in those days, there was only one way to go—you played along to get along. On those other priors in Randy's rap sheet, there isn't any doubt as to his guilt. He was all the things they said he was when it came to those crimes. But I can swear on any Bible you got handy that he wasn't a murderer."

"How do you connect to him?" I asked.

"Randy didn't have much in the way of family," Pearl said. "His grandmother worked two, sometimes three jobs to earn the paycheck of one. I knew his uncle, and when he was healthy, he would ref some of the high school basketball games. But he didn't last long enough to help keep Randy on the right side of the law."

"And his mother?"

"Dead."

"Any brothers or sisters we can reach out to?"

"They're scattered all over the country," Pearl said. "And if we found any of them, doubt they would care much. The only one who did was Mo Hastings."

"I remember him," I said. "Worked for the parks department. Used to be a gangbanger back in his day but got scared straight and stayed that way, far as I know."

"He did," Pearl said. "And he tried to help steer as many kids out there as he could away from a wasted life. He spent a lot of time with Randy. Gave him a place to sleep when he needed one, bought him a meal here and there. Had me talk to the boy a few times, using me as an example of the kind of life you can have if you can beat the street."

"What was your read on Randy?"

"Tried to come off as tough, like all street kids do," Pearl said. "But I didn't buy it. Deep down, he was scared of what he didn't know. He was looking for the easy out, because that's what they see each and every day. Fast money, flash cars, quick scores, and all the drugs you can pump into your body. He was polite enough, but I knew my words didn't make a dent."

"Mo didn't seem to have much luck in that department, either," I said.

"It wasn't from lack of trying," Pearl said. "He did as much as anyone could, and it broke Mo's heart when Randy was sent away on the murder rap. He kept telling me there was no way that boy killed that girl. No way."

"Did you look into it?"

"As best I could," Pearl said. "Jury says guilty and the judge slams that gavel down, there isn't much anyone can do. Even back then, signed confession and all, something about the case just didn't feel right. But who was I to go up against the great Eddie Kenwood?"

"You still keep in touch with Mo?" I asked.

"We would meet now and then," Pearl said. "Less and less as the years went on. He came to see me a few times in the hospital when I got hurt. But back then, as you well know, I wasn't much in the mood for visitors."

"With good reason," I said.

"Then, when news broke about the DA unwrapping all of Kenwood's cases, Mo gave me a call," Pearl said. "He asked if I would take a look at the Randy Jenkins case. He had heard that me and you take on a job now and then, and he asked me to make it right. I told him I would."

"Where's Mo hang his hat these days?"

"He lives in the Bronx," Pearl said. "Up near Tremont Avenue. But he won't be there long."

"Why not?"

"He's got cancer," Pearl said. "Terminal. He thinks at best he's got one month left, if that."

I nodded and stayed silent for a few moments. "You ever reach out to Randy over the years?" I asked.

"I went up to see him a few times," Pearl said. "But after I got shot up, I stopped. That guilt's on me. I write him letters every few weeks, but that don't help ease the burden."

I sat back and closed my eyes. "None of the weight is on you, Pearl," I said. "If Randy is guilty, then it's on him. If he's innocent and locked in a cell for no reason, then it's on Kenwood."

"There's only one way for us to find out," Pearl said.

"I should go upstate and visit with Randy. Get his side of the story. You good with that?"

"Was counting on it," Pearl said. "So, you'll ask the chief for the case?"

"I'll talk to him," I said. "Rest easy on that score. And there's someone else we should have a sit-down with, someone I never thought I would see again, let alone go up against."

"Kenwood," Pearl said.

I stood and looked down at the scattered folders. "That's right," I said. "Eddie Kenwood. Mr. Homicide himself."

11.

UPPER WEST SIDE

APRIL 2006

I TURNED THE CORNER AT SEVENTY-FIFTH AND AMSTERDAM Avenue, running fast, my gun in my left hand, held low against my leg. Pearl was on the other side of the street, also in full pursuit. We had been driving around in an unmarked when the call came over the radio, break-in at a clothing store near the Fairway Market on Broadway. Two black males, both armed, rifled the register and pistol-whipped the owner and were last seen heading downtown.

We'd been the closest in the sector and had responded to the call. I had rounded the street, Pearl riding in the passenger seat, our eyes on the crowded sidewalks. Pearl was the first to spot them. "Up there on the right," he said. "The two looking over their shoulder like they're expecting company."

"I'll move the car two blocks up," I said. "Then we go after them on foot. That work for you?"

"I'm wearing my felony fliers," Pearl said with a smile. "No way those two fools can outrun me with these babies on my feet."

"Okay, I'll play along, Pearl," I said as I maneuvered the car around a double-parked FedEx van. "How fast are you exactly?"

"I'm Superman-fast," Pearl said. "Just like my man Muhammad Ali. There was a time he was on a plane and the flight attendant asked him to put on his seatbelt. And Ali smiles and says to her, 'Superman don't need no seatbelt.'"

"And what did the flight attendant say?" I asked, angling the car toward the corner, tossing a police placard on the dashboard and a red light on the roof.

"She told him, 'Well, Superman didn't need no plane, either,'" Pearl said, swinging open his passenger-side door and jumping out.

I was quick to follow.

They made us as they were about to cross against the light on Broadway. They turned left, the glint of steel in their hands visible to passersby. They sprinted away from Broadway and back toward Amsterdam, me and Pearl in hot pursuit, our shields out, hanging on chains around our necks. We pulled our weapons out of our hip holsters and held them firm against our thighs.

Pearl and I split up; I took the north side of the street and he took the south, and we chased them past Amsterdam and onto Columbus Avenue. "The park!" I shouted to Pearl. "They're going to try and make the park."

It was an unseasonably hot and muggy spring day, and my thin sweatshirt was stained with sweat. I wanted to avoid a street shoot-out and figured the two thieves would be aware of that and use it to their advantage. They were on my side of the street, about fifteen feet ahead of me, and I was closing in. From the corner of my eye, I spotted Pearl crossing the street and moving in ahead of them. With a little luck, we would have them cornered from both sides.

The two spotted Pearl in front of them and could sense me behind them. They skidded to a halt, and the taller of the two reached out and grabbed an older woman holding two grocery bags. He wrapped an arm around her neck, the groceries spilling to the street and sidewalk, fruits and vegetables rolling in all directions. He lifted his gun and pressed it against the woman's waist. She was short, thin, and frightened. The second gunman stood behind his partner and aimed his gun at Pearl.

I stepped closer to the gunman and his hostage, my gun still resting against my thigh. "Take a beat," I said to him, "and think for a minute. Right now you're looking at an armed-robbery charge. Taking a hostage brings this to a whole other level. That's not something my partner and I can let happen."

"You stay where you are," the gunman said to me. "Or I take this bitch out right before your eyes. That something you want to see happen?"

I took a deep breath and looked past the two shooters and the hostage. Pearl was standing close enough to the second gunman to take him down, if needed. The pedestrians surrounding us had scattered, seeking shelter behind mailboxes, inside storefronts, and behind parked cars.

I turned to look back at the gunman. He was thin and wiry, with a runner's build, and was wearing tight jeans and a cutoff T-shirt. He was breathing heavy and sweating profusely, his skin glistening under the glare of a warm sun. The woman he was holding close to his body, a shaky .38 caliber jammed against her right rib cage, stared at me with trembling lips. "I'm going to make this easy for you," I said to him, loud enough for Pearl to hear me. "We're going to take baby steps, you and me. First, I'm going to holster my gun. That's just to show you I'm not looking to get in a gunfight. That work for you?"

The gunman stared at me for a few seconds and then nodded. "Be more than a baby step," he said. "Be a major step to us all getting the fuck out of here."

"Now, that's going to be my move," I said. "In return, you got to make yours. Still with me?"

"And what would you want that to be?"

"I'm not going to ask you to toss your gun away, nothing like that," I said.

"That's good," he said. "Because bullshit like that won't work on me."

"I just want to make it easier for us to talk," I said. "So keep the gun in your hand. Just move it away from the lady's side. Because from where I'm standing, she looks about ready to faint. And neither one of us wants to see that happen. What good is a hostage if she's crumpled up in your arms like a rag doll?"

"I'll think about it," the gunman said, giving a quick once-over to the trembling woman. "Meantime, put that gun back where you said you were going to put it."

I moved my weapon away from my leg and slowly jammed it into my hip holster. As I did, I moved a few steps closer to the gunman. "I did my part," I said to him. "Now it's your turn."

Police sirens were raining down on us from all corners, RMPs squealing to a stop, uniform cops taking their positions behind their vehicles. "I see you called in your friends," the gunman said.

"I didn't call anybody," I said. "Let's just keep this where it is: between you and me."

The gunman's hands began to twitch as he slowly moved the gun away from the woman's side. I held his gaze and waited as his partner turned away from Pearl to look back at his accomplice. Pearl had moved even closer to the second man, who was dressed in a sweatshirt, running shorts, and high-tops. Pearl had holstered his weapon as well. I inched closer to the gunman. Pearl and I were both near enough to the two to make our move.

The gunman with the hostage—his gun now resting by his side, the woman still clutched in front of him—turned his head and took a quick glance at the patrol cars surrounding the street.

Pearl and I rushed the two gunmen at the same time, catching both off guard, neither expecting such a sudden and dangerous move. Pearl caught his man at chest level, barreling into him like a linebacker taking down a quarterback. The man folded like a chair under Pearl's weight and force, his gun sliding out of his hand and skidding against a fire hydrant.

I shoved both the woman and the gunman to the ground, leaving my feet and doing all I could not to harm the frightened hostage. The gunman landed first, his head bouncing against the cracked pavement, his gun sliding off his fingertips. The woman rested on top of him, her weight and mine holding him in place. I jumped to my feet, kicked the man's weapon a safe distance away, pulled my gun, and aimed it at the stunned suspect. I kept my eyes on him and reached a hand out for the hostage. She took it and slowly lifted herself to her feet. "Go to one of the uniform police officers," I said. "They'll take care of you."

I waited as she made her way to a patrolman, walking on unsteady legs and falling into his embrace. I looked down at the gunman and nodded. "You know what to do," I said. "On your knees, hands behind your back."

"You conned me, I admit," the man said, as he rolled over and used his hands to help him to his knees. "Didn't see your move coming."

"It played out better this way, didn't it?" I asked. "Hostage is unharmed, and you get to walk away without a murder rap tacked to your record."

I pulled my cuffs, slapped them on the gunman, and lifted him to his feet. Pearl stepped up next to me, holding his prisoner by the arm; the man's hands were shackled behind his back. "Was wondering when you were going to make your move, partner," Pearl said. "I could have read a book all the time I was waiting out there, baking my ass off in the sun."

"Sorry for the delay," I said, smiling at him. "I was a bit distracted by the gun this clown had jammed against some poor woman's ribs."

"I hope you had a Plan B ready," Pearl said. "Just in case your Lawrence Taylor tackle didn't pan out as it did."

"I did," I said, starting to walk toward one of the RMPs, my prisoner in tow. "I was going to walk away and let you handle it."

"No big deal," Pearl said, following me with his man in cuffs. "I would have put a pin in this drippy loser and then taken your man out before either one of them could blink."

My prisoner glanced at Pearl and then turned to me. "I'm surprised they let wack jobs like the two of you out on the street," he said. "With guns and badges to boot."

I smiled at him. "I wonder about that myself some days," I said.

12.

UPPER WEST SIDE

MOMENTS LATER

THE FIRST TIME I SAW EDDIE KENWOOD WAS WHILE ME AND PEARL were walking our two prisoners to a parked RMP. He came up on my left side and tapped the top of my shoulder. "I'll take it from here," he said.

I turned to look at him. He wore a light-brown jacket, tan slacks, and scuffed black tassel loafers. He had his hands on his hips, a gold shield clipped to his waistband, and a curved smile on his face.

"Take what exactly?" I asked.

"The two losers you and your partner slapped the cuffs on," he said.

I ignored him and opened the rear door of the patrol car. I nudged my prisoner toward the backseat and was preparing to ease him into it when Kenwood stepped in front of us, his right hand on the door. "I guess you didn't hear me," he said. "These two belong to me now. So hand them over and we'll all go happily on our way."

"This is our collar and it's going to stay our collar," I said, inching closer to him. "And not you or anybody else is going to stop that from happening."

"I'm guessing you don't know who I am," Kenwood said, still flashing his curled-lip smile.

"You should also be guessing I don't give a shit," I said.

"Well, you should," Kenwood said. "Both you and the black guy should take notice of who you're talking to before you start running your mouth."

"Which black guy would that be?" Pearl asked. "The one with the badge or the two in cuffs?"

"I'm Eddie Kenwood," he said, keeping his eyes on me. "I'm a gold-shield detective, and neither of you is. So, hand over the two perps and get the fuck out of my way."

"Get back in your car, Gold Shield," I said. "Me and Pearl take these two in, book them, and fill out our paperwork. You want them after that, run it by the chief, and if he feels the need he'll hand them to you. That's how it's going to work. The *only* way it's going to work."

"And what if I decide that's not the way I want it?" Kenwood said. His voice was rising, and his pale skin was now tinged with red blotches. "What if I want to take them right now? What happens then?"

"Then one of us is going to bleed," I said, stepping closer to Kenwood.

"I've seen you around," Kenwood said. "You and the black guy. You're both up-and-comers, at least that's what I hear. Would hate to see anything get in the way of that."

"You call me the black guy one more time, and there will be plenty to get in the way of that," Pearl said. "Like a possible homicide, if you catch my drift."

"You're making a mistake," Kenwood said to me. "A major-league mistake at that."

"It's mine to make," I said. "Now, me and Pearl would like to get back to work, if it's all the same to you. And we can't do that unless you get the fuck out of my way."

Kenwood held his stare for a few moments and then backed away from the car door. "I'm not going to forget this," he said.

"It would be a mistake if you did," I said. I tucked my prisoner into the back seat and Pearl did the same with his from the other side of the car.

"We'll run into each other again," Kenwood said, starting to walk away from the car. "I have no doubt about that. And when that day comes, it's going to be bad luck for you and your partner. You can make book on that."

"Hey, Kenwood," I said, waiting as he turned around to face me. "I read about that last big bust you made, the kid from Inwood. It was in all the papers. I have to be honest, there was a lot in there that might spell trouble, but nothing in it that even came close to closing in on murder."

"Maybe that's why you're running through the streets chasing low-end bangers and I'm the lead guy in homicide," Kenwood said, the smile returning to his face. "Catch you later, losers."

I nodded. "Unless we catch you first," I said.

13.

161 MADISON AVENUE

AUGUST 2017

THE OFFICES OF THE ACCOUNTING FIRM OF CURTIS, STRASSMAN, and Randolph were on the seventh floor of a building tucked in the mid-30s. They were plush, large, and well furnished, with expensive artwork hanging on the walls as you exited the elevator. An attractive receptionist greeted me as I stopped by her desk, which was covered with thick manila envelopes, a blinking phone bank, and two large vases full of fresh flowers.

She took my name and placed a call to David Randolph's office, listened, nodded, and clicked off the connection. She looked up at me and smiled. "Mr. Randolph's office is the first door on your right," she said, pointing down the long corridor.

I found the door, knocked, and walked in without waiting for a response. Randolph was sitting behind a large mahogany desk, half-listening to a phone call, waving me in with his right hand and pointing to a seat across from him. He was in a shirt and tie, his suit jacket hanging on the shoulders of a leather rolling chair. He hung up the phone, stood, and walked toward me. "I'm sorry to have to meet you under such sad circumstances," he said in a voice that was clearly trained for just such occasions. "Jack was a very special person. I miss him dearly. We all do. Men like him are difficult to find and impossible to replace."

"But you did replace him," I said. I sat in a comfortable thick red leather chair and crossed my legs. "Or so I was led to believe."

"We filled the job, Mr. Rizzo," Randolph said, stepping back behind his desk. "Out of necessity. But it will never be the same here without your brother."

"Were you Jack's supervisor?" I asked.

"More or less," Randolph said. "I recruited him to the firm. And I did his end-of-the-year evaluations. He worked on a number of accounts, not all of them under my supervision, but, yes, if he answered to anyone it would be to me."

"Were there ever any issues between the two of you?" I asked.

Randolph leaned back into his chair, gently rocking it, and smiled. "Are you here as a detective," he asked, "or a grieving brother?"

"I'm no longer on the force," I said. "As I'm sure whatever research you did on me revealed. And I didn't come here to cry on your shoulder, if that's where you think this is going."

"Then, why, may I ask, are you here?"

"Curiosity, more than anything," I said. "Jack and I weren't particularly close the last few years, so I didn't really know much about the work he did. And his son, Chris, is living with me now, and he's a smart kid who asks a lot of questions. Most I can answer. Some I can't. Figured you might help me out in that area."

"What sort of questions?"

"What accounts my brother worked on," I said. "How involved he was with his clients. Were the clients handed to him by you or the other partners or was Jack allowed to go out and solicit his own. Like that."

"Not sure what use such information would be either to you or to your nephew," Randolph said. "And, to be completely up front, most of what you're asking about needs to be kept confidential. We never discuss our clients."

"So the information stays between you and the client," I said. "And, of course, the IRS."

Randolph gave me a weak smile. "They are part of the process, I'm afraid," he said. "And never a pleasant one."

"I'm guessing Jack came up clean in that area," I said. "He was a stickler for the rules, and I can't imagine he would do anything to put himself or his clients in IRS crosshairs."

"No," Randolph said, shaking his head. "That is a safe assumption. Jack's files were impeccable, never a discrepancy."

"That hold true for the rest of the firm?"

Randolph stopped rocking and leaned closer to his desk, his hands resting flat on the shiny surface. "I agreed to meet with you, Mr. Rizzo—"

"It's Tank," I interrupted. "Just Tank."

"As you wish," Randolph said. "I agreed to meet with you, Tank, to express my sorrow and the firm's over the death of your brother. I also was open to answering any pertinent questions you might have regarding Jack's time with us. But discussing firm business does not fall under that category. I assume you received the personal contents of Jack's office?"

"Chris tells me they arrived at the house the same day as the funeral. Along with a nice flower arrangement. Thoughtful. And efficient. Cleared the decks before anyone had a chance to check out my brother's office."

"Other than the personal materials, there was nothing there for anyone to, as you say, check out. What was left were client files and work Jack was doing for the firm."

"That's something I'll never know," I said. "Seeing as how it was cleared out before I could take a look for myself."

"It's procedure, I assure you," Randolph said. "Nothing more sinister to it than that."

"Does your firm have a high turnover rate?" I asked.

"No more than most firms in our field," Randolph said. "It's a very competitive business, as you can imagine."

"If someone does leave, and for the sake of this conversation let's say they leave here still breathing, do you make an effort to keep them on?" I asked. "Offer them a salary bump, a bigger bonus, corner office, more vacation time—that sort of thing?"

"If we feel the employee is of value and worth keeping," Randolph said, "then of course we would do all we could to keep him on our team."

I could tell from his manner that he was growing tired of my questions. As any seasoned detective will tell you, that's the perfect time to zero in on the answers you came to hear.

"Did my brother have to sign a nondisclosure form in order to work with your clients?" I asked.

Randolph nodded. "All members of the accounting staff do," he said. "It's standard protocol."

"Does the nondisclosure also cover talking to the feds?" I asked.

Randolph stood, his hands balled into fists, his face flushed red, glaring at me. I figured him to be a guy who had never thrown a fist in anger in his entire life, but if he were, he'd be swinging lefts and rights in my direction.

"I'm afraid, Mr. Rizzo—"

"It's Tank," I said, smiling.

"Either way," Randolph said, "it's time for you to leave."

I stood, turned, and started toward the door, not bothering to reach out a hand for him to shake. "You're right," I said, looking at him over my shoulder. "I've taken up enough of your time. Besides, I shouldn't be bothering you with these questions. I have a pal downtown who'd be happy to give me all the answers I need. And all it will cost me is a nice bottle of wine."

"And who might this pal be?" Randolph asked.

"The U.S. Attorney," I said.

14.

VISITING CENTER, ATTICA CORRECTIONAL FACILITY

THE NEXT DAY

RANDY JENKINS KEPT HIS HANDS FOLDED AND RESTING ON A small counter, leaning forward and staring at me through a double-glass partition. He was sitting on a thick aluminum chair, wearing a prison-issued olive-colored top and bottom, white socks, and thick-soled flip-flops. Several minutes passed before either of us spoke. He looked at least ten years older than he was, but his body was workout hard, and the areas of his arms that were visible were lined with prison tattoos.

"So, you the one Pearl's always talking about in his letters," Randy finally said. "From the way he describes you, I thought you might be a brother, not a white guy."

"Me and Pearl are brothers," I said. "Color's got nothing to do with it."

Randy smiled. "Try selling that line of shit behind these walls," he said. "Those Aryan boys will slice you like a piece of ripe fruit."

"There are quite a few on the outside of these walls feel that same way," I said. "Lucky for me and Pearl, we don't give a shit about any of them."

Randy leaned closer to the glass and lowered his voice, the words taking on a sudden weight. "Just got Pearl's last letter," he said. "In it, he says you're going to do what you can to get me out of here. Now, something like that's a heavy lift. I heard tell you were a great cop and all back in the day, but how you expecting to pull off something like that? I ain't in here for no overdue parking ticket. I'm in on a murder one, and there's no easy walk on that count. And it's even harder if you got the color skin I got."

"You've been doing too much hard time for me to sit here and sell you a line of shit," I said. "It is not going to be easy. You checked off every box on the murder-suspect board: multiple priors; you not only knew the victim, you were the last one seen with her before she died; you signed a locked-down-tight confession; you had a connect-the-dots criminal lawyer who took the case because his number was called; and in the courtroom you looked and acted exactly like the prosecutors wanted you to look and act—guilty."

"That's all true," Randy said. "And yet here you are, sitting across from me. Now, why would you make the trip from the big city if you have your doubts?"

"I needed to see you and hear it for myself," I said. "Before I take this on full throttle, I need to believe, without a hint of hesitation, that I'll be out on those streets busting hump to free an innocent man."

"Me telling you I didn't kill Rachel won't get me very far," Randy said. "Stop any con in the yard and he'll try and sell you that same line. But I don't know how else to convince you other than with those very words—I did not kill Rachel."

I nodded. "How about we start with a couple of building-block questions. Why did you sign the confession?"

"That detective was going to get it out of me one way or another," Randy said. "He was not going to let me out of that interrogation room without my signature on that piece of paper. Not alive, anyway."

"Eddie Kenwood," I said. Randy stiffened at the mention of the name. "He wasn't the one who busted you, though, am I right? Two plainclothes detectives were the ones who brought you in. But he caught the case. How did that come to happen?"

"The two plainclothes were getting ready to process me," Randy said. "Then Kenwood called out their names and they went into another room, the three of them. A few minutes later, they were gone and I was sitting there, looking up at Kenwood. He told me I belonged to him now."

"What'd they nab you for?" I asked. "The two plainclothes."

"Cocaine possession," Randy said. "Back in them days, I sold some, and what I didn't sell, I used."

"When did you first know that you were the one Kenwood was putting the finger on for Rachel's murder?"

"A few minutes after I was taken into the interrogation room," Randy said. "He told me Rachel had been found dead and he knew I was the one that killed her."

"Did you ask for a lawyer?"

"Would it have done any good?" Randy asked.

"No," I said. "But it does matter if you asked for one."

"Kenwood never brought it up," Randy said, "and neither did I. Besides, any lawyers I ever had weren't of much use. What they saved me in expense, they cost me in prison time."

"Had you ever met Eddie Kenwood until that day?"

"No," Randy said. "I'd heard his name mentioned more than a few times. And I knew he was one of those badges who only nabbed brothers and pinned heavy prison sentences on their ass. Rachel knew him, though."

"Rachel?" I said. "How did she connect to Kenwood?"

"He'd come around to see her now and then," Randy said. "She was a pretty girl, you know? He'd stop by her place looking for any information she could pass his way. Sometimes that was all he wanted. But sometimes he would want more."

"So she puts out for Kenwood, and in return he doesn't bust her for cocaine possession," I said. "That the long and the short of it?"

"Pretty much," Randy said. "He'd bruise her up some, too. He liked to go at it rough. That was his thing, at least with Rachel."

"The connection between Rachel and Kenwood ever come up at the trial?"

Randy shook his head. "No reason that it would. Kenwood made Rachel one of his CIs. And you can't bring a confidential informant's name up in court."

"Who else knew about Rachel and Kenwood's connection?" I asked.

"Most anybody in the neighborhood," Randy said. "Kenwood didn't need to bother hiding it. Who were they going to run off and tell?"

I stayed quiet for a moment. "Back in the interrogation room," I said. "Did Kenwood lay a hand on you? Did he use physical force to get you to sign the confession?"

"He would have if he had to," Randy said. "He paced around the room, acting like a fighter waiting for the bell to ring. I was a kid still, but I'd been around long enough to know a man like Kenwood gets what he wants from somebody like me. Held true then. Holds true now. I read the papers and so do you. Tell me, what the hell's changed from when I first was sent up to today?"

I leaned back in my chair and took a deep breath. I glanced around the drab room, the colors on the wall a faded white, the cement floors cold and stained, the windows small, barred, and barely giving a glimpse of the outside world. I'd been inside many prisons in my life, visiting friends and even some family. I find the inside of these places to be where time goes to die and takes along with it many an inmate.

It is difficult in one short meeting to determine if a man sitting on the other side of a glass partition is guilty of the crime of which he was convicted. Makes it harder when I believe each of us, any of us, under the right circumstances, is capable of taking another life. So I didn't know—not for sure, anyway—as I prepared to leave that visiting center whether Randy Jenkins was an innocent man framed for a murder he did not commit. I wasn't sure whether he was cold-blooded or just someone who happened to be in the wrong spot at the worst time.

But I did know Eddie Kenwood. I knew he had plenty of dirt under his nails and he didn't care who he convicted or why, as long as there was another "closed case" placed next to his name. To me, that made Eddie Kenwood as guilty as any man doing time behind the walls of this prison.

But I did come out of that visit with a piece of information I didn't have before I drove up: a connection between Kenwood and the victim. That wasn't in any of the files or trial transcripts I had read. Now, that could end up being nothing more than a bad cop forcing a young woman to do what he wanted in order to stay out of a jail cell. Or it could just be the missing piece that would help flip the lid on Kenwood.

I pushed my chair back and knocked my knuckles against the glass. "You'll be hearing from me and Pearl," I said. "We'll keep you updated."

"So you're taking on my case?" Randy asked.

I nodded. "I'll meet with the chief of detectives and get him to assign it to me and my crew. Then we'll get to work. And if you're as innocent as you say and we catch a little luck, we'll figure a way to get you out of here."

Randy and I stood at the same time and stared at each other for a few moments. There were tears streaming down the sides of Randy's face. He took a deep breath and then asked, "What makes you so sure? What makes you so damn sure?"

"There anybody in here you can trust?" I asked. "In your cellblock, in the yard, anywhere? Anyone?"

"Not a damn soul," Randy said.

"Well, now you got somebody on the outside you can trust," I said. "And if you're right, then I'll make it right. You have my word on that, and that's all you'll need."

15.

GREENWICH VILLAGE

CHRIS WAS BOUNCING A BASKETBALL, STANDING ON A CORNER, waiting for the light to turn green. He had taken notice of the dark sedan parked across from the playground but had been too distracted by the three-on-three basketball game he was in the middle of with two new friends to give it much attention. He placed the ball under the crook of his right arm, gave a slight tug to the white towel resting around his neck, and wiped the sweat from his face and forehead. Tank had been right. The neighborhood was friendly, and there were plenty of kids his age up for a game of basketball or playground chess. It had been easy for him to blend in, and it made Chris less apprehensive about the new school he would be starting in a few weeks.

The light changed and Chris began to slowly cross the street, once again bouncing the ball against the pavement. The day was hot and humid, summer not yet giving in to the demands of the encroaching fall season, yet the streets were still crowded as late afternoon was creeping toward evening. Chris heard the footsteps closing in on him before he had a chance to turn his head. He stopped bouncing the ball, reached the curb, and then turned to face them. He looked up at the two men standing in front of him, both wearing suits much too heavy for the day's weather. They smiled at him, and the taller of the two reached out a hand and rested it on top of Chris's sweat-soaked Knicks T-shirt. "You got a minute for us?" he asked.

"Not until I know who you are and what it is you want," Chris said.

"It has to do with your dad," the shorter man said, still smiling as he spoke.

Chris looked from one to the other. "What about him?"

"Look, how about this?" the taller man said. "We walk up to that shop over there, the three of us, and we grab a couple of cold drinks and have a nice little talk. That work for you?"

Chris leaned against the side of a parked red Subaru and shook his head. "This works better," he said. "You came here to say something, say it."

Both men shrugged and eased off the curb to position themselves on either side of Chris. "Have it your way," the taller one said, leaning against the car, close enough to Chris for him to smell a heavy dose of his cologne.

"What are your names?" Chris said. "If you want me to talk to you, I need to know your names."

"I'm Franklin," the taller of the two said. "My sweaty friend to your left there, his name is Jeff."

"And you both knew my dad?" Chris asked.

"That's not what I said," Franklin said. "I never met the man. Sorry to hear he died, but him and me never crossed paths."

"But what we came here to say has to do with him," Jeff said. He took out a thick white handkerchief, unfolded it, and wiped at his neck and forehead. "Not to mention you, too."

"What is it?" Chris asked.

"It's more a question of who is it," Franklin said. "Your uncle, the ex-cop, the one who took you in. He might be looking to poke his nose in places it don't belong. That wouldn't be a smart thing to do. Not for him and not for you."

"But you're telling me instead of him," Chris said.

"That's right," Jeff said, casting a glance to his right and left. "We figured a guy like him, he's not going to pay attention to what we have to say. Like most cops, he'll take a step back and come at us hard, ready to do a head-to-head. You can't reason with guys like him."

"Look, your dad died, and that sucks," Franklin said. "You're left in the lurch and you want answers. Only in this case, there's only one answer. He and your mom died in a car accident. It's sad. It's tragic. But it happened. And that right there is the beginning, middle, and end of the story. There's no more to it."

"But if that ex-cop uncle of yours starts sniffing around places he don't belong and asking questions he shouldn't be asking, then people might get hurt," Jeff said.

"Was it an accident?" Chris asked. "Did they die because they were driving on a bad road during a snowstorm?"

"No doubt about it," Jeff said.

"Then why are the people who sent you so worried?" Chris asked. "My uncle has never said anything to make me think otherwise. I have to learn to live with it. No easy thing, you know?"

"I can imagine," Franklin said, nodding. "But that goes down a lot easier if he eases up on the questions and stops snooping around your dad's old company. That sort of shit makes people nervous."

"Is that what you want me to tell him?" Chris asked.

"Would be a nice start," Jeff said.

"You want me to mention we might get hurt, too?" Chris asked. "My uncle? He's used to getting threats. He's not used to me getting them. Not sure if you know this, but I'm the only family he has left. I don't know how he'll take hearing something like that."

"Look, smart-ass," Franklin said, moving away from the car and standing over Chris, his shadow helping to shade out the sun. "You pass the word. How he takes it means shit to me. So long as he hears it. We clear, you and me?"

Chris nodded and watched as Franklin and Jeff turned and started the walk back to their car. Only once they were out of his line of sight did he fall to his knees and begin to shiver. He leaned his head against the front fender of the parked car and closed his eyes, letting the full force of fear overtake his body.

16.

PETE'S TAVERN

THE NEXT DAY

I SAT IN A BACK BOOTH ACROSS FROM RAY CONNORS, THE CHIEF of detectives and my friend for many years. I always chose the same booth when I could, the one with a photo on the wall above it of a previous owner shaking hands with an elderly James Cagney, my all-time favorite actor. Ray and I were both movie buffs, and back in the days before binge-watching TV shows became the norm, we were weaned on the great gangster movies of the thirties and forties. We each had favorite films and actors—Cagney and Bogart topped both our lists, with Edward G. Robinson and John Garfield coming in close behind them.

Ray glanced over at Cagney's photo and smiled. "Even as an old man, he still had that smile and that attitude," the chief said. "He was one of a kind, he was. I read an article a year or two back—they were going to do a remake of *White Heat*, and I'm thinking, they must be out of their minds. Who could ever top Cagney's Cody Jarrett? Name one guy working today who could pull a role like that off."

"Probably some TV actor neither of us has ever heard of," I said.

"And most likely never will," the chief said.

Pete's Tavern first opened its doors in 1864 and is the longest-operating saloon in the city. Legend has it that O. Henry wrote "The

Gift of the Magi" sitting in the second booth off the East Eighteenth Street entrance. There's a plaque on the wall of the booth marking the spot. I used to come here quite a bit during my years on the job—the burgers are top-shelf, the tap beer served cold as a winter morning, and the waiters are fast and efficient. It smells the way an old bar should.

These days, the patrons are a generation younger and hipper than either me or Ray and there are as many women flocking to the bar as there are men, which suits us both fine. Now, when we meet up for a meal, Ray and I prefer lunch as opposed to dinner, since you can actually have a conversation in daylight hours. Once the sun settles, the noise meter hits the red zone.

"Nice to get out of the office," Ray said, after putting in his order for a bacon cheeseburger with the works, a side of sweet potato fries, and a large diet soda. "And nice to put something in my stomach other than that organic shit my wife is telling me to eat. If I never have another Greek yogurt in my life, I'll die a happy man."

I matched the chief's order and handed the waiter our menus. "We keep eating lunches like the one we just ordered, we won't only die happy, we'll die young."

"Let's just hope it takes more than one of these meals to do the trick," the chief said.

"So, I'm guessing you read the two files I sent over. Otherwise we wouldn't be sitting here," I said.

"What?" the chief said. "I need an excuse to break bread with an old friend? But, yes, I did read through both files. Twice, as a matter of fact."

"And you think I'm biting off more than I can chew," I said.

"That's true, I do think that," the chief said. "But I also think that won't matter to you. You're going in on both whether I back you or not."

"Let's take it one at a time," I said. "Start with Randy Jenkins. Where are you on that one?"

"Same place we're at with all of Kenwood's cases," the chief said.

"The DA has asked that we reinvestigate as best we can all his closed homicides."

"He was top gun in that arena," I said. "He had to be putting away six-to-eight long-term sentences a year, easy. That would total out to a small room full of case folders."

"Fifty-six at last count," the chief said. "That's not including the ones that have already been dismissed due to new evidence and DNA results."

"So you were going to hand my crew one of these no matter what," I said. "You don't have the manpower to handle that kind of load on top of all the new cases coming in."

"I was thinking of handing you more than one," the chief said, pausing as the waiter rested both our platters in front of us. "But I need to rethink that, since you have this other case that's going to take up more than half of your time."

"Let me put my feelings for Kenwood on the table," I said. "You know me and him were never on the same wavelength. The same with Pearl. Neither one of us would piss on the guy if he were on fire. He came on the job dirty and only got dirtier as the years went on. And he didn't pay any price for putting innocent young men behind bars for double decades of time. In fact, he got promoted. More than once. What I don't know and am almost afraid to ask is, was he acting on his own, or were there others in on it with him? I mean was there anyone— the brass, the prosecutors, judges—that knew what his play was?"

The chief stayed silent for a few moments, pouring ketchup on his fries and burger and taking a long pull on his soft drink. "I would love to tell you the answer to your question is no," he said. "But the God's honest truth is I don't know. Is it possible? Yes. He could have had someone on the inside, maybe more than one someone, who knew what he was up to."

"What would be in it for them?"

"A conviction is a conviction, Tank," the chief said. "You know that well as I do. To some people it doesn't matter much if the guy sitting on the other side of the table is guilty or not."

"In other words, as with every case we work, don't trust anybody," I said.

"Nobody but me and the ones on your team," the chief said. "It's the safest route to take, especially when it comes to Eddie Kenwood. He's still got a lot of friends in the department, those still on the job and those off."

"You must have crossed swords with him once or twice," I said. "Would be hard not to, I would think."

"Let's just say we're not friends," the chief said. "And leave it at that for now. But hear me when I tell you—watch your back on this one. There are great cops, good cops, average cops, and those just looking to put in their twenty and cash in on a pension. That covers about eighty percent of the force. Then you got the twenty percent that are bad. To my way of thinking, Eddie Kenwood is at the very top of that corrupt little pyramid."

"You're starting to make me think looking into my brother's accident is going to be a cakewalk," I said.

"Don't kid yourself," the chief said. "That one could turn out to be even worse."

"What do you know about the firm he worked for?" I asked. "Besides what was in the file?"

"On the outside, they are as they appear to be," the chief said. "A high-end, big-time white-shoe accounting firm. They have a long roster of A-list clients, most, if not all, coming to them with seven-figure bank accounts. They pay their bills, keep their accounts clean, and don't do anything that might draw the attention of either the SEC or the U.S. Attorney."

"Okay," I said, nodding, "what about on the inside?"

"The shoes are a shade darker," the chief said. "I'm working off rumors here—there's been no solid evidence to this point for us to go anywhere near them legally. But if even half the rumors are true, what they pull in illegally is a dozen times more lucrative than what they claim on the legal end."

"So, how come nobody's been able to touch them?" I asked. "They've been around for years. You don't just decide to go dark overnight."

"It's not from lack of trying, let me tell you," the chief said. "They've been on our radar for at least five, six years. With the Southern District, even longer. We've sniffed around a lot, tried to dig out one or two disgruntled former employees, but nothing came of it. As good as they are at making money, they're even better at covering their tracks. And then Jack came along, and he started to shed some light on their operation."

"Jack?" I said, not bothering to hide my surprise. "I only thought he was planning to blow the whistle. I didn't know he had already taken his first steps."

The chief nodded. "Your nephew's files all point to that," he said. "But he wouldn't have any way of knowing that your brother was already talking to the U.S. Attorney. I didn't know myself until I started reading through the files. I put in a call to Dee Dee Jacobs and she filled me in."

"How long had he been talking to them?"

"Not long," the chief said. "They were just going through the preliminaries. The basics—would he wear a wire, xerox statements, would he be willing to testify. But he gave them more than enough to have them sit up and pay attention. Last time they all met was four days before his accident."

"The firm must have suspected something," I said. "Maybe they put a tail on him or wired up his phone. Dee Dee runs a tight ship, so I wouldn't look to her office to drop a dime on my brother."

"Not likely," the chief said. "They may be a white-shoe firm, but they wear black gloves. These are not your meek-accountant types by any means."

"I know from what Chris dug up that they cook the books," I said. "And they invest money for a few shady characters. How much deeper than that does it go?"

"We're talking money from drug cartels and the Russian mob, dirty money that's dry-cleaned and stored in waterfront condos and car dealerships, real estate agencies, any other place where it's easy to shell your money."

"That's not something the partners would want their employees to know."

"I'm guessing not," the chief said. "Too much of a risk. The top two layers of the company are in on it for sure and making too much money to complain. From the middle tier on down, they're just accountants paying the clients' bills and mailing out their tax returns."

"And somehow Jack got wind of what was going on," I said.

"He was working his way up the masthead," the chief said. "Probably got close enough to see what was going on and clearly didn't like it."

"He must have done something to tip the partners, lead them to suspect he was talking to someone outside the firm," I said.

"It doesn't take much, Tank," the chief said. "Could be as simple as leaving a piece of paper in the Xerox machine, a stray email open on a laptop. Or maybe they just decided they could no longer trust him. These guys don't stay in business by being careless. They survive by being ruthless."

I pushed away my platter, leaned back in the booth, and stared at the chief. "How far can I get with what's in Chris's file?"

"There may be enough for a search warrant," the chief said. "But that'll get you nowhere, since you won't know what the hell to search for. You're going to need help on this one, Tank. You'll need someone working with them on the inside and you'll need some muscle on the outside. I'll do all I can from my end. But it's going to take somebody with bigger muscles than mine to break through that wall. And that's where the U.S. Attorney comes in. You get Dee Dee on your side with this, she'll be a big help."

"I'll reach out to her," I said. "As far as the inside guy, I'm a step ahead of you on that one."

"Anybody I know?"

"Tramonti," I said. "If they're as corrupt as we think, then they'll jump at the shot to handle Carmine's money. It's no secret he's a made man, deals only in cash, and wants his money parked where no one can touch it. And if there's a hiccup along the way, he's not going to run to the cops with a complaint."

"It's also no secret that the two of you know each other," the chief said. "And they need dig only just below the surface to know you date his daughter."

I shrugged. "They probably know all that already," I said. "They'll see what we want them to see—an old-school gangster looking to hide some cash. The last person on earth a guy like that would share that info with would be an ex-cop like me, friend or not. And me keeping company with his daughter would be even less of a concern. You cut to the quick, chief, he's still mob and I'm still cop."

"Good call," the chief said. "How much of his money is he going to put up?"

"Not a nickel," I said with a smile. "He's here to help us out, gain their trust, dangle other old mob guys with pockets full of cash in front of their eyes. But he's not going to risk his own dough."

"You need six figures going in for them to take a meeting," the chief said.

"He'll have money," I said. "It just won't be his."

The chief smiled back and he finished his soda. "So, you were already planning to go see Dee Dee. Hit her up for a loan."

"She's someone we both know and trust. I can't handle this just with my crew and Carmine. This is new terrain for me. I'll need a guide to help me navigate the waters and I can't think of anybody better."

"You'll get no argument from me," the chief said. "Just go in with your eyes open. On *both* cases. Kenwood's not going to take a step back any more than the guys at Curtis, Strassman, and Randolph are. They won't care you're an ex-cop or about Chris, Connie, or anyone on your team. There's a lot at stake for everybody involved, and when that's the case, more often than not, people get hurt."

"There's more at stake than you imagine," I said. "The Jenkins case puts me up against a guy I'm ashamed to call a cop, and one of us is no doubt going to bleed before it ends. But the one involving my brother could ruin me, Chief."

The chief stayed quiet for several moments, letting my words settle in. "Ruin you how, Tank?" he finally asked. "What exactly are you afraid of?"

I slid two twenties under my platter and eased my way out of the booth. "I hope like hell you never find out, Chief," I said, shaking his hand. "I hope to hell no one does."

17.

U.S. ATTORNEY'S OFFICE, SOUTHERN DISTRICT, LOWER MANHATTAN

THAT SAME DAY

I WAS OUTSIDE THE U.S. ATTORNEY'S OFFICE, WAITING FOR HER closed-door meeting to conclude. While I walked in small circles in the large reception area, I sipped the room-temperature bottle of water I'd been offered by an assistant—much to her annoyance. A desk piled with folders clearly needed her full attention. As a rule, city cops and the feds don't mingle well. The atmosphere has improved since the horror of September 11 brought on a reluctant sense of unity among all branches of law enforcement, but still there are remnants of distrust. Federal agents are higher on the pecking order than city cops, both in salary and prestige. I never met a cop who didn't feel the feds were overrated and nowhere near as good as we were at cracking cases, and the reverse no doubt holds true, as well.

The feds dress better, have bigger budgets, and carry more weight inside a courtroom and with the public at large. Don't believe me? Think about this: What scares you more, an RMP pulling you over on a traffic stop or an FBI agent ringing your doorbell? They tend to have years more education and can claim jurisdiction over any case a cop has been working.

None of this ever bothered me while I was on the job, and I enjoyed my time on joint task forces. From my way of thinking, we were all there to do the same job, and who got paid what or who got their suits from Brooks Brothers and who got them from Men's Wearhouse made little difference to me. I was there for one reason only—to crack a case.

But cops, like anyone in any other profession you can think of, love to piss and moan. And when they do, there is no one—aside from a defense lawyer—with a bigger bull's-eye on their back than a federal agent. Me and Pearl were having a drink one night with Gio Fernandez, one of the best undercovers we ever worked with, when he started regaling the packed bar with the story of his adventures with four FBI agents. "They called me in to help them execute a warrant," Gio said. He was short, muscular, with a shaved head that gleamed under the bright lights of the bar. "I meet them up by Jo Jo's—you know, the bar up on Lenox. I drive up in my beat-up Oldsmobile, wearing a Yankees long-sleeve T and a pair of Levi's. These four suckers jump out of a black SUV with tinted windows, each one looking like they were there for a *GQ* photo shoot."

"All under forty and in great shape, right?" Pearl asked.

"Exactly," Gio said. "I mean, they looked like fuckin' Tom Cruise, if he were four inches taller and a Protestant. Anyways, in place of a suit jacket, they're each wearing a blue windbreaker with FBI written in large letters across the back. Then one of them pops the back lid of the SUV and pulls out four sledgehammers. Can you believe that shit? We have to go to the boss to voucher extra gas money while we're on a stakeout, and these fuckers hand out sledgehammers like they're working on a construction crew."

"Why do you need a sledgehammer to execute a warrant?" I asked Gio. "Not to mention four of them."

"That's exactly what I was thinking, standing there scratching my Puerto Rican ass and wondering what the hell these guys were planning," Gio said. "Keep in mind, it's not even six in the morning, nobody—and I mean nobody—on the street except for a couple of junkies on the nod, huddled in a corner. The feds walk over to me, hand me the warrant, and the leader of the pack asks, 'How do you want to handle this?'"

Gio paused to take a long pull on a longneck bottle of beer. "I look at the warrant and turns out we're standing right in front of the building. It had one of those glass doors. I suggest we just kick in the door and make the grab. Odds are the guy they want is sprawled out on a bed or a couch, sleeping off a drunk. 'Just watch out for pit bulls,' I told them. 'You know how these fuckin' dealers love those pits.'"

"Got a scar on my left leg to prove your point," Pearl said.

"I'm about to head toward the door when the leader of the pack reaches out a hand, holds me in place, and hands me a sledgehammer. I was about to argue but figured, what the hell, ain't my show, you know? I'm just along for the ride. So I take the sledgehammer and walk up to the door. Now, keep in mind, I don't know jack shit about sledgehammers. I can barely hammer in a nail. Asking me to take down a door with a sledgehammer is asking for a boatload of trouble."

"Did you bang on the door with it?" I asked.

"Better than that, Tank," Gio said. "I stepped close to the door and got into my batting stance, crouching down like Derek Jeter. I pumped the sledge around a couple of times and then swung it hard as I could against the glass."

"Hit a home run with that swing?" Pearl asked. "Or did you miss, like you do at our softball games?"

"I went for the fences, Pearl, when I should have been going for a single," Gio said. "I swung the sledgehammer so hard, it flew from my hand and went right through the glass. I'm watching it fly through the air into the apartment, and where the fuck does it decide to land? Right square in the center of the suspect's bed. There the guy is, sleeping with legs apart, a sledgehammer two inches from his package. That woke his ass up in a hurry."

"That had to fuck him up," I said.

"Here's the best part," Gio said. "The four feebs are standing around me, stunned. Then one of them says, 'What did we just do?' I looked at him and said, 'We? Where you getting that "we" shit? What, you got a mouse in your pocket? All I see and all everybody popping eyes out of their windows sees is FBI. And that ain't me, suckers. I ain't wearing no windbreaker.'"

"And you did help them get the man they came to get," I said. "They can't deny that."

"And I got to keep the sledgehammer," Gio said. "All in all, not a bad way to start a new day."

18.

U.S. ATTORNEY'S OFFICE, SOUTHERN DISTRICT, LOWER MANHATTAN

MOMENTS LATER

I WALKED INTO THE U.S. ATTORNEY'S LAVISH IF CLUTTERED OFFICE and was immediately greeted by a wide smile and a warm embrace. Dee Dee Jacobs had been in the office for a month shy of two years and was, in the words of the great Southern writer Harry Crews, "kicking ass and taking names." She was building a national reputation as a driven prosecutor, handing out indictments and subpoenas like Halloween candy.

Dee Dee was five foot four if she wore heels. She was in her mid-fifties but looked a decade younger. Her blond hair was long and curled at the sides, and her body was toned from a boot-camp workout routine and a low-fat, low-carb diet she had been following since I first met her twenty years ago. She had only one bad habit I knew of: She drank coffee to excess, more than a dozen cups a day. As a result, Dee Dee was always wired and never tired.

"It's been a long time, Tank," she said, sitting now behind her desk and gesturing me to sit across from her. "Too long. Way too long."

"It doesn't feel that long," I said. "Maybe because I read about you in the papers practically every day and see your pretty face on cable news nearly every time I switch on my TV."

Dee Dee shrugged. "The price to pay for putting scumbags where they belong."

We first met when she was a green prosecutor working out of the Manhattan DA's office. Back then, me and Pearl were just starting to bring down some heavy hitters, and since we were new and Dee Dee hadn't been there long enough for the DA to figure how to work her in, he assigned her to our cases. Over the years, we worked more than twenty cases with Dee Dee—clean, solid convictions. In court, she was as solid as me and Pearl were on the streets.

"Just the other day, I was just thinking about a case we worked on," she said. "The Bossano murder trial. You remember that one?"

"Hard to forget a stuttering hit man," I said. "Arresting him was the easy part. He had killed two wiseguys on 109th Street in East Harlem. By the next day, there was a citywide BOLO out. While that was going on, me and Pearl were relaxing over a nice meal at Patsy's. With you and that chubby guy with the high-pitched voice you were dating."

"He wasn't much of a date, but he was and is one terrific carpenter," Dee Dee said. "If you said the word 'screw' to him, his mind went in an entirely unintended direction."

"He ate well, as I recall," I said. "While all you wanted to know was why the hell me and Pearl were enjoying a meal instead of searching for a killer. We told you not to worry, we'd have him in cuffs before the night was out. And we did."

"He kills two guys on 109th Street," Dee Dee said, "and he goes off and hides in an apartment on 108th Street. And you guys acted as if you knew that all along."

"We did," I said. "It was his mother's place, and every Sunday, like clockwork, Bossano had dinner with his mother. Never missed a Sunday. Not even when every badge in the city was looking to nail his ass."

"Remember what he asked when we went in to take him?" Dee Dee asked, a smile creasing her pretty face.

"He asked if he could have his dessert first," I said. "And if it would be okay not to cuff him in front of his mother."

"So we were sitting at a kitchen table, eating homemade cannoli and drinking espresso with a stone-cold killer and his sweet little mother," Dee Dee said.

"We could have been there for the lasagna if we didn't have to drop your chubby boyfriend off first," I said.

"Ex-boyfriend," she corrected.

Dee Dee stood, walked over, and poured out two cups of coffee from a large silver dispenser. She handed me one and sat back down behind her desk, taking two long sips of the hot liquid. "The chief filled me in on the cases you're planning to take on," she said.

"Kenwood needs to go down," she continued. "On him, I need all the help I can get. If you and your crew help nail his ass, I'll be happy. There's plenty of problems there, though, Tank."

"Such as?"

"He can't be touched unless we prove he planted evidence or got those confessions in an illegal manner," Dee Dee said. "Right now he collects his full pension and can't be prosecuted. On paper, his arrests hold. He can point to the Manhattan DA's office for the convictions. If the cases smelled bad, they should have been the first to notice."

"You ever handle one of his cases?"

Dee Dee shook her head. "I like to think I would have figured them to be wrong, but I can't say for certain. He had locked-down confessions from the mouths of felons with multiple convictions. Most prosecutors wouldn't have batted an eye."

"If Randy Jenkins is innocent, me and my crew will prove it," I said. "And if I can put Kenwood's fingerprints on even a shred of the evidence, then I'll make sure you and the chief will be the first ones to see it."

"Watch your step with Kenwood," she said. "He's like a New York City rat. If he's cornered, he goes for the throat."

"What about the accountants?" I asked. "I heard you were working with Jack. How far along did you get?"

"Not very," she said. "He came to us three, four weeks before he died. He gave us some information but not enough to build anything solid."

"Were they on your radar before Jack talked to you?"

Dee Dee nodded. "We were looking their way for about a year," she said. "They keep their business tight and clean. At least on the surface. But I don't need to tell you these bastards are dangerous and deadly. They'll do anything to keep up the racket they've got going."

"Like murder my brother and his wife," I said. "Based only on suspicion."

"Like murder anyone who gets too close to their business," she said. "And they'll make sure their prints are nowhere near the scene of the crime."

"My crew's good," I said. "But a lot of this is white-collar work. I need somebody who can cut through all that and get to what they're really doing."

"I know you do," Dee Dee said. She opened the top drawer of her desk and pulled out a thin yellow file and handed it to me.

"One of yours?" I asked, opening the file and skimming through the bio.

"One of my best," she said. "He can help navigate the waters, and he's as good with a gun as he is with financials."

"How will you square him with your office?"

"It helps I'm in charge," she said. "Most times I get to ask the questions and not the other way around. But in case it comes up, all anyone needs to know is he's on an undercover assignment. Which, in fact, he is. He's also not stepping into this blind. He's been looking into their operation for a few months. He'll help you navigate your way through their waters. He will report to you and back to me."

I looked down at the name typed in bold across the top of the résumé. "Bobby Gregson," I said.

"Was a lawyer before he decided to pin on a badge, so he'll help you in that arena, as well," Dee Dee said. "Now, I know how you hate to work with anyone you don't know. But I know him, and that should carry some weight with you."

I nodded. "If he's got your stamp of approval, Dee Dee," I said, "then that's good enough for me."

I rested my coffee on her desk, closed the folder, and stood, ready to leave. I looked over at Dee Dee and smiled. "I'm not going to keep anything from you," I said. "We work same as we did when we were younger and faster. So, up front, you should know I'm sending in someone to plant money with the firm. Be a good way for us to track how they move the cash handed to them."

"Not a bad play," Dee Dee said. "So long as it's someone who knows what he's going up against."

"Carmine Tramonti," I said.

Dee Dee nodded. "Old mob guy going in to piece away some money. He'll pass their smell test, I'm sure of it. How much are you going to have him invest?"

"One hundred and fifty thousand," I said. "But it won't be his money he'll be handing over."

Dee Dee stood and walked around her desk to my side. "I'm taking a guess it's not going to be your money, either," she said.

"Not a chance," I said. "I was thinking federal money. It wouldn't be the first time your office put cash on the line. Besides, once we nail these guys, you'll get it back, to the penny. Plus, you'll have your guy there tracking it along with my crew. It's a no-brainer."

"It's a lot more than a no-brainer, Tank, and you know it," Dee Dee said.

"You're right," I said. "It's a favor. From one friend to another."

Dee Dee stared at me for a moment and then shrugged. "If I'm going to risk my neck putting federal money in anyone's hands, I can't think of anyone better than an old wiseguy like Carmine."

"Thanks for the help, Dee Dee," I said, heading for the door. "It's great to be working with you again."

"Same goes for me, Tank," Dee Dee said. "I want to bring these bastards down, and Bobby's the best one to help you get that done. But there's something you should know about him before you two get working on the case."

I turned to look at Dee Dee.

"It was back when he was working his way through law school," she said. "It didn't last long, and from what I know it was never serious."

"What is it, Dee Dee?" I asked.

"Bobby Gregson dated Connie," Dee Dee said.

19.

GREENWICH VILLAGE PLAYGROUND

THE NEXT DAY

I LEANED AGAINST A CHAIN-LINK FENCE, PEARL IN HIS WHEEL-chair next to me, both of us watching Chris and five of his friends playing a game of three-on-three. Chris was dribbling the ball when he saw us standing there, and he waved and gave us both a smile. He then drove to the basket, stopped short, and passed the ball to a wide-open wiry kid a few inches taller. The kid sank a twelve-foot shot, turned, and did a Steph Curry shuffle as he collected high-fives from his two teammates.

"Glad to see some things don't ever change," Pearl said. "Kids still imitate the great pros. Just like you and me did in our day."

"Yeah, but that kid's Curry shuffle was a whole lot better than your Darryl Dawkins Chocolate Thunder dunk," I said with a smile. "You came close to breaking your hand whenever you tried one of those."

"I couldn't help myself," Pearl said, grinning at the memory. "I loved those dunks—from Dr. J to Dominique Wilkins to Connie Hawkins. They were a ton of fun to watch and just as much fun to try and do."

"They had a Clyde Frazier name for you at the courts we played on, didn't they?" I asked. "What the hell was it?"

"Shuck and Stick," Pearl said. "That was me. If I had a few more inches and a whole lot more talent, you'd have courtside seats at the Garden and I'd be playing out the string with my Knicks."

The ball came bouncing up against our end of the fence, and Chris ran over to fetch it. He picked up the ball and walked closer to us. "You up for a game of H-O-R-S-E?" he asked me. "Pearl can keep score."

I glanced over at Pearl, then turned back to Chris. "Are you sure you want to go up against me?" I asked. "I never lose at H-O-R-S-E. It's my go-to game."

"Take it, Chris," Pearl said. "It *was* his go-to game, back when Bloomberg was still mayor. His go-to has got up and gone."

Chris's friends waved their goodbyes as I took the ball from him, dribbled toward the foul line, and sank a fifteen-foot jumper. "Your shot," I said, bouncing the ball back to him.

Chris made the shot, hitting nothing but net, and we were off. "You seem to have made quite a few friends in the neighborhood," I said, getting ready to take my second shot.

"I guess so," Chris said. "But I think it might be better if I keep to myself more, at least until this thing with my dad's firm is finished."

I stopped bouncing the ball and brought it up to the crook of my right arm. "You don't need to do that," I said. "Spending time with your friends is a good way to take a break from all the computer work you're doing for us. Besides, we're bringing in someone to help you with that. Free up some more of your time."

"It's not about the work," Chris said. He seemed suddenly hesitant, nervous, his eyes glancing up and down the quiet street.

"What, then?" Pearl asked. He moved his chair closer to the far side of the basket.

"It's nothing," Chris said. "I just thought it would be better if I spent more time digging into my dad's firm. That's all."

I went over to Chris, put my hand on his back, and walked him over to Pearl. "There's more to it than that," I said. "Did something happen? Something that me and Pearl should know about?"

Chris lowered his head and then looked up at both me and Pearl.

"I should have told you," he said. "I was going to, but I didn't want you to worry. You're dealing with so much already."

"Told me what?" I asked.

"It happened a couple of days ago," Chris said, speaking slowly and in a low voice. "Two guys came to talk to me after our last game."

"Talk to you about what?"

"My dad," Chris said. "They didn't say for sure, but I think they work for the same people my dad worked for."

"Why didn't you tell one of us?" I asked. "Stuff like that happens, you can't sit on it."

"I know," Chris said. "I thought it was a one-time thing."

I looked into Chris's eyes. "It's my job to worry about you," I said. "Pearl's, as well. And for you to worry about us. We're family, and the best way to stay family is to look out for one another. You're the only nephew I have, and I don't plan on losing you. I'll do anything not to let that happen."

"I don't want to lose you, either," Chris said. "I love living with you, with Pearl. I love the guys and Connie and Carmine. When I first got here, I didn't think I would last a week. Now I can't imagine my life without you. I'm sorry. I should have told you."

"Let's write it off as a rookie mistake," I said. I reached over and held Chris close to my side.

"Those two guys, they show up only that one time?" Pearl asked.

"Just to talk to me, yeah," Chris said. "But I've seen them drive around here a couple of times. They sit there in the car for a while, keep the engine running, and then pull out of the parking spot. I think they're trying to scare me. See how long I can take it before I ask you to back off working the case."

"Is it working?" I asked.

"I am scared," Chris said. "I don't want anything to happen to you and to Pearl. And if that means walking away from the firm, maybe that's what you should do. I'll have to learn to live with what happened to my mom and dad. Accept it. As long as you're safe."

"Nobody's walking away," I said. "They're bad people and they need to be chased down. That's what me and Pearl have always done. It's too late for us to stop now. I know you worry about us, and I love you for it. Not only for that but for a lot of other reasons."

"Same goes for me, little man," Pearl said.

"But know this, too," I said. "If someone comes after you, it's the same as if they were coming after me or after Pearl. There's no difference. They reach for one of us, they're reaching for all of us. And I will always be there for you. Always. Never forget that."

I let go of the basketball and watched it roll toward Pearl. "We still need to finish our game," I said. "Unless you just want to call it now. I'll take the win any way I can."

Chris looked at Pearl. "Do you think I can beat him?" he asked, smiling.

"Shit, son, *I* can beat him, and I'm in a wheelchair," Pearl said.

So, for the next hour, Chris and I played two games of H-O-R-S-E and one of Twenty-one. And in that short period of time, he was allowed to be a kid again, in the company of men he loved and trusted. He was a teenager free of worry, enjoying a lazy summer morning.

20.

THE BROWNSTONE

LATER THAT DAY

MY TEAM WAS ASSEMBLED IN THE LARGE LIVING ROOM, SOME sitting on the couch, others sitting on folding chairs, two leaning against a wall. Pearl was in his wheelchair, next to the wine-barrel table, where the two case folders had been spread out. Connie had the restaurant send over large platters of food and was passing around plates filled with lasagna, broccoli rabe and sausage, and linguini in a white clam sauce. There was more than enough wine to go around and, for Chris and Pearl, all the root beer they could drink.

I stood in the center of the room, took in the faces of the group, and got down to the business at hand. "We've never tried to take on two cases at the same time," I said. "At least not two that were as difficult to crack as these will be."

Carmine rested his platter on the fireplace mantel, slapping a few crumbs off his shirt. "They're hard cases, beyond a doubt," he said. "But to put it in its simplest terms, we need to get one guy out of prison and then we need to toss an accounting firm in one. A break-out and a break-in, if you will."

"Chris started the computer work on the firm," Carl said. "He found out as much as he could, but these guys know how to hide their tracks pretty well."

"We need to go in deeper," I said. "Get into their database and break through their firewalls. Any equipment you need to make that happen, you got."

"With a firm like that, it'd be nice to have an inside man," Bruno said. "Not somebody who works there. From what I read in those files, they are double careful about who they hire. Their background checks run deep. So our best bet is a client. Someone they want and someone they think they can trust."

"You're looking at him," Carmine said.

"They'll expect you to invest some money with them," Alexandra said. "Six figures at the start and build it up from there."

"And that they will get," Carmine said.

I saw Connie standing in a corner, shaking her head. "Relax," I said, more to her than to the group. "Not a nickel of it will be Carmine's money."

"Tank went and found us a money honey," Pearl said, smiling. "One with subpoena power to boot."

"It seems the U.S. Attorney's Southern District office has had their eye on the firm for quite a while," I said. "They haven't been able to flag them on anything as yet, so whatever we can do to speed that along would be most welcome."

"And they'll front the money for Carmine?" Carl asked.

"Dee Dee Jacobs wants these guys caught, and she has the resources. And we're not asking for a fortune. One hundred and fifty thousand to get the ball rolling. Carmine will know how to take it from there."

"I'll check in with my clients," Alexandra said. "See if any of them have their money with this firm or if they know anyone who does."

"How do you do that, exactly?" Chris asked. "Won't they get suspicious if you start asking about their accountants?"

"I don't ask," Alexandra said. "I read their fortune and tell them that a place or a company where they keep their money may be doing more than just investing it. Then I sit back and let them do the talking."

"The U.S. Attorney is giving us something else besides money," I said. "Or, in this case, someone else."

"Somebody to keep an eye on us?" Bruno asked.

"Someone to work with us," I said. "Someone who knows the terrain and the players and has been tracking firms like this since he joined the office."

"You're bringing in a fed," Carmine said. "That's like walking on hot coals, Tank. Sooner or later, you're going to get burned."

"I have no choice in this, Carmine," I said. "If I want their help and their money, we need to add one of theirs to our team. And we have to trust him until he gives us reasons not to."

"You'll all be doing the bulk of your work on the firm and their operation," Pearl said. "Me and Tank will focus on the Jenkins case."

"To me, that seems an even tougher nut to crack," Carl said. "The guy confessed and he got convicted. And no one has raised a hand to say he wasn't the one that did it."

"And we're going up against a thick wall of blue that we know from experience doesn't budge in the slightest," Pearl said. "It's a heavy lift, I grant you."

"Working off the fact that Jenkins didn't commit the murder, someone else did," I said. "And we need to find that someone else. We work it like a cold case. Forget Jenkins. Our job is to find Rachel's killer. That's the way, the only way, we get Randy out of prison."

"The killer could be someone Randy knew," Chris said. "Someone he hung out with in the neighborhood. Rachel and Randy were dating, right?"

"More like friends with benefits," Pearl said. "Depending on which day of the week it was. But Randy isn't the only one who connects to Rachel."

"Eddie Kenwood was pretty tight with her, as well," I said.

"That ties the detective who pinned the murder rap on Randy to the victim," Pearl said. "That doesn't happen very often, at least not in my experience."

"More than half of the unsolved homicides committed against one or both people in a relationship is done by a friend or someone they see on a regular basis," Chris said.

"Where'd you pick up that nugget?" I asked.

"Saw it on a rerun of a *Law & Order: Criminal Intent* episode the other night," Chris said.

"Do you know the agent the U.S. Attorney is assigning to your team yet?" Connie asked.

I looked across at her and smiled. "Yes, I do," I said. "His name's Bobby Gregson. He joined the feds after he passed the bar exam. Dee Dee trusts him, which means, for now at least, I trust him."

"A lawyer *and* a fed," Carmine said. "I'm already breaking into hives."

"Chris can dig up some background information on him in case anyone's curious," I said. "Anything more than what's on the Web, you can ask Connie. She knows him, or so I've been told."

"*Connie?*" Carmine said, turning to face his daughter. "How do you tie up with him?"

"I don't," Connie said. "At least not in the way you're thinking. We were in school at the same time, him at the law school, me taking some business courses. Sometimes we would have a coffee or a drink after class. Then he would go his way and I would go mine."

"I never heard him mentioned before," Carmine said.

Connie looked at me as she answered. "There was nothing more to it than that," she said. "So there really wasn't anything to mention."

I held her look for a moment and then rested my wineglass on a side table. "Let's get to work," I said to the team. "We've got cases to crack."

I turned and walked past them and out of the room.

21

CENTRAL PARK ZOO

"THANKS FOR MEETING ME HERE," CARMINE SAID TO DAVID Randolph. Both of them watched a grizzly bear prowling along a series of makeshift rocks and stones. "I'm not big on doing a face-to-face in somebody's office, as you can imagine."

"I admit, I was a bit taken aback by the choice of locale," Randolph said. "But as I learned from my earliest days in business, you go where the client tells you."

"Just as long as the client has money," Carmine said, giving Randolph a gentle tap on the arm. "Am I right?"

"I wouldn't be here, Mr. Tramonti, if I had any doubt about your financial situation," Randolph said.

"Then we're clear why we're here," Carmine said. "I've got some money I want parked. Cash only. I might have a few friends in the same situation. We want to hold on to the money we have, watch it grow, and give as little of it away as possible. I suppose that would make you my go-to guy."

The day was hot and muggy, and they walked alongside mothers pushing strollers and older couples stopping to watch the polar bears and seals. "It all depends, Mr. Tramonti, on how much money you wish to invest. Dealing in cash is not as easy to accomplish in my world as I imagine it is in yours."

Carmine stopped and turned to face Randolph. "First, lose the Mr. Tramonti," he said. "It's Carmine. Second, if you're just going to be tossing shit, the monkey section is that way. I came here to talk business. I thought you did, too. If I'm wrong, let's end this little chat right here and now and we can both be on our way."

Randolph looked at Carmine for a few seconds and then nodded. "How much were you thinking of investing?" he asked.

"Six figures at the start," Carmine said. "Since we're new to each other. That gives me a chance to see how you operate and how good you are at making my dough grow. It also gives you a feel for me, whether I'm someone you want around or not. Sound good to you so far?"

"It's a fair and balanced offer," Randolph said. "And one I expected."

"All right, then," Carmine said. "Let's keep walking and you tell me how this works."

"Before I get to that part, may I ask a question?"

"Shoot," Carmine said.

"Is the cop, or ex-cop, who keeps company with your daughter and is a regular in your restaurant the reason you chose my firm to invest your money in?" Randolph asked.

"You did your homework," Carmine said. "That scores some points with me. Now if you were thorough in your work, you would know a guy like me never tells a cop or an ex-cop nothing about where he keeps his money or where he parks it. I don't ask him where he keeps his cash and I don't expect him to ask me where I keep mine. We clear?"

"And why my firm?"

"Because your firm's dirty," Carmine said. "Which means you won't ask too many questions I don't have to answer. Now can we get on with it or not? Give me the lay of the land."

"It's very simple, really," Randolph said. "You open an account with the firm, either under your name or under an LLC we can set up for you out of Delaware. Once that's done, we select the best possible avenues in which to, as you say, park your money."

"What kind of profit margin are we talking about?"

"With an initial six-figure investment, we can deliver an eight percent return in your first year," Randolph said. "The same holds true for any other investors you point our way."

"How much of that goes to you and how much goes to the government?" Carmine asked.

"The firm takes five percent of profits," Randolph said. "And there's no cap. We secure your investments and keep them away from prying eyes."

"Which means what when it comes to me paying taxes on the dough?"

"Your balance sheet will show a loss," Randolph said. "A minimal one, but enough that you wouldn't be required to pay any amount beyond our fee."

"And how do you make that happen?" Carmine asked.

"That's our business," Randolph said, his voice taking on a harsher tone. "And it stays our business."

Carmine glanced at him and smiled. "It may be your business, Randolph, but it's my money. Now, I'm not looking for a step-by-step on how you duck the government. Just knowing some of the logistics will make me a happier man."

Randolph paused and then said, "Your money will be invested in overseas companies and placed in banks that will know you only by a number, never by a name. We spread the money around and it is constantly on the move. Think of it as an assembly line. Makes it difficult to trace and even more difficult to track. Does that satisfy your curiosity?"

"For now," Carmine said. "Let me ask you this. Let's say for one reason or another I get caught in a jam and need to get my hands on the cash fast. How quick can you turn it back to me? And does it come back to me clean or does it set off a few loud bells and whistles?"

"You can have your money back the day you ask for it," Randolph said with calm assurance. "It can be done one of two ways. If you wish to leave your cash in the investments we've selected, we can pay you out of our discretionary fund. There will be no interest charged if you return it to us within three months. Otherwise, there is a slight fee but one so negligible you'd barely notice."

"Trust me, Randolph," Carmine said, "unless the fee is zero, I'll notice it. What's the second way?"

"We pull the money out of the investments and hand it back over to you," Randolph replied. "We liquidate the LLC, and both the company and the money disappear, as if neither were ever there."

"You make it sound as easy as me making a veal Milanese," Carmine said. "Hope it plays out that way. How soon can you get me set up?"

"From the time you hand over the money," Randolph said, "a little less than a week."

"And how does that work, exactly?" Carmine asked. "Me handing over the cash. Don't expect me to waltz into your firm and drop a few large envelopes stuffed with money on your desk."

"That won't be necessary," Randolph said. "Once you've made your final decision and have the money in hand, you send a text to this number." He reached into his jacket pocket and handed Carmine a folded sheet of paper. "Don't use your cell phone or one belonging to anyone connected to you. Get a burner. You will then receive a return text with a location. Someone will be waiting there to receive the money. It would be wise if you were not the one delivering the cash. Choose an employee or, better yet, a courier, one you've never used before and don't plan on using again."

"In other words, I stay under the radar," Carmine said.

"Exactly," Randolph said. "You and I will never meet again. At the zoo or anywhere else."

"If that's your way of keeping my money safe and sound, I'll play along," Carmine said. "But there would be one circumstance where you and I would need to meet again. Face-to-face."

Randolph stopped and turned to Carmine. "And what would that be?"

Carmine slid his hands into his pockets and stepped in closer. "If anything were to happen to my money," Carmine said in a low voice. "If it were to suddenly go into the wind or I find out all those profits you promised me turned out to be Bernie Madoff bullshit. That's when that would be."

"I assure you such a meeting won't ever be necessary," Randolph said, his calm veneer fading away, a nervous inflection in his words. "Your money will be safe, and you will be pleased with the profits you earn and the lack of exposure you encounter."

"I hope that's the case," Carmine said. "Otherwise, it's back to the zoo you and I go. Only this time, only one of us will be standing outside the grizzly bear's den looking in."

Carmine nodded at Randolph, turned, and began to walk slowly toward the Fifth Avenue exit.

22.

TRAMONTI'S

THAT SAME DAY

I SAT ACROSS FROM CONNIE, WATCHING HER PICK AT A HALF-EATEN Caesar salad. I was content nursing a glass of Averna on the rocks. The restaurant staff was busy setting up tables for the soon-to-arrive lunch crowd.

I checked my watch and glanced at Connie. I couldn't help but notice the concerned look on her face. "I know you're not happy about me asking for your dad's help," I said. "But he's not just the only one I could trust, he's the only one I knew with the know-how to pull it off."

"I get that, Tank," she said, her voice low and barely audible. "And if he didn't want to get involved, he wouldn't have done it. And, to be honest, helping you out on your cases this past year has brought more energy back to his life. I didn't realize how much Dad missed being around the action. It was all he'd known since he was a kid running numbers for the local bookies."

"There's a 'but' coming my way," I said, trying to lighten the mood. "I can feel it, rushing in at any minute."

"The 'but' is he can get hurt," Connie said. "He was beaten up pretty badly earlier this year when he helped you chase down that drug dealer. Now he's going up against a firm that seems to play as rough as any dealer or mob crew, if not rougher. If in fact they had your brother and his wife killed, that means they will do anything to protect what they have. That scares me, Tank. Scares me for my dad. Scares me for Chris, Pearl, and the others on the team. And it scares me for you."

"It's not a case I ever envisioned working," I said. "But there's no stepping back from it for me. I'm aware of the risks going up against these guys' posses. Your dad is, too. But he's been moving around large amounts of money all his life. He understands the ins and outs of that business a lot better than me. He'll know how to keep them on the hook. Trust me, I would rather be out banging heads with a high-end dealer or taking you on a nice vacation. But Chris laid this on my lap, and I can't ignore it."

Connie reached out a hand and placed it on top of mine. "I never expect to talk you or my father out of doing anything you set your minds to," she said. "I learned that lesson a long time ago."

I sat back and nodded, letting the brief silence give us both a chance to take a deep breath. "Let's not forget, on this one, it's not just my team working the case. We got the U.S. Attorney in on it, as well. We have her full support. She's assigning your old pal Bobby Gregson to work with us. Under the table, so no one but us knows about it."

"Have you met him yet?" Connie asked.

I shook my head. "Maybe you can tell me a little about him."

Connie's face flushed a bit, and she moved her hand away from mine. "It's been years since I've seen him," she said. "Didn't know he was a fed. Last I saw him he was planning on practicing law."

"You downplayed it when I first brought up his name," I said. "But there was more to the two of you than an occasional cup of coffee and glass of wine."

"I got caught off guard," Connie said. "Plus, you saw the way my dad reacted. Thought it best to keep it simple. Which, in fact, it was."

"So, you did date him," I said.

"We were friends, Tank," Connie said. "Nothing more. Bobby was working for a cable company, helping to pay his way through law school. I was taking classes during the day and helping out here at night. There wasn't much time for serious dating. Though I don't see how any of that will help you work this case."

"Just trying to get a better picture of the guy, seeing as how we're going to be working together," I said.

Connie brushed a few strands of hair away from her face and smiled. "There's more to it than that, Tank," she said. "You're not worried about working alongside a fed you've never met. You're worried about working next to an old boyfriend of mine."

"You don't want to go there, we won't," I said. "But he'll be part of my team, on this case at any rate. And odds are better than even you two will be seeing each other. So I need to make sure you're okay with that."

"There's no reason not to be okay with it," Connie said. "We never got to the point where it was considered a real relationship. We were friends for a period of time. Then he went his way and I went mine."

"What brought it to an end?" I said.

"It kind of faded away," Connie said. "One day he was too busy to meet up. Another day, it was me who couldn't get away. I suppose if we wanted to be together, we would have figured a way to work all that out."

"Any regrets?"

Connie reached for my hand. "I love the fact you're jealous, Tank," she said, a wide smile on her beautiful face. "It's a side of you I've never seen. But there was never anything serious between me and Bobby. We were two friends with busy schedules who met now and then to relax and forget about work. And it ended because, well, that's how it was meant to go. There's no bad blood, no regrets, and no what-ifs."

"I didn't mean to come off as jealous," I said. "I never thought we'd have to talk about one of your boyfriends, let alone me having to work alongside one."

"Bobby was never my boyfriend," Connie said. "Not in the way you're thinking in that cop head of yours. And there aren't any other boyfriends out there for you to fret over. Most of the time I wasn't interested in anyone looking my way. And on the rare occasions I was, one glare from Carmine scared them away."

"I'm sorry it took me so long, Connie," I said.

"To do what?"

"To be with you," I said. "It should have happened long ago. I let the job get in the way, and I regret that now. All those years where we could have been together, instead of loving each other from a distance. That's on me."

"It happened when it was meant to happen, Tank," Connie said. "We're together now, and that's all that matters."

I looked at her and smiled. "Then, just so I'm clear, you're not still carrying a torch for Bobby Gregson?"

Connie laughed as she slid out of the booth. "You mean that Brad Pitt look-alike you're about to work with?" she said. "Not a chance."

23.

BRYANT PARK

WHEN YOU WORK A COLD CASE, YOU ALMOST ALWAYS START WITH the victim. At least I do. You trace the victim's patterns, personal habits, close friends, possible enemies. You work it right up to the night of the incident, slowly putting the pieces of the crime together until a clear picture emerges. That's how me and Pearl mapped it out whenever we caught a cold one. But this time, with Randy Jenkins, we had to approach it from a different angle.

It wasn't a cold case, at least not officially. As far as the system was concerned, this baby was closed and solved. The victim was dead. The perp doing hard time in a brutal prison. Which meant we needed to find the real killer and then prove it was him and not the one who confessed to the murder.

To make our task even harder, we were going back nearly twenty years. We were working a blank slate, not knowing if the killer was still in the city or even the state. We didn't know if he was already put away for another crime or string of them. We weren't even sure if he was still alive. So I figured the best place for us to start was with Zeke Jeffries.

Zeke was now in his late sixties and weighed about forty pounds more than he did back when he was making a name for himself on the basketball courts of New York City. Zeke was a playground legend, from the Harlem summer leagues to Greenwich Village pickup games. He could out-rebound, outscore, and outplay anyone he went up against. And he had highlight-reel moves. When word spread that Zeke Jeffries was going to be in a game, it wouldn't take long for a crowd to materialize. Even pro ballplayers came out to watch him, and when they were bold enough to match up against him, they would be left breathless and defeated.

As great as Zeke was on the city playgrounds, he could never make the move to the NBA. He caught a few cups of coffee with the Knicks and the Pistons but could never adapt his skills to the pro level. He was a one-man team, and that played well on cement but not on the hardwood. Zeke saw enough money from the bets that were laid down in his favor to not have to worry about paying his bills or having a nice place to live. He earned pocket money, just never real money. When Zeke's legs surrendered to the abuse heaped on them by the cement courts of the city, he was content to move from court to court, telling stories about his playing days and listening to the street gossip. Before long, there wasn't any activity, legal or otherwise, happening from Lower Manhattan up to the Heights that Zeke Jeffries didn't know about. As great a storyteller as Zeke is—and, believe me, there are few better—he's an even better listener, and he remembers everything. Pearl used to always say, "If you blow a dog whistle, Zeke will hear it before the damn dog."

I spotted Zeke sitting on a park bench, a cold beer wrapped in a paper bag cradled in his right hand. He was checking out the comings and goings in one of his favorite parks, a short distance from the main branch of the New York Public Library, another of his regular Midtown haunts. He smiled when he saw me approach. "Long time, old friend," Zeke said. "Nice of you to make your way up here to check on my beat-up ass. Sit yourself down and tell me how my man Pearl is doing, before we get down to any business you came to discuss."

"What makes you think I have business to discuss?" I asked, sitting down and shaking his hand. "Maybe I just wanted to come check on you and see how you're doing. Would that surprise you?"

"Enough to kill me," Zeke said, laughing. "Shit, men like you and Pearl always got business going. Now, tell me, how is he?"

"He's dealing with it," I said. "Some days are harder than others, but Pearl's never been one to raise a white flag, even though there were times when he came close."

"Working cases with you will do him more good than any doctor he could see or any medicine he could take," Zeke said. "And having him live with you, well, that was a slam-dunk idea. You been a good friend to him, Tank. There ain't no doubt about that."

"He's been an even better friend to me," I said. "And I'm not going to bother asking you how you knew he was living with me."

"Same way I know you two are nosing into the Randy Jenkins case," Zeke said. "Looking to unlock what's been sealed for close to twenty years."

"Did you know Jenkins before he got pinned for the murder?"

Zeke took a long swallow of the beer and nodded. "Saw him around now and then," he said. "Him and a group of his friends used to come watch me play."

"He run with a tough crowd?"

"Name one kid his age didn't think he was tough," Zeke said. "They caused some noise, and one or two of them got jammed up. Jenkins himself did a few spins, one in juvie and two in state, as I remember. But if you're asking me if he was the type looking to lay blood on his hands, I'd have to say no to that."

"Well, somebody killed that girl," I said, looking out at the small parade of people passing by. "And if it wasn't him, we need to find out who, and fast."

"No way he took that girl's life," Zeke said, shaking his head. "Not from what I know and from what I heard."

"He confessed to the murder, Zeke," I said. "And he got himself convicted in court. If me and Pearl are going to get him out of that hole, it might help if you could share what you know and what you heard."

"First off, that boy had a mad crush on Rachel," Zeke said. "If he could ever get his shit together, the two of them had a shot at making a life for themselves."

"They were both on the pipe back then," I said. "That wrecks your mind. Makes who you think you love one minute your biggest enemy the next. You know that well as I do."

"They were playing around with it, I give you that," Zeke said. "But they weren't hooked. Not like some of them zombies walking the street. They were fighting hard to get off it, Tank. As much as they may have wanted it, that's how much they wanted off it."

"If you were me and Pearl, who would you be looking at?" I said.

Zeke finished off his beer and laughed. "Don't go sticking no badge on my hip. I ain't cut out for any of that shit."

"Just for argument's sake," I said.

"I'd have me a few suspects," Zeke said. "The cop who took him down, for one."

"Eddie Kenwood," I said.

"He was as dirty as an oil rag," Zeke said, not bothering to hide his disdain. "He put away lots of young men, and not all of them were guilty of the crimes he laid on their names."

"A number of his cases have been overturned already," I said. "The men he sent up were set free."

"That don't make up for it, Tank," Zeke said. "How do you give a man back twenty years he spent in a cage for no reason?"

"You don't," I said. "Now, Kenwood knew Randy from the street, and I heard he had warm eyes for Rachel."

"There's truth to that," Zeke said. "He was on the prowl for her, for sure. And what Kenwood wanted, he took. And there was no one around that could stop him. Looking his way would be my first move."

I nodded. "Anybody else?"

"There was another guy who also had eyes for Rachel," Zeke said. "That Rachel was one fine-looking young girl, the kind most men would give their all for a hot sheet jump and a roll."

"A gangbanger or a wannabe?"

"He had his hands in all sorts of shit," Zeke said. "Sold dope.

Boosted cars. Cranked out a few ladies on the street. And if you put some cash in his pockets and gave him a name, he would waste a guy. Jack-of-small-trades and master of none."

"Is he still walking or is he in prison?" I asked.

"Last I heard he was still around," Zeke said. "Cleaned his act up a bit, or as clean as a guy like him will ever be. Over the years, he's been in the system more than he's been out of it. These days he's got himself a cover job, bouncer at one of the all-night titty clubs downtown. Place ain't got a name, but somehow folks seem to know where it is. Never been there myself, but I hear you can get anything you want once you step onto those sticky floors. And he's the guy that gets it for you. Now, I ain't telling you he might have done in Rachel. I'm just saying it would not surprise me."

"You got a name, Zeke?"

"Livingstone," Zeke said. "J. J. Livingstone. You go looking for him, Tank, go in ready to do battle. He spent all those years in the joint lifting weights and popping that muscle shit. Guy makes Stallone look like a hand puppet."

I patted him on the knee and stood. "Appreciate the help, Zeke," I said. "Anything I can throw your way?"

"A couple of Knicks tickets once the season starts would do me a world of good," Zeke said. "Bad as they've been these past years, I might start pushing my ass into the gym and get myself back into playing shape. Can't do worse than that sad bunch."

"I'll get a few games to you," I said. "Maybe me and Pearl will go with you. We'll make a night of it."

I turned and started to walk away. "Hang on a second, Tank," Zeke said. "There's something else you should know. Heard it for the first time myself not too long ago."

"What is it?"

"About that cop Kenwood," Zeke said.

"What about him?" I said.

"Word got to him that you and your bunch are looking to clear

Jenkins," Zeke said. "That didn't sit too well with him, as you can imagine."

"Wouldn't expect it to," I said.

"He's still got friends with badges on the job," Zeke said. "And he has a rough crew of ex-cops working for him now. They're a nasty bunch, so you and Pearl watch your backs."

"They can come looking for us," I said to Zeke. "We're not hard to find."

"They're not coming to talk you out of it, Tank," Zeke said. "They're coming to take you and Pearl down."

24.

THE BROWNSTONE

THAT NIGHT

PEARL HAD THE CREW ASSEMBLED IN THE LARGE LIVING ROOM by the time I walked in, Bobby Gregson by my side. I stepped in front of Bobby and introduced him to each member of the team. He shook hands with each and saved Connie for last, giving her his widest smile. "Been a long time," he said to her. "Nice to see you again."

"Same here," Connie said, eager to let the awkward moment pass as quickly as possible. "Thanks for coming in to help out."

"Wasn't my call," Bobby said. "But if we nab our targets in the end, that makes it worth it."

I walked over to the bar and poured myself a glass of wine from an already opened bottle of Biondi Santi. I looked over at Bobby. "Red or white okay by you?" I asked.

"It'll do," Bobby said. "Unless you got Dewar's somewhere on that bar. Then I'll have that instead. Neat."

I handed Bobby his drink and turned to face the team. "Bobby's been looking into the accounting firm my brother worked for," I told them. "So I'll let him start us off."

Bobby faced the room. "Think of them as a two-tier operation," he said. "The bottom rung is made up of folks looking to invest their money, pay their taxes, and, with a little luck, see some profits fall their way. The top rung is what we've been looking at. That's where the big money is, and it all comes from people with a lot to hide—drug dealers, mob guys, white-collar thieves, grifters, casino bosses looking to hide their skim. The firm always turns a profit for their clients, but those profits are hidden in offshore accounts and overseas banks."

"What's their end?" Bruno asked.

"The usual five percent fee per client," Bobby said. "But I suspect they skim quite a bit more off the top for themselves. Haven't been able to prove that end of it yet."

"Are you here to work with us or to spy on us?" Alexandra asked. "Be good to know that from the start."

"I can see this is going to be a friendly crew to work with," Bobby said, taking a sip of his drink.

"They don't know you yet," I said to him. "And what they don't know, they don't trust. That has to be earned, and you just got here."

Bobby was in his mid-forties, tall, and in workout-solid shape. He kept his dark-brown hair trimmed short and came off as relaxed and composed. Me and Pearl exchanged a glance, and we were both thinking the same thing: There had to be some mettle to this guy in order for Dee Dee to choose him to come work with us.

"What Tank says is true," Bobby said to them. "Except for Connie, none of you know me, and she hasn't seen me in the longest time. But if you want to catch these guys, you're going to need my help. You may think you can take the firm down without me. Thinking that would be boneheaded. It might also get you killed."

Chris stepped away from the corner wall he was leaning against and walked up to Bobby. "Have you read the files I worked on?" he asked him.

Bobby nodded. "More than once," he said. "I'm sorry about what happened to your parents. And you did a great job poking holes in the car-accident scenario they came up with. But going after them for killing your parents is only one way we can nail them and, to be honest, maybe not the best way."

"I don't care that they keep money in offshore accounts and don't pay taxes," Chris said. "Maybe you do, but not us. We want them . . . I want them for killing my mother and father. The rest of it means nothing to me."

"We need to get them for the rest of it, for all of it, to pin them for the murder of your mother and father," Bobby said.

"How you figure that?" Pearl asked.

"There's three partners who own the firm," Bobby said. "There were, at last count, a dozen associates with knowledge of their under-the-table business."

"Fifteen," Carl said. "Last time we checked their personal rankings, three more junior members got booted up to senior level."

"Okay, then," Bobby said, "fifteen. We nab them on the tax fraud, drug-dealing, money laundering, they each face a minimum of twenty years in prison. And not a country-club medium-security place. Flat-out hard federal time."

"And how does that get us to where we got them on killing my parents?" Chris asked.

"Because when they're facing that kind of time," I said, "up against a prosecutor like Dee Dee Jacobs, then one of them, if not more than one, will be looking to do a flip."

"And in order for Dee Dee to make that flip happen," Bobby said, "she'll need to know who ordered your parents killed and why."

"What happens to the ones who flip?" Chris asked. "Do they just get to walk away clean?"

"Depends on who it is," Bobby said. "If it's one of the associates, they might have caught wind of what went down with your mom and dad but were in no position to give that kind of an order."

"And if it's one of the partners?" Chris asked. "One of the ones who did give the order to have my mom and dad killed? What happens to him if he cuts a deal?"

I reached over and put a hand on Bobby's arm and then stepped in closer to Chris. "In that case, there will be two deals," I said to him. "The one that Dee Dee gives him. And the one I'll give him."

Chris stared at me, tears forming at the edges of his eyes. "What's the difference between the two?"

I leaned over and put both hands on Chris's shoulders. "Dee Dee's lands him in prison," I said. "Mine puts him in a coffin."

25.

ONE POLICE PLAZA

THE CHIEF OF DETECTIVES, RAY CONNORS, SAT BEHIND HIS LARGE wooden desk, his spit-polished shoes resting against an open drawer, sipping from a large container of Dunkin' Donuts iced decaf. I was across from him, pacing between his desk and the large windows that looked out at the congested streets of Lower Manhattan. Chief Connors glanced at an open folder on his desk and then looked up at me. "Doesn't surprise me that Kenwood still has a few friends on the job," he said. "It shouldn't surprise you, either. What does put me back on my feet is that he's still tight with some ex-cops that are eager to do his bidding."

"And there might be a few loose cannons on his side in the DA's office that block me from digging deeper on the Jenkins case," I said.

"Some of the active cops that like Kenwood know him only by reputation," the chief said. "A hard-charging detective with a long string of notches on his conviction belt catches the eye of a lot of cops. Especially the ambitious ones. That doesn't mean they're willing to risk their job and their pension doing some dirty work for him."

"I'm not too worried about the ones who kneel at Kenwood's altar," I said. "They only know about the convictions, not how he got them. And not even reading about the overturned ones in the papers is going to sway them one way or another. The ones that have my attention are the ones off the job, who worked with Kenwood and may have helped him get those false confessions. The more Kenwood cases get overturned, the more likely their names will pop up on somebody's radar. And that might be all the incentive they need to come after me and my crew."

"We've been keeping tabs on Kenwood for a while now," the chief said. "He plays golf and does a little sailing when the weather's nice. He splits his time between a house in Nassau County and a small condo down in Boca. Lives within his means. If he made under-the-table money, he's good at keeping it off our radar."

"He's not tied in to the mob in any way," I said. "If he were, I would have caught wind of it from Carmine. But we both heard the talk about him shaking down mid-tier dealers and pimps, clearing about three, maybe four hundred a week. There was never any proof, but it wouldn't be a stretch for it to prove out to be true."

"He probably did do those things, but that's not what drove him. Kenwood's a hot-tempered guy whose reputation is being sullied, day in and day out, in the newspapers and the DA's office," the chief said. "That means more to him than anything. When he left the department, no one had a higher homicide closeout rate. He sees himself as a Hall of Famer. Messing with that just might be enough to put him over the edge."

I turned away from the window and looked at the chief. We had known each other since I joined the force, and he was one of the most honest and honorable men I knew. He was fair but tough, demanding and dedicated both to his work and to those he considered his friends. "Well, Chief," I said to him, "if I clear Randy Jenkins, he'll do more than go over the edge. He'll come gunning for me, and he'll have his ex-cop goons by his side."

The chief smiled. "And it doesn't sound to me like that bothers you all that much," he said. "But it's not going to look good for the department overall if that were to happen."

"How do you think it looks now, Chief?" I asked. "One case after another of Kenwood's getting overturned. City forced to pay out millions in settlements to men who had their lives ruined by a detective who looked only at skin color to link them to a crime. And for what? To see his closed-case rate rank higher than the next guy in the bureau? To me that's a stain that won't wash out easy."

"Don't read me wrong, Tank," the chief said. "I want to nail the piece of shit much as you do. But right now, legally at least, we can't touch him. His pension is secure, as is his health plan. He's still claiming all his convictions are on the square. If you want to point a finger, look to the prosecutors. They're the ones who convicted the guys. He merely got them to admit to their guilt. I don't buy it and neither do you. But there are quite a few who do."

"We'll take it one step at a time," I said. "He'll tumble eventually. Once those walls start closing in, he'll put away his golf clubs and ditch the boat shoes and make his way to me. But for now I've got to clear Randy Jenkins."

The chief picked up a second folder from his desk, opened it, and scanned the rap sheet of J. J. Livingstone. "He's nobody's idea of a role model, I'll give you that," he said. "And he knew both Jenkins and the victim. He's worth a hard look. He's had his finger in all sorts of street business, wouldn't be a shock if it reached all the way up to murder."

"There's one other reason to line him up as one of our suspects," I said. "Aside from the violent temper and him maybe having a sweet spot for Rachel."

"You pick this up from your talk with Zeke?"

"He pointed me in the right direction," I said. "Look for yourself. On his rap sheet. His third bust, for a breaking and entering. The collar went to a still-new-on-the-job uniform patrolman."

The chief flipped over several pages and ran his fingers along a page of an old 61, the report a cop types up detailing how an arrest went down. The report ends with the patrolman's signature. The chief read the name typed just above the signature and then sat back in his chair. "Eddie Kenwood got the collar," the chief said, looking from the page to me. "That ties him to Livingstone."

"Does more than that, Chief," I said. "Kenwood got the case tossed three days after he filed the papers. Went to the higher-ups and told them Livingstone had agreed to be a confidential informant and that having him on the streets as a CI was better than letting him do a spin for a minor offense."

"Which means Livingstone owed Kenwood," the chief said.

"And that Kenwood owned Livingstone," I said.

26.

CHURCH OF ST. FRANCIS OF ASSISI

I NEEDED A QUIET PLACE TO CLEAR MY HEAD AND ARRANGE MY thoughts, and this peaceful and beautiful church is one of my havens. The original church, on Thirty-first Street between Sixth and Seventh Avenues, was built in 1844. It was then demolished and rebuilt in 1892, with a mix of marble brought over from Italy and trucked down from Vermont. In 1928, what was then the largest mosaic in America was first shown to the public in this church; its 1,600 square feet feature Mary along with beautifully rendered scenes from the life of St. Francis and other saints from the religious order he founded.

You don't need to be a deeply religious man to admire St. Francis or, for that matter, throw a prayer his way. His goals were simple—help the poor and those in need. And those that followed in his footsteps executed the mission he laid out for them. During the height of the Great Depression, for example, the Friars doled out bread and alms, feeding as many as four thousand hungry and desperate New Yorkers in a single day. Toss in the fact that St. Francis is also the patron saint of animals, and that makes him my favorite saint. Not far behind him is St. Jude, the patron saint of lost causes and cops—where I qualify on both accounts.

I often make it a point, either coming into the church or before leaving, to stop in the courtyard and reach a hand to touch the bronze statue of St. Francis. His right heel, knees, and hands all shine from the millions of fingers that have rubbed them over the years.

I sat in a pew in the back of the small church, taking in the beauty and the silence, as I contemplated the tasks before me.

I needed to either clear Randy Jenkins or prove to myself and everyone on my team that he really did commit the crime for which he stood convicted. The fact that an innocent man was possibly spending double decades behind prison bars sickened me. Anyone I slapped the cuffs on deserved it. I sent a lot of men to prison and a few to the morgue, but all had earned that fatal ride. And the fact that the hideous shadow of Eddie Kenwood hovered over this case made it that much more crucial I get to the truth of the matter. It is no secret that cops like me, Pearl, and Chief Connors harbor a deep dislike for the criminals that prey on the powerless, taking what little they have and leaving blood and ruin in their wake. But our hatred for dirty cops runs even deeper.

A hood does not take an oath to obey the law and protect the innocent from harm. But a cop is held to a higher standard, or should be. Once they cross the line and walk down a path that lines their pockets or inflates their reputation at the expense of those without recourse, they cross into my red zone. To my way of thinking, a dirty cop is the lowest and vilest form of criminal. He abuses the trust that's placed in him by the public he has sworn to protect. Eddie Kenwood was now my enemy and I was his, and only one of us could come out of this battle unscathed.

The danger posed by the accounting firm that set my brother up also brought with it significant and potentially lethal challenges. Now, I wasn't walking into that minefield blind. But these guys were pros and had been above the reach of the law for many years. The feds hadn't been able to nail them, despite their best efforts. I had to wonder about the level of success I would have.

It was a company of tightly held secrets. And I was a man who feared his dark secret would one day be exposed. They would go to any lengths to keep their machinations off anyone's radar. And they would not hesitate to bring harm to me or any member of my team. All to protect their profits.

And their secrets.

Would I be willing to do the same? How much did I fear the revelation that could come out about me while working this case? These people had the means to dig into my past. They would look to attack us at our weakest points, exposing parts of our lives that had for good reason been hidden away. Jack and my parents were the only ones who had known my secret, and now they were dead. I told Connie the reason Jack and I didn't speak was that he had seen me kill a man. But I didn't go any deeper into it than that and she didn't ask. But that didn't mean my secret was safe and tucked away forever. A long-held secret can be exposed in a blind moment, coming out and revealing itself when you least expect it. It was a fact I had chosen to ignore for many years. But I knew that at this time, with this case, against these particular adversaries, I could no longer allow myself that luxury. I believed without a doubt, as I sat there in that silent church, that what I had kept hidden for so long would soon be divulged to all who knew and loved me. I would be powerless to prevent it. I simply needed to learn to live with that sad fact.

I stepped out of the pew, genuflected, and walked out of the church toward the courtyard. I stopped in front of the statue of St. Francis and rested a hand on his knee. I said a silent prayer, asking for forgiveness and for courage. I stayed there for what felt like a long time, my eyes looking into the sculpted eyes of St. Francis.

I was a man of action and violence standing in a sun-drenched courtyard seeking solace and wisdom from a man of peace and love.

27.

GRAND CENTRAL TERMINAL

THAT SAME DAY

EDDIE KENWOOD STOOD UNDER THE BIG CLOCK IN THE CENTER of Grand Central Terminal, his back resting against a side of the information desk. He was in a T-shirt and gray shorts, his hair thinner than when he had been an active detective and his stomach surrendering to the daily routine of cold beer and whiskey chasers. He looked at the two men standing in front of him and slapped his hands together. "Let's get to it," he said to them.

"You want to talk here?" the tall and leaner of the two asked. "Might be better if we go to the Oyster Bar, no? Grab us some littlenecks and a couple of cold ones."

"I didn't drag my ass down here to grab a meal with you, Arthur," Kenwood said. "Tell me what you and Pete came to tell me. And then you can go down to the Bar and eat all the raw fish you can stand."

"Tank and that crippled partner of his are digging into the Randy Jenkins file," said Pete. He was older than his partner, with a shaved head and wearing a tight black muscle T and jeans torn at the knee. "Went in and asked for the case from Connors is what I heard."

"Why that one in particular?" Kenwood asked.

"Not sure," Arthur said, shrugging.

"Have they reached out to anyone yet?" Kenwood asked.

"They've only been on it a couple of days," Pete said. "They might have connected with one of their old street informants, but that's not going to get them far. They have to dig up a doer from seventeen years back. That's no easy feat."

"I don't give a damn how many hurdles Tank's got to jump over," Kenwood said. "He's the type that doesn't stop until he gets what he's after. Trust me. I know that bastard better than either one of you."

"Maybe so," Arthur said. "But even with the chief running cover for them, it's a heavy lift. They have to prove the guy who confessed and got convicted for the murder didn't do it and dig up the one who did. I don't care how good Tank is, I don't see how he cracks this baby open."

"Don't be so quick to brush them off," Kenwood said. "Especially when it's my ass and not yours that's in the ringer."

"The DA's office is taking a second look at all your closed homicides," Pete said. "Why's this one got your ass tied in knots?"

"Besides, what do you care if they find the guy?" Arthur said. "Just like with all the others, they release the con, pay him out seven figures, and two, three days later everybody moves on, business as usual. You still sit back, collect your pension, and live your life."

"That might be true on them other cases," Kenwood said. "But not with this guy Tank. Him and Pearl catch some luck and pin the murder on someone other than Jenkins, they're not going to be happy to see it end there. If that happens, then they'll come looking for me, and I'm not in any mood to give those fuckers that chance."

"Okay, then," Pete said. "What are you thinking of doing about it?"

"Stop them now," Kenwood said. "Don't give them a chance to get anywhere near the case."

"You better go looking for somebody else," Arthur said. "Passing off some information your way is one thing. Going after a couple of retired badges is another matter. And I'm not in this to piss away my pension, let alone risk some jail time of my own, just to cover your greasy tracks."

"You take my money, you take my orders and follow them," Kenwood said. "And you're both in too deep to take any back steps now."

"My advice?" Arthur said. "Keep a clear head. Tank and the chief go back a gang of years and they're tight. Something happens to either him or Pearl while they're working this case, you don't think the chief is going to come looking at you hard?"

"Let him look all he wants," Kenwood said. "Something goes down, I won't be anywhere near where it happens. And besides, where's it written it has to be Tank that takes the hit? He's got himself some half-ass crew helping on the cases come his way. I even hear he's got his brother's kid living with him, and he still spends cozy time with the looker runs that restaurant he hangs out in. There are targets everywhere you look."

"I would steer clear of the girlfriend if I were you," Pete said.

"And why is that?" Kenwood said. "Because of her old man? I gotta shit my pants because of some past-his-prime wiseguy?"

"Past his prime or no, Carmine Tramonti was a high-end mob boss," Pete said. "And with a guy like him, you touch his family, he'll do all he can to make sure a bullet gets sent your way."

"Not if my bullet hits him first," Kenwood said. "Hard to get off a shot when you're laid out in a coffin."

"You make a move like that, it's going to piss off lots of people," Arthur said. "None more than Tank himself. He'll figure you for that in less time than it would take him to pour a cup of coffee. And he'll come straight at you."

Eddie Kenwood moved away from the information desk and looked at the two men and smiled. "I wouldn't have it any other way," he said. "No matter how all this shakes out, it's going to come down to him coming after me and me going after him."

"There must be some real bad blood between the two of you," Pete said, "if you're looking to take him down as bad as all that."

"I'm not planning on taking him down," Kenwood said. "I'm planning on bringing him in, handcuffs and all."

"For what?" Arthur asked.

"For murder," Kenwood said. "I'm going to arrest Tank Rizzo for murder."

28.

LITTLE WEST TWELFTH STREET

EARLY THE NEXT MORNING

I STOOD NEXT TO BRUNO, OUR BACKS AGAINST A POWER-WASHED brick wall, both of us drinking coffee from hot containers. I looked up and down the street and marveled at the change that had come over the area that still bore the name of the Meatpacking District. "My pop would flip if he saw what this area has turned into," I said. "Middle of the night, this was once the most active part of the city. Meat trucks lined up and down these blocks, streets lit up as if it were the middle of the day."

"Some of the old iron awnings are still left," Bruno said. "Only instead of beef, they're fronting shops moving high-end clothes and restaurants selling grilled cheese for what a pair of pants used to cost. Things are meant to change, Tank. Whether we like it or not."

I looked at him and nodded. "I used to come down here with him some mornings during the summer months. It was like walking into another world. There were all these lights blaring down, and lines of rusty barrels, holes poked into their sides, were set up three deep on each street. They were packed up with the remains of wooden crates and lit to burn."

"What for?"

"For breakfast," I said. "Around sunup, the workers took a break.

Tables were set, filled with fresh-baked Italian bread, sliced red onions, tomatoes. Then one of the guys would start slicing thick hunks of meat off the hanging hindquarters. They would jam them onto skewers and grill them over the fires. Once the meat was cooked, you grabbed yourself a slab of bread, put the steak on it with all the fixings, and you chowed down."

"Great way to start a day," Bruno said.

"I've never had a better breakfast than I did back in those days on these streets," I said.

The street was partly deserted, a few late-night stragglers making their way home after too many drinks and possibly drugs if they hit the right after-hours clubs. Down a side street, just off the corner, a thick door swung open; through the haze of smoke that filtered out, I saw three women emerge, led by a tall, muscular man in a black tank top and leather pants. "There's our guy," I said.

Bruno and I ditched the containers in a nearby garbage can and headed toward the door. The muscular man helped each girl into a waiting sedan and watched as it moved away from the curb, turned at the corner, and headed uptown.

He spun around when he heard me and Bruno approach. "You're too late," he said in a harsh manner. "We're closing up. If you want to see the girls dance, you'll have to come back tonight."

"We're not here to see anyone dance," I said. "We're here to see if you might be able to help us out."

"Help you out how?" the muscular man asked. He was in solid shape, upper body like chiseled stone, both hands closed into tight fists as he walked slowly toward us.

"Some straight answers on a few questions," I said. "Nothing more."

He looked at me and then turned his attention to Bruno, staring at him for a few moments. "You were a fighter, am I right?" he asked him. "Not small time, either. You were a main-event guy. Or am I thinking of somebody else?"

"I fought in the Garden a few times," Bruno said. "Other places, too."

"You were pretty good, if I recall," the muscular man said.

"Good, yes," Bruno said. "But not good enough."

"And who's the guy with you?" he asked. "Your trainer?"

"My name's Tank," I said. "You seem to know Bruno here. And unless I'm way off base, you're J. J. Livingstone. We came to talk to you about Randy Jenkins."

"Randy Jenkins?" Livingstone said. "Man, I haven't heard that name in the longest time. Last I heard, he was still eating his meals off of tin trays."

"Still is," I said. "But word is, before he got roped into a murder rap you and him ran with the same pack of friends."

"Maybe so, maybe not," Livingstone said. "Either way, why do you and the wannabe champ here give a shit?"

"Because I don't think he did what they say he did," I said. "And I think you might know a little more about that situation than we do."

"The dude confessed, did he not?" Livingstone asked. "And a jury agreed. There ain't much more to speak about beyond that."

"Every CI I had on the streets got cut loose from something they could have got prison time for," I said. "It's part of the deal. They give me information I wouldn't otherwise get, and I clear them of a crime they might have got sent away for."

"Figured you for a cop," Livingstone said. "You got the look and the manner. But why you telling me this?"

"Because you were one of Eddie Kenwood's CIs," I said. "So I'm just curious what information you passed his way to give him enough rope that he cut you free on something you might have done."

"We're done talking," Livingstone said. "I got nothing to say to either of you two sad sacks."

"Randy Jenkins was a friend of yours," I said, stepping closer to Livingstone. "But you let a lowlife like Kenwood jam him up."

"And you did it to a brother," Bruno said. "Which makes it that much worse."

"But maybe you had your reasons," I said. "You were pissed. After all, Rachel had her eyes on Randy and never glanced your way. It's enough to make a guy jealous."

"I don't know what the fuck you're talking about," Livingstone said, his voice taking on harsher tones, his body twitching and bracing for action, the short leash he had on his temper about to snap.

"Or maybe you decided to go down another street," I said. "If you couldn't be with Rachel, then no one could. She was either going to be yours or be nobody's. So maybe you're the one who iced her. Then you ran to your pal Kenwood and snitched out Jenkins."

"Kenwood didn't give a damn who he put away," Bruno said. "One black guy in jail is just as good as the next to him."

Livingstone stepped closer to me and Bruno and started to circle us both. I watched as he crouched down and raised his fists to chest level. "You can turn and walk away," he said through clenched teeth. "Or you can stand your ground and bleed. I'll leave it up to you."

"Think it out, Livingstone," I said. "You might be able to take me. Been a while since I've been in a street brawl. But if you did indeed see Bruno in the ring, you know your chances with him are slim to none at best."

"I said I saw him fight," Livingstone said. "I didn't say I saw him win."

Bruno stepped away from me and toward Livingstone. His hands were at his sides, his body poised, relaxed. Livingstone lunged and swung a right fist toward Bruno, who leaned back and dodged the blow. Bruno then landed two powerful punches, short and contained, to the sides of Livingstone's right shoulder. The blows made his knees buckle.

Livingstone took a deep breath and then bum-rushed Bruno, landing against the front of his stomach. Bruno braced for the hit, his knees bent, and held Livingstone at bay by throwing two brutal uppercuts. One landed against the front of the bigger man's chest, the second caught him in the throat. Both punches were enough to send Livingstone to his knees, gasping for breath.

"I think you've had enough," I said to Livingstone. I walked over to him and helped lift him to his feet.

"Take deep breaths," Bruno told him. "The pain will fade in a minute or two."

"Now that we got that out of the way," I said, "I figured how you can help us and, at the same time, help yourself."

Livingstone gazed at me through glassy eyes, rubbing at his chest and throat. "And how's that?"

"One more question for you first," I said. "Does Kenwood still stay in touch with you? Look to you for information?"

Livingstone nodded. "He comes around once or twice a month," he managed to say between gasps for air. "He still likes to keep his nose in what's going on. Talk is he's the bag man for a couple of active units that take from dealers and pimps, and he pockets a share of the profits."

"That makes it that much easier for me and for you," I said. "You don't know us yet, so you'll have to take our word you can trust us. Now, we don't know you well, either, but I'm willing to give you a chance. But if I even get a hint you were the doer of that girl and let Randy take the rap, I'll jam you in ways you didn't even think existed. That come through to you?"

Livingstone nodded. "What do I have to do?"

"Simple," I said. "From this second on, you're no longer Eddie Kenwood's confidential informant. You're mine. You pass on to me anything he tells you and we'll tell you what to pass on to him. Clear?"

Livingstone caught his breath and looked at me and Bruno. "I didn't kill Rachel," he said in a low voice. "Yeah, I had a thing for her. Shit, everybody did. She was sweet as sweet could be. And I knew she wouldn't make time for a guy like me. But I wasn't the one to bring harm to her."

I patted Livingstone on the shoulder. "I believe you," I said.

"One more thing before you go," Livingstone said.

"What is it?"

"Randy Jenkins didn't bring harm to her, either," he said.

29.

HOSPITAL FOR SPECIAL SURGERY

LATER THAT MORNING

I SAT IN A CROWDED WAITING ROOM, PEARL FACING ME, CHRIS to my left. Pearl had been doing his physical therapy at the brownstone, but he needed to be checked out by his doctor once a month. I looked around the room and could sense that Pearl was growing impatient. He hated waiting, and he hated being prodded and probed by doctors even more. I was happy Chris asked to come with us. He and Pearl had grown close in the months we had all been together, with Pearl becoming one more uncle to help ease the boy's transition to his life with me.

"What do the doctors do to you when you're in there?" Chris asked Pearl.

"The usual," Pearl said. "Blood pressure, blood work, see if my arms are getting stronger from the exercise routines. They're good at what they do. I'm the one that's a pain in the ass to them."

"I can swear to that," I said.

"You know," Pearl said to me, "might not be a bad idea to get yourself checked out, seeing as how we're here anyway. Be a good thing for the docs to take a look at that lung and see if it's healing up proper."

"You're the one with the appointment, Pearl," I said. "Not me."

"That won't matter to Doc Cantor," Pearl said. "He's known us both for years. He'd be more than happy to take a look and a listen."

"What's wrong with your lung?" Chris asked.

"I took a bullet to the rib cage same day Pearl got hurt," I said. "It put a little dent in one of my lungs. Nothing major, just enough to get me to retire. It doesn't bother me most days."

"But it does on some," Pearl said. "Now, I know that's a fact. Be nice for the doctor to know about it, as well."

"We got a lot on our plate at the moment, Pearl," I said. "I need to focus on what's in front of me."

"All the more reason for you to get checked out," Pearl said. "We're tackling two big cases at the same time, and you need to be at your best. I'll do what I can, but stuck in a wheelchair I can't offer you the best backup. Chris here is great at what he does and he adds a lot to the team, but he's still learning and still a boy. And the rest of the team, good as they are, look to you to lead the way."

"There's nothing to worry about on that score," I said. "I can handle it. The way you're talking, might as well be me sitting in that chair instead of you."

"I heard you come back from your run the other morning," Pearl said. "You were gasping for air."

"That's because I had just run seven miles," I said. "And, in case you hadn't noticed, it's hot and humid out. That takes a lot out of you, no matter what shape your lungs are in."

"All the same, it would make me happy to have Cantor give you the once-over," Pearl said. "Give me peace of mind."

I glanced at Chris and could see the concern etched on his face. "Okay," I said. "When the nurse calls your name, I'll ask if he has time to take me, as well. If he does, I'll chuck the clothes and put on that silly gown they give you and let him have at it."

"Fair enough," Pearl said, giving Chris a wink and a smile.

"Now that we got that out of the way, how about we talk about where we are on these two jobs," I said. "Unless you want me to check in with my dentist before the day is done."

"This new guy, Gregson, seems to know his business," Pearl said. "He's been working the computers with Chris here, and they're finding a lot of open lanes on the accounting firm. These guys spend their days and nights moving money from one place to another. Makes it hard to keep track and shows why no one has nabbed them at it. At least not just yet."

"With Carmine handing them some cash to invest, we'll be able to get a clearer picture of how they operate," I said. "I'm not as worried about that part of it."

"Which part does worry you?"

"These guys are hooked up, Pearl," I said. "They can hide it all they want behind the white-shoe firm with the fancy office. But they do serious business with the Russians, the cartels, some of the Italian crews. Toss on top of them the Wall Street high-rollers and some politicians with deep pockets, and you're looking at a group of people who will not let anyone get in the way of their profits."

"Which means the firm must have a team of their own set aside to deal with anyone that starts casting a curious eye into their business," Pearl said. "I mean beyond big-league law firms and high-powered PR agencies."

I nodded. "They got a fixer, for sure," I said, "and, on top of that, a crew that gets paid to do their dirty work. Whether they farm these guys out from the mob or the cartels or whether they recruited them on their own, we don't know. But they are out there, and soon as they get a sniff of us going after them, they'll start looking our way."

I glanced over at Chris and saw him hanging on our every word. "It looks like we're going to be here for a while longer," I said to him. "The doc must be running late. You want to grab yourself a soda and a snack?"

Chris shook his head. "These people killed my mom and dad," he said in a low voice. "And I need to know as much about them as you do. And the more I know, the more I can pass on to Bobby, and together we can dig up what we can from our end."

"If they got coverage to go with all that cash," Pearl said, "then we're going to need more than the current crew. We need to go deeper, a lot deeper, if we're going to take these vipers down."

I nodded. "And let's not forget Eddie Kenwood," I said. "He's got some muscle on his end, as well."

"How much cover can the U.S. Attorney give?" Pearl asked.

"In court, if we give her enough to hang both Kenwood's team and the accounting firm, she will nail their ass to heavy prison sentences. But out on the street, she's limited."

"And the chief?" Chris asked.

"He will help as much as he can," I said. "Especially when it comes to fingering the dirty badges and come takedown time. The rest is up to us."

"Which leaves us with who?" Pearl asked.

I took a deep breath and sat back in my chair. "Alban," I said. "Alexandra's cousin. He's got the manpower and the means. And he's not afraid to go after anybody that stands in his way."

"Reaching out for a guy like Alban is going to cost plenty," Pearl said. "His crew can fight, no doubt about it. And they are fearless. But at the end of the day, they expect to leave the battlefield with full pockets."

"Then we'll make sure they do," I said. "That accounting firm has got lots of money stashed. We'll help the feds take down as much of it as we can. But if at the end of the day we come up short a few million here or there, who's going to complain?"

"Sounds like a good enough idea," Pearl said. "Plus, combined with whoever the chief and Carmine bring into the mix, it gives us a lot more firepower. But what makes you so sure Alban will come in on it with us?"

"Because it won't just be business with him," I said. "It will be personal, and when it hits that stage with a guy like Alban, there's only one thing to do."

"What?" Pearl asked.

"Stand back and let the blood flow," I said.

30.

TRAMONTI'S

Bobby Gregson sat across from me, both of us nursing large cups of cappuccino. "I haven't been here in the longest time," Bobby said. "Not since I was . . ."

"Dating Connie," I said.

"Is that what this is about?" Bobby asked. "This is why you asked to see me? To talk to me about Connie?"

"That was one reason," I said. "What went on back then between the two of you, that stays between the two of you."

"That's very kind of you," Bobby said.

"But I'm in her life now and she's in mine," I said. "I just want to make sure our working together doesn't complicate that."

"I don't see why it would," Bobby said. "I'm here to do a job—one I didn't ask for, by the way. And if I wanted to make time to see Connie, I wouldn't need an assignment to help me do that. A dinner reservation would have done the trick."

"She still likes you," I said. "And it wouldn't be a stretch to figure you feel the same way. And no one ever forgets their first love. The one you let get away stays with you forever."

Bobby sipped his coffee and shrugged. "Who says I'm the one who let her get away?" he asked.

"You tell me," I said.

"Connie was a good friend to me," Bobby said. "I didn't have many of those back then, not with working a full-time job and going to law school. It was nice to sit with her late at night in an empty diner and be able to forget about work and school, for a few hours at least. She was easy to talk to and even easier to like. And maybe if I were smarter and not as focused on the work, I would have made a move to take it to the next step. But I wasn't and I didn't."

"What about now?" I asked.

Bobby smiled. "I'm here to work with you, Tank," he said. "Bring down a firm that deserves to be brought down. But I'm not going to hide from Connie just because she's seeing you. She wants to talk to me, we'll talk. She wants to have a cup of coffee, that's what we'll do, just like I'm doing with you. I'm not going to hide. If that doesn't sit right with you, then that's something you're going to have to learn to live with."

I stared at Bobby for a few moments. My hands were wrapped around my large coffee mug and I struggled to keep a lid on my temper. "You want to have coffee with her, that's fine by me. You want to talk over old times, again not a problem. That I can live with. But you making a move on Connie won't be something I will just let happen."

"I have no plans for it to head in that direction," Bobby said. "But if something like that were to happen, I would think Connie deserves to have as much say in the matter as either one of us."

"That's right," I said. "She would."

"How about we focus on the case in front of us for now?" Bobby said. "The sooner it gets resolved, the sooner I get out of your hair. Fair enough?"

Carmine came up behind me and Bobby, signaling to a passing waitress for three more cappuccinos. He slid in the booth next to me and across from Bobby. "I miss anything?" he asked.

"Just shootin' the shit," I said. "Getting to know a little bit about Bobby here."

"Looks like it went well," Carmine said. "I don't see any guns on the table and there aren't any bloodstains on the floor."

I waited as the waitress brought three fresh cappuccinos and rested them in front of us. She took away the two empty cups. "I'm going to see Dee Dee tomorrow," I said.

I was eager to shift the conversation back to work. The talk with Bobby had rattled me. I wasn't quite sure if that was his intent or if he was seriously looking to reconnect with Connie. I knew I could trust him working on the team. Dee Dee wouldn't have sent him my way if there was any doubt to that fact. But to suddenly have a potential suitor for Connie unnerved me a bit. I knew she loved me as much as I loved her. But, still, his presence left me with an uneasy feeling. And that was something I had never experienced when it came to me and Connie.

"See her about what?" Carmine asked.

"She's going to give me the money for you to open your account with the firm."

"Finally, I get to play with tax dollars," Carmine said.

"It's enough to get you started, and then it's up to you to sell them the idea that this is a drop of what you plan to bring their way," I said to him. "They have to believe you're going to be a mob rainmaker. They'll be holding six figures but need to be leaving the meeting seeing seven."

"I've called around since I met with Randolph," Carmine said. "They got some mob money tied in to their firm already. Mostly East Coast and down South."

"Anybody you know?" Bobby asked.

"*Everybody* I know," Carmine said. "But there's still a few more out there with plenty of cash to invest. Don't worry. I know how to sing songs guys like these accountants like to hear."

I looked at Bobby. "I'm also going to let Dee Dee know I'll be reaching out to some people for help on this case and on another one I'm working. Figured I should also tell you, make sure you're aware and are on board with it."

"I imagine some of these people have criminal records," Bobby said.

"Not some," I said. "All of them."

"Such as?"

"Well, I guess you figured out by now, Carmine's old running pals aren't recruits from a seminary," I said. "The firm knows the players out there as well as we do. We can't be bringing in ringers. They have to be the real deal."

Bobby nodded. "Makes sense," he said. "Old-timers with a lot of money angling for a fresh place to put it. And any name Carmine brings in they don't know, they can run by some of their other mob investors."

"Exactly," I said. "You couldn't do this working out of the U.S. Attorney's office. Too many hurdles to jump over. But with us you can. Gives us instant credibility, and the more cash we flash and the more clients Carmine brings in, the deeper we can get into their business. That'll mostly fall on your shoulders. So you need to work closely with Carmine and his associates."

"Now, my guys are not going to be doing backflips when they hear one of the team is an active federal agent," Carmine said. "It was hard enough to convince them to trust Tank, and him they knew. You they don't."

"To make it easier, I'm going to ask Dee Dee to give anyone we bring in blanket immunity," I said. "Are you good with that?"

"That's up to Dee Dee," Bobby said. "But Carmine's crew has been on the sidelines for a while now. Most are either retired or tied up in legit businesses. I don't see a problem giving them a pass."

"It's not just Carmine's buddies I'm reaching out to for help," I said.

"Who else, then?"

"Alban and his crew," I said.

Bobby pushed aside his cappuccino cup and leaned in closer to me and Carmine. "Are you fuckin' serious?" he asked. "Those guys will slit your throat if you look at them funny. They steal everything they have, they work cons and hustles in every borough of the city, and if you pay them enough they'll kill anybody you want. Now, tell me, Tank, why the fuck do we need them on our side? And why the hell would Dee Dee or the chief consider giving these guys immunity?"

"You've been dancing around these accountants for well over a year," I said. "And you're not any closer to sniffing an indictment. We're going to go in and not only try to pin a murder on them, we're going to bring their entire operation crumbling to the ground. They're not going to roll over and let that happen. They'll come at us just as heavy. And they're not going to be sweet and gentle about it."

"Which means what?" Bobby asked. "You bring in a team of lifters and thieves to help you out? From what I know about Alban and his gang, they don't lift a finger unless there is something coming back their way. And if you ask me, immunity isn't what they're going to be looking for."

"Immunity and twenty percent of the dough we confiscate gets handed over to Alban," I said. "It may not be enough to bring him to our side of the table, but it will get the conversation started."

Bobby sat back, took a deep breath, and stayed silent for several moments. "This is a lot to take in," he finally said. "I need some time to think it all out."

"Fair enough," I said. "You got a lot more at stake than either me or Carmine. You're still on the job and moving up the ladder at a rapid pace. Coming in with guys like us is risky. I'm out to bring the ones who killed my brother and his wife down. And I'm not particular about how I get it done. It's not the same for you. You work on this and it comes out right, you score quite a few points in the Southern District. But if it goes south and word gets out about how we operated, then your elevator ride will come to a screeching halt. You're right to take some time before you jump in."

"You want to see these guys go out of business, am I right?" Carmine asked. "You've been trying it your way, the legal way, and that will work eventually. But it will take years and frustrate the shit out of you. These guys are always moving three steps forward for every two you take. Our way may not work, but if it does, they'll come crashing down in a week, maybe two tops. And you'll have your page-one bust."

"Along with a heavy body count," Bobby said. "There are never any winners when you have that to consider."

"That's where you're wrong, Bobby," Carmine said. "There's always a winner with that kind of brawl."

"Yeah, tell me who."

"The ones still alive," I said. "They take home the gold."

31.

RIVERBANK STATE PARK

THE NEXT DAY

I STOOD NEXT TO PEARL, BOTH OF US LOOKING OUT AT THE twenty-five-yard pool at 140th Street in Harlem. Just beyond the pool, the large expanse of the Hudson River and the New Jersey piers and high-rises were visible in the distance. The pool was packed, a perfect place to ward off the onslaught of the August heat wave the city was grinding its way through.

"You sure he'll show?" Pearl asked. "J.J. could be playing us. Doing his best to balance the ball between us and Kenwood."

"I don't think J.J. would lie about something like this," I said. "He knows we knew Boyd from when we worked in the sector years ago. Besides, he didn't give up much. All he told us is Boyd was one of Kenwood's stoolies back when he was on the job. Tossing name after name at Kenwood is what kept him out of jail."

"But then he gives Kenwood a name that doesn't map out the way he planned," Pearl said. "And next thing old Boyd knows is Kenwood sends him away for a ten-year stretch on the one crime he probably didn't commit."

"It was a harsh lesson learned by Boyd, for sure," I said. "But not one that was lost on Livingstone, either."

Billy "Little Napoleon" Boyd was a hardcore criminal. He mugged and shot his way from Washington Heights to Harlem and even ventured into Brooklyn terrain belonging to other gangs, always on the lookout for a score and a target to take down. He began his life of crime just out of his teens and, despite a few stints in prison, never sought another way of life. He was protected for years by Eddie Kenwood, feeding him information that led to arrests that helped pad the gold-shield detective's résumé. Then Billy pointed a finger at the wrong target, a criminal protected by another corrupt badge. That brought an end to the arrangement.

He came onto our radar last night, after J.J. overheard Kenwood and a few friends talking at one of the tables at the club where he worked. One of the men mentioned Boyd's name in relation to the Randy Jenkins case and was quickly shut down by Kenwood. "Change the subject," Kenwood told the man. "The guy convicted of that murder is in jail, right? Let it rest where it is."

We spotted Boyd walking at the other end of the pool, checking out the action, clearly on the prowl for business. He was older than I remembered and a bit thicker around the middle. But he still had that street swagger, a short, now middle-aged man trolling the dark side of a doomed life.

I grabbed the handles of Pearl's wheelchair and we eased our way in Boyd's direction. He was gazing down at two teenagers lounging by the edges of the pool as we approached. "Looks to me like the real Napoleon got the better deal," Pearl said as Boyd turned our way. "He went from Paris to the island of Elba. You, on the other hand, moved from prison to our little island here by the river."

"I never did quite understand why they called you Napoleon," I said. "I get the 'Little' part—you're both short enough to be the last ones to know when it's raining. But that guy ran a country. All you did was run against the law."

"How I got the name is my business," Boyd said. "As is everything else I do. We got nothing to talk about, assuming it's talk that brought your asses out here."

"I am glad to see the passage of time hasn't mellowed you out, Little Nap," Pearl said.

"How about we let the kids have the pool and we step away and have ourselves a little chat?" I said.

"And what do I need to talk to you two losers about?" Boyd asked. "It ain't like you're on the job anymore. Not unless NYPD is short on cops in wheelchairs."

"Randy Jenkins," I said. "We're here to ask you about Randy Jenkins and the murder he didn't commit."

We both caught the look in Boyd's eyes. They flickered and darted from one face to the other, sweat starting to form on the top of his lip and on his forehead. He clenched and unclenched his hands, and he bounced up and down on his legs like he was about to shoot a free throw. "That name don't mean shit to me," he managed to say.

I moved away from Pearl's wheelchair and closer to Boyd. The concrete was wet and slippery from the water splashing out of the pool. "Think harder," I said. "You lived in the same neighborhood. The same playgrounds. Might have bumped into each other here and there."

"And maybe it was you that flagged his name for your boy Eddie Kenwood," Pearl said. "That was what you did back then, right? Gave up names to Kenwood in order to keep your tiny little ass out of jail."

"Kenwood didn't care who killed Rachel," I said. "All he wanted was a signed confession, didn't matter to him whose name was on it. And that's all you needed to give him—a name."

"You two must be smoking that new brand of shit been making the rounds," Boyd said. "If that's all you came to talk to me about, you might as well turn around and take your crazy talk somewhere else. It ain't working here."

"You had a rep yourself for being rough with the ladies," I said. "Or am I wrong?"

"Maybe you tried a run at Rachel and got turned away," Pearl said.

"Pearl's got a point," I said. "Low-expectation little dick like you walks around making like he's Denzel, can't help but bring a chuckle instead of a moan to any woman."

"Guys like you have to pay or get nasty to get close to a woman," Pearl said.

Boyd lifted his balled hands and stepped closer to Pearl, his eyes bulging, body taut with tension. "You crippled son of a bitch," he said. "One more word and I'll toss your wrinkled ass into the pool. Watch you drown with them dead legs of yours."

Pearl smiled. "Come and give it a shot, Napoleon," he said. "I'll put fifty to your one that I'll have your neck snapped before you even lift me from this chair."

"And in case Pearl's off his game," I said, "count on me to finish what he started."

Boyd kept his place, his anger still at full boil, casting a glance at the crowded pool. He took a deep breath and backed away from Pearl. "I'm done with you both," he said. "You've taken up enough of my time."

"You run back now and let Kenwood know we're on the hunt," I said. "And we're not only going to nab Rachel's real killer. We're going to do one better."

Boyd swallowed and looked at both me and Pearl. "What would that be?"

"We're going to nail Kenwood and any badge, off or on the job, that went in with him," Pearl said.

"You get all that?" I asked. "Or you need me to write it down for you?"

Boyd nodded. "I got it, Tin Badge," he said. "And I'll pass it on. Kenwood likes to have a good laugh."

I walked up to Boyd and smiled. "One more question," I said, "before me and Pearl let you get on with whatever sorry business you need to attend to."

"Make it a fast one," Boyd said.

"Can you swim?" I asked.

Before he could answer, I grabbed Boyd by the collar and the top of his jeans and dragged him toward the edge of the pool. The move took him by surprise and brought all pool activity to a halt. Soon as I had him close enough, I tossed him in. I walked back over to Pearl and we both watched as Boyd kicked and slapped his way from the deep end over to the closest edge, gripping the side with both hands. He glared at us, breathing heavy and coughing out spurts of water.

"Well, guess we learned something with this little visit," Pearl said.

"What's that?" I asked.

"Napoleon can't swim," Pearl said.

32.

U.S. ATTORNEY'S OFFICE, SOUTHERN DISTRICT

THAT SAME DAY

I DECIDED TO BRING CHRIS WITH ME FOR MY MEETING WITH Dee Dee Jacobs. He was the primary reason I'd chosen to go after the accounting firm, and I thought it was important for the two to meet. Chris was more than just my nephew. He was now a valuable member of my team. He could travel the dark zones of the Web with skill, unhindered by firewalls and security locks, doing a deep dive into files thought to be securely sealed. He didn't work alone. He was part of a nationwide network of like-minded teenagers, each spending countless hours looking to solve cold cases or bring attention to situations that would eventually require legal intervention. They modeled themselves after the Vidocq Society, a group of professionals from various fields formed some decades back, who worked together to try to solve long-neglected crimes.

Chris was also a victim.

All the evidence suggested his parents were murdered by the firm, and I thought it only right that Dee Dee have the chance to put at least one face to the many crimes committed by the accountants I was looking to bring down. I was asking her to extend beyond the boundaries of her office, actions that could cost her the position she had worked so hard to earn if I failed to prove my case or broke the law in the attempt, and I wanted her to know it was worth it.

"I see you brought along a bodyguard," Dee Dee said, smiling at both me and Chris as she stepped from behind her desk when we entered her office. "And a young one at that."

"This is Chris," I said, introducing them. "My nephew. Jack's son."

Dee Dee put out a hand and Chris shook it. She held on to his hand and looked at him. "I'm very sorry about what happened to your parents," she said. "We're doing all we can to get to the facts of the matter and, if they prove out, put the guilty ones where they belong. In jail."

Chris nodded. "The facts prove out," he said in a strong voice. "They killed my parents. Thank you for the help you're giving us. It means a lot to me."

Dee Dee let go of the handshake, looked at me, and then moved back behind her desk. "Has Bobby been a help?" she asked as she sat down.

"You mean Connie's old boyfriend?" I said with a smile. "He's been working with Chris mostly, doing a tight money trail. I figure he's sent you daily reports on what they've uncovered."

"He has," Dee Dee said. "But, like with any good agent or cop, what he doesn't say interests me as much as what he puts in a report."

"I'll let Chris fill you in on that," I said. "But first I have to ask you a huge favor. And if, in any way, you feel it will compromise you or your office, then say no. There'll be no hard feelings."

"Let me see if I can guess," Dee Dee said. "I already put in the request for Carmine's front money. That gets you an inside man."

"It's money worth lending," I said, giving her a smile. "One hundred and fifty thousand in cash is more than enough to get the ball rolling."

"Handed over to a onetime crime boss," Dee Dee said.

"These guys are primed to be on the lookout for an undercover. Carmine's old school, and that gives him cover and offers them comfort."

"And he wants to bring these guys down," Chris said. "Carmine says they're the kind of thieves that give criminals a bad rap."

Dee Dee couldn't hold back a laugh. "I never thought he and I would agree on anything, but he does have a point. These guys think just because they're wearing Brooks Brothers suits and eating at private clubs that they stand apart from most criminals. That they can hide behind the façade they've built. And those are the ones I hate the most. The ones who hide their true intent by wearing a mask of civility."

"I figure no one in your office knows who you're handing over that amount of cash to," I said. "Other than you and Bobby."

"It's an undercover operation, and I don't need to disclose the name of the one going deep," Dee Dee said. "But I better get the cash back, one way or another."

Dee Dee got up from her chair and walked to a small fridge, opened it, and pulled out three bottles of Snapple iced tea. She handed one to me, one to Chris, and then went back behind her desk. "Didn't think either of you wanted coffee," she said. "And that's all I keep in the fridge."

"I wouldn't have minded a coffee," I said.

"Drink your tea," Dee Dee said, giving Chris a smile and a nod. "And let me hear about this favor."

"This firm will be sending heavy hitters my way," I said. "It puts my team and me in jeopardy. Now, we can handle a few, but not a full onslaught if it comes to that. So I need to bring in some of our own."

"Your own what?" Dee Dee asked.

"Guys who can help take down whatever gets sent our way," I said. "Some of them will be from Carmine's old ranks. They can be a help, no doubt, but I was looking for more. Younger, stronger, and dangerous."

"Which leaves us where?"

"With Alban," I said.

Dee Dee looked at me for a few moments and then sat back in her chair. "It's a major risk," she said. "You get Alban and his band involved and there will be bloodshed. A lot of it."

"There's going to be bloodshed whether they're in it or not," I said.

"Has he agreed to help?"

"I'm meeting with him soon," I said. "Wanted to run it by you first."

"If they go in—and there's no guarantee they will—it will cost money," Dee Dee said. "Alban doesn't make any move that doesn't end with cash in his pockets."

"Anything he gets comes out of the firm's dirty stash," I said. "That is part of the offer. But only one part."

"What's the other part?"

"You know a family member is part of my crew," I said.

Dee Dee nodded. "The psychic," she said. "She helped you take down that dealer a few months back."

"That she did," I said. "Brought in some of her friends and relatives and they did some major damage."

"But she didn't bring in Alban and all he comes with," Dee Dee said.

"She didn't need them then," I said. "But we need them now."

"And you think she can convince him?"

"She needs to tell him a story," I said. "That will convince him."

"What kind of story?" Dee Dee asked.

"My mom and dad weren't the first people these guys have had killed," Chris said. "They've killed a lot of people, hurt a lot of people."

"Give me an example," Dee Dee said.

"Two years ago, a woman named Sasha Buttera was found in an alley in Lower Manhattan," I said. "She'd been raped, beaten, and left for dead. It was one of those stories that gets buried in the Metro section of the *Times* and is a page-one tabloid story for a day, maybe two."

"I remember reading about it," Dee Dee said. "A few leads, a few suspects, no arrests. The girl lived, as I recall."

"If you call it living," I said. "She's home, with her parents, needs full-time medical supervision. She doesn't remember much about the night, only that she was working at an early holiday party and left when things were starting to wind down. Her supervisor told her she could leave, that they would handle the cleanup."

"She was followed out of the party by a man, an older man. He rode down with her in the elevator," Chris said. "He wished her a great holiday when they got out of the building."

"That was so nothing suspicious would pop up on any surveillance cameras the building might have in place," I said.

"The cops still would have questioned him," Dee Dee said.

"They did and came away with nothing more than a guy leaving a party same time as Sasha," I said. "She headed in one direction. He walked off in another."

"But you don't think that's how it ended?"

"I think he doubled back and followed her," I said. "The streets down this part of the city are dark at night—you can't even see shadows, let alone someone walking close behind you. I think he dragged her into one of the alleys on a side street, attacked her, and left her there to die."

"Two days after the girl was found, one of the partners at the firm of Curtis, Strassman, and Randolph left the country," Chris said. "He worked out of their London office for three months."

"Which partner?" Dee Dee asked.

"Strassman," Chris said.

"How does he connect to the girl?"

"The apartment where the party was held is a condo owned by an LLC based in the Channel Islands," I said. "A place that, as you know, is famous for laundering money."

"The LLC is in the name of a real estate executive in Nevada," Chris said. "That, in turn, is owned by a banker in St. Louis."

"Peel the onion for me," Dee Dee said.

"Go back far enough, which is what me and Bobby did, and the condo is owned outright by Curtis, Strassman, and Randolph," Chris said.

"How do you know Strassman was at the party?" Dee Dee asked.

"The condo is used only for business and party purposes," I said.

"That night's event was for junior associates, secretaries, and interns. One of the partners is required to attend. That night it was Strassman's turn."

"And Sasha Buttera was working as a waitress for the catering firm hired to serve food and drinks at the party," Chris said.

"And what makes you so sure Strassman was the one who raped and beat Sasha?" Dee Dee asked.

"Strassman has a drinking problem," I said. "He's had three DUIs in the last six years. And he thinks of himself as a ladies' man. A rough kind of ladies' man. A deep dive into his background does not paint a pretty picture."

"And the only thing Sasha does remember is an old man grabbing her from behind and dragging her into an alley," Chris said.

"Would you call Strassman an old man?" Dee Dee asked.

"I wouldn't call him young," I said.

"And how does Alban fit into all this?" Dee Dee asked.

I leaned in closer, resting my Snapple on Dee Dee's desk. "Sasha is Alban's wife's sister," I said. "He'll want money to step into this skirmish, you're right on that score. That he'll take from the firm. He'll also want their blood. It might make him a nightmare for you. But it makes him a perfect partner to have on my side."

33.

INWOOD HILL PARK

LATER THAT NIGHT

EDDIE KENWOOD LEANED AGAINST THE SIDE OF A LARGE OAK tree, hands thrust inside the pockets of a worn pair of blue jeans. He watched quietly as three men in dark clothing dragged a bloodied and beaten J. J. Livingstone closer to him. They were just off the park entrance on West 215th Street and Indian Road. It was dark and the park was deserted, the lights from the street shrouded by the thick leaves from the many low-hanging branches that circled the area.

Inwood Hill Park is where, according to city legend, Peter Minuit purchased Manhattan Island from Native Americans for an armful of trinkets and beads. It is also said to be the last remaining primeval forest on the island. But neither of those factors mattered much on this night.

"Lift him up," Kenwood said to the three men, "and rest him against the tree. The two of us need to have a little chat."

J.J. was hoisted, and his large body was slammed against the side of a massive tulip poplar tree. One of his eyes was swollen, and blood streaked down the sides of his face. His right hand was broken and dangled by his side. His left arm hung at an angle. He had trouble breathing, his nostrils crusted with dried blood, and both lips were swollen. Eddie Kenwood walked over to him and stood inches from his battered face.

"You got caught, J.J.," Kenwood said. "That's what happened. You tried playing one side against the other and you got caught. All this time, all these years, I figured you were one of the ones I could trust, and then you go out and burn me."

"I don't know who's been filling your head with that bullshit," Livingstone managed to say, blood spurting out of his mouth as he spoke. "I'm not playing on any side but yours."

Kenwood shook his head. "That's not what they're saying on the street, J.J. They're saying you're playing ball with Tank and Pearl. If that's true, it puts you up against me."

"I wouldn't play you that way," J.J. said.

"But you did talk to Tank," Kenwood said. "Or is that part bullshit, too?"

"He came to talk to me," J.J. said. "Stopped and asked a few questions. None of them had to do with you."

"Who did they have to do with?" Kenwood asked.

"That kid from back in the day," J.J. said. "Randy Jenkins. The guy they said killed Rachel."

"The same guy Tank is looking to set free," Kenwood said. "He knew you and Jenkins used to run together?"

"That ain't no secret," J.J. said. "We was from the same neighborhood, same street. Who else you gonna run with other than the ones you know? That don't mean I knew jack shit about what happened that night."

"If Tank knew you were running pals, then he also put two and two together and figured you had the hots for Randy's squeeze," Kenwood said. "The girl he killed."

"I knew her, that much he could zone out on his own," J.J. said. "But there wasn't no love between me and Rachel. She was with Randy. At least some of the time. You don't mess with another man's lady. No matter how you might feel about her. You keep that shit to yourself."

"Then how does Tank move from you to Little Napoleon, do you figure?"

"Tank and Pearl were cops," J.J. said. "Like you. Doesn't take much to piece us all together. And if they couldn't, maybe one of their street connections pointed them in his direction. It sure as shit wasn't me. I swear it to you, Eddie."

Kenwood nodded and stepped away from J.J. "I would like to believe you," he said, glancing at the three men waiting off to the side. "I really would. It would make it so much easier if I could. But I have to be honest. The fact is, I don't. Sorry to say, J.J., but that's really bad news for you."

"I've been true to you all these years," J.J. pleaded. "Why would I go and turn you out now? I don't owe Tank and Pearl. They haven't done shit for me. But you have. You covered for me, got me a job, and put me on your roll. And I earned the cash you sent my way. My information was tight, that you have to admit."

Kenwood glanced at J.J. and smiled. "That is on the money, no doubt. If it weren't, you would have been long gone by now. I would have pinned a homicide on your ass faster than you could flex a muscle. But it still doesn't mean you aren't double-dipping, collecting from both me and Tank in return for telling what you know and hear."

"I'm on your side with this shit that's about to go down," J.J. said. He smelled an opening, a last chance at a way out, a long shot at making it to another day.

"Do you know, J.J., what will happen to you if one word of that turns out to be smoke?" Kenwood said.

"Bet your ass I do," J.J. said. "And I'm not playing you. No way I even think of going down that street. What I said, I mean."

Kenwood walked around, head down, hands still in his pockets. The three men stood nearby, arms folded across their chests, awaiting instructions. Kenwood stopped, turned, and moved closer to J.J. "I think I figured a way you could prove it to me," he said. "It would show me whose side you're really on. If you're up to it, that is."

"Anything, man," J.J. said. "Just name it."

"I mean, the fastest way would be for my three amigos here to drag your ass to their warehouse and drop you into a vat of acid," Kenwood said. "That gets you out of my hair and me out of yours quick, easy, and—for me, at least—painless. The other option is a bit more complicated and I would need to set you free, give you the time and space to get it done."

"Just tell me what it is," J.J. said, his voice cracking from strain and fear. "I swear to you, whatever it is, it will get done."

"Are you sure, J.J.?" Kenwood asked.

"A hundred and fifty percent," J.J. said.

"But you don't even know what it is I'm going to want you to do," Kenwood said. "How can you be that certain you'll get it done?"

J.J. swallowed hard and looked straight at Kenwood. "I'll do anything for you," he said. "Anything."

Kenwood stayed silent for several moments and then nodded. "All right, then, J.J.," he said. "I'm going to go out on a limb and trust you. I'm going to give you a chance to prove yourself to me. A final chance."

"Great," J.J. said. "That's great to hear. Now, tell me, what do you need me to do?"

"I want you to kill Tank and Pearl," Kenwood said.

J.J.'s eyes were moist from the heat and the beating, and his body tensed when he heard Kenwood's request. He kept his focus and tried to maintain some form of composure.

"I saw a little hesitation there, J.J.," Kenwood said. "If you're not up to it, no worries. We'll go the other way, be easier on everybody."

"No," J.J. managed to say. "I'll get it done."

"Get what done?" Kenwood asked. "I want to hear it from your lips."

"I'm going to kill Tank Rizzo and Pearl Monroe," J.J. said, the words coming out in a rush.

"Plan it out the right way, think it out before you move on it," Kenwood said. "I got a surprise in store for my old pal Tank, and I want to lay that on him before you go and take him and his crippled pal out."

"What sort of surprise?" J.J. asked.

"One that will rock Tank's world," Kenwood said. "One that's going to rip him apart and show everyone who he really is."

"But you still want me to kill him, right?" J.J. asked.

"You bet your ass I do," Kenwood said. "And after I hit him with my news, he'll probably welcome the bullet."

"So, I wait on you," J.J. said. "I'll scope the job out and then sit back until you give the word."

Kenwood nodded. "We'll be on our way. Wait ten minutes and then move your ass out of here, as well. You got important work you need to get started on."

"I won't let you down," J.J. said.

Kenwood looked at J.J. and shrugged. "It doesn't matter to me either way. If you kill them, you get to live. If you don't, you die in their place. It's a win-win for me."

J.J. stood against the tree and watched Kenwood and his three accomplices disappear into the darkness of the surrounding woods. He closed his eyes and lowered his head. "Win-win for you," he whispered to himself. "But a lose-lose for me."

34.

SEVENTY-SECOND STREET
IRT STATION

ALBAN LOOKED OUT AT THE SUBWAY TRACKS AS WE APPROACHED. He was wearing dark glasses and had a German shepherd by his side, the handle of the leash resting casually in his right hand. I walked between Chris and Alexandra, checking out the few passengers awaiting the next downtown train. It was late in the morning and rush hour had long since faded. Alban stood with his back against a poster of an upcoming Denzel Washington movie, hands at his side, his massive and muscular body relaxed and at ease. He was in his late forties and had been running his crew going on two decades now, having replaced his father in the leadership role.

They made a chunk of their money out of the many psychic parlors found throughout the city. The rest they earned through theft and scams. They were the finest pickpockets to be found and cleared a good five thousand dollars a week lifting wallets and purses. Alban owned at least three dozen chop shops in Queens and Brooklyn and parts of Nassau County, where a dozen cars a day were lifted off the streets, stripped bare, and then crushed into storage metal. The parts would then be sold off for cash, good for a total yearly six-figure haul for his crew.

They lived by a code of silence and secrecy. It is difficult to determine how many members of the gang there are. I've heard as many as
six hundred and as few as a hundred working out of New York City
alone. There are hundreds of members in every major city in the States
and hundreds more spread throughout Europe, as well. And they are
all, men and women, among the deadliest fighters anyone could encounter, a sharp blade their weapon of choice. "Nobody, and I mean
nobody, is better with a knife than Alban's bunch," Carmine once told
me. "The Sardinians are a close second, but even they would take a step
back. It would be one of the only times I would bet on a knife over a
gun."

I had worked with a few of them some months back. Alexandra
recruited a handful to help me take down a major Washington Heights
drug dealer. They were fearless and were often hired out to help settle
gang disputes. In return, they would be given a piece of the winner's
street action and free rein to work on his turf.

They kept a low profile, living on the outer edges of the city's five
boroughs. They worked under a blanket of darkness and anonymity.
There was nothing they wouldn't do for money, but they always kept
their word and never betrayed a trust.

I had known Alban for many years, going back to before I became
a cop. He started hanging around the neighborhood when we were
both still in our teens, even though I knew he didn't live anywhere near
there. His aunt ran a psychic parlor a few blocks from where I lived,
and his father sent Alban there in the late afternoons to help clean up
and then get her home safe. He usually had some free time, since his
aunt liked to keep the parlor open late, and he often made his way to
the playground, watching us playing either basketball or softball. He
always stood on the other side of the fence and never once asked if he
could join in. The other kids in the neighborhood ignored or shunned
him.

We were in the middle of a pickup basketball game one late-
summer afternoon when one of the guys my friends and I were up
against started making cracks at Alban. "Watch your pocket money,"

he said, sneering over at Alban. "First chance this bastard gets, he'll rob you clean."

"Focus on the game," I said.

"My dad told me if you look into a gypsy's eyes long enough, he'll steal your soul," another kid said.

"My soul he can have," the first kid said, bouncing the ball and edging closer toward Alban. He stayed quiet, standing on the other side of the fence, his dark eyes taking it all in without the slightest show of emotion. "My money is a whole other issue."

"He's not bothering anybody," I said. "He's watching the game. Nothing more."

"You his bodyguard now, Rizzo?" the first kid asked. "Or you just got a thing for gypsies?"

The kid's name was Tony Nanna. He was in his mid-teens like the rest of us, but he fancied himself a tough guy, helped by the fact his father was doing a long stretch in prison for murder. "Your team's down six points," I said. "And we got money riding on how it ends. Now, you want to play it out or not? Get your mind off the gypsy. He's not why you and your friends can't buy a basket."

"He's jinxing us, this bastard," Tony said. "That's why we're not hitting our shots. We were doing fine until he showed up and started staring at us."

Tony tossed the ball against the fence and moved toward Alban. "Ain't that right, gypsy?" he said. "Because of you, we're going to owe these losers money. How about this? Since you're the reason we're losing the game, how about you make good on the bet? Pay them for us and we'll be square."

I stepped in between Tony and Alban, my back resting against the fence. "We didn't make a bet with him," I said. "We made one with you."

"Let him come over," Alban said, speaking for the first time. "Maybe he can fight better than he can shoot a basketball. If he beats me, I'll pay off his bet. If he loses, he gives me all the money in his pockets."

I turned and looked at Alban and smiled. "What's your name?" I asked.

"Alban," he said.

I looked back at Tony. "I'll go in on it," I said. "You beat Alban, we'll each give you five dollars. But if you lose, you pay him *and* you pay us, too."

I glanced over my shoulder at Alban. "That work for you?" I asked him.

"Yes," Alban said.

Tony stood still for several minutes, clenching and unclenching his fists. "You picking a guy like him over us?" Tony said to me. "A stranger over a friend."

"You're not my friend," I said. "I see the way you roughhouse with the younger kids in the yard during recess, pushing them around for no reason. But you know what I've never seen you do?"

"What?" Tony asked.

"Get in a fight with somebody who can stand up to you," I said. "That I've never seen. It sounds like Alban here is giving you a chance to do just that."

"I'm not going to fight just to make you happy," Tony said. "I got better things to do with my time."

"And one of those things is paying up on what you owe," I said.

Tony turned to face me, his eyes looking at the cracked cement around the rim of the basket. "I don't have the money on me," he said. "None of us do."

"You came here looking for a game and it was your idea to put money on it," I said, inching closer to him. "Instead, you played me small, Tony. You played me and my friends small."

"I thought we would beat you," Tony said.

"Great plan," I said. "Too bad it bit you in the ass."

"I'll pay up next time I see you," Tony said. "Give you enough to cover you and your friends."

I stared at Tony and then turned to look at Alban. "What do you think?" I said. "Think he'll keep his word?"

Alban nodded, giving Tony a hard look. "He better," Alban said. "Unless he wants to meet up with me again."

"You hear that, Tony?" I said. "You welch on our bet and Alban here is going to come looking for you to collect and maybe even kick your ass."

"Why's the gypsy care so much?" Tony asked. "What does he get for going out of his way?"

I looked at Alban and he glanced back and smiled. "A friend," he said.

Tony ponied up what he owed two days later. I never played another game of basketball with Tony, but I did make a friend in Alban. The friendship continued even in the years I was a cop and he was taking on more of his father's responsibilities. Me and Pearl never went after his action while we were on the job, and Alban always steered clear of our sector when we were in uniform and plainclothes. Besides, me and Pearl weren't looking to bust pickpockets and fortune-tellers. We went after big game and hardcore criminals who spent their days and nights looking to do serious damage to innocent people.

And Alban was a help to us. He had eyes and ears in every neighborhood in the city. If the information was important, Alban made sure it made its way to us. He also kept his people clear of the drug trade, realizing early on that that end of the business led to an early death or a long prison sentence, neither of which was of any interest to him.

On our off-hours, we would get together occasionally and play chess at one of the downtown parks. Basketball is the prime playground game in New York, but in the dozens of small parks dotting the city streets, hidden amid the noise and the foul smell of bumper-to-bumper traffic, chess games were played round the clock. Men, women, teens, and preteens played for fun, cash, or bragging rights. And when it came to chess, Pearl and Alban were both A-level players.

"It's a game that can make you better at everything you do," Pearl would say. "That's a pure fact. I'll let Alban here tell you why."

"You need to be three moves ahead of your opponent," Alban would say. "Think the way he thinks and be prepared to respond to the moves he's going to make. If you're really good, you'll know his moves even before he does. In your kind of work, that kind of thinking keeps you alive. We always need to know what's coming."

When Chief Connors first called to offer me a chance to work on a case that had been collecting dust, he gave me permission to put together my own team, and the first member me and Pearl chose was Alexandra Morrasa, Alban's cousin. "She's like me," Alban said. "She can be trusted, and she will never let you down. Not ever."

Now I needed his help avenging my brother's death. At the same time, it would allow Alban the opportunity to get justice for his wife's younger sister, Sasha.

That's one other thing, one very important thing, I have in common with Alban: We both have a strong thirst for revenge.

35.

SEVENTY-SECOND STREET IRT STATION

MOMENTS LATER

A LBAN LOOKED AT ME AND SMILED. ALEXANDRA REACHED OVER and gave him a long and warm embrace. Then he looked down at Chris. "And who might this young man be?" he asked me.

"This is Chris," I said. "He's my nephew. And he's the main reason I asked to meet with you."

Alban put out a hand and Chris shook it. Then Chris asked, "Okay if I pet your dog?"

"Nothing would please him more," Alban said. "His name is Zeus."

Chris crouched down on one knee and began rubbing the dog's head and neck. Zeus responded by nudging himself closer to Chris.

"How's the blind-man routine working for you?" I asked Alban. I couldn't help but notice how happy Chris was with Zeus. I hadn't seen that wide a smile on his face since he first came to live with me.

"A blind man with a dog is invisible to most people," Alban said. "Means I can see everything I need to see without being seen. Plus, there's always the occasional kind soul who drops some money in that cup by my feet."

"You must have a hundred ways to turn a buck," I said. "And I'm guessing only a handful are legal."

Alban nodded and smiled. "Most likely that's true," he said. "But you didn't come to see me to pick up tips on how to shake a dollar from a tree. So what can I do for you, Tank?"

"My brother, Jack, worked at an accounting firm," I said. "Curtis, Strassman, and Randolph. He died earlier this year, and that's how Chris here came into my life. My brother and his wife were killed in an auto accident. Or at least that's what the firm would prefer us to believe."

"And you think it goes darker than that?" Alban asked.

"All the way to murder," I said. "Chris is a bit of a crime buff and has a triple-A computer rating. He put most of the pieces together. Enough of them, at any rate, to convince me to look into it."

"What have you found so far?"

"These guys are top-to-bottom dirty," I said. "They come off legit at first glance, but the deeper you dive into their operation, the more you find that accounting is only the tip of a corrupt iceberg. They funnel money for the cartels, hedge funds, drug dealers, pretty much anyone who wants to move cash and stay off the radar."

"And what have you done about it?" Alban asked.

"I brought in the feds, Alban," I said. "Before we go any further, I need you to know that and be comfortable with it. The U.S. Attorney, Dee Dee Jacobs, is a friend. She assigned one of her guys to my team. She's also fronting six figures for me to get someone on the inside to get a firsthand look at their operation."

"Who are you sending in?"

"Tramonti," I said.

"Seems like you have your bases covered," Alban said. "Feds on one end. Carmine and some of his crew on the other. Your team standing in the middle."

"I'm coming to you for two reasons," I said. "They killed my brother and his wife, so they're not afraid to get blood on their hands to keep what they got going. They get a whiff of what I'm up to, they will not hesitate to bring my team down."

"What's the second reason?"

"Coming in with us will give you a chance to get even, too," I said.

Alban removed his glasses and shrugged. "Me?" he asked. "I've got no beef with any accounting firm. We bury our money. We never hand it over to anyone. Especially anyone we don't know or trust."

"This goes deeper than cash," I said. "This one is personal. Just like it is for me."

"How personal?"

"Sasha Buttera," I said. "Your wife's kid sister. She's still under medical care, am I right?"

"Yes," Alban said. "Not that it's doing any good. That young woman will never be the same again. Neither will my wife."

"The apartment she was working in the night of the attack belongs to the accounting firm," I said. "The guy who did damage to her, the one who skipped town, he's a partner in the firm. They got him out of town and covered his tracks."

Alban put his glasses back on and looked out at the arriving subway, watching passengers exit and enter. He waited for the train to pull out of the station and then turned to face me.

"What's your end goal?" he asked.

"Bring the firm down," I said. "Let the feds take the ones they can send away to prison—that'll justify their involvement. Leaves the rest to my crew, Carmine's team, and you and your guys."

"I heard you were working on a case," Alban said. "Trying to get a guy out of prison and bring in the real killer. Which puts your ass up against that dirty cop from a few years back. Guess I heard wrong."

"No, you heard right," I said. "We're on that case, too."

Alban looked at Chris and handed him the dog's leash. "If it's okay with your uncle and you're up to it, would you like to take Zeus for a walk outside?" he asked. "Truth be told, he hates being down here. He likes the street action."

Chris took the leash and glanced at me. "Go ahead," I said. "Alexandra will go with you. When you're done, meet us over by the hotdog place on the corner. We'll catch up with you there."

I leaned against the wall next to Alban and watched Chris, Alexandra, and Zeus walk down the platform and out of the subway station. "Thanks," I said. "That was nice of you. He seems to really like your dog."

"I never trust anyone a dog doesn't like," Alban said. "They can sniff out the bad faster than a hundred cops. But if you're good and on the level, they'll be by your side every step of the way. Sounds like that boy's been through a lot in a short period of time."

"He has," I said. "And now he's knee-deep in a case dealing with the death of his parents. Not exactly the ideal situation for a teenager in mourning."

"You should think about getting him a dog," Alban said. "It might go a long way toward healing his hurt. Would be a good thing for you, too."

"I got Pearl living with me now," I said. "And Chris. Now you want me to add a dog to the mix?"

"Just one more member of the team," Alban said. "Might come in handy. You never know."

"If I promise to get Chris a dog, will that seal our deal?" I asked, smiling.

"They treated Sasha like she wasn't even human," Alban said. "They beat her, raped her, then beat her again. Then left her to die in a filthy alley. That's a debt that cannot go unpaid."

"I know," I said. "We bring them down any way and in every way. You'll get immunity from the U.S. Attorney. They'll go ahead and work it like they work every case. They'll hit these guys with subpoenas and all sorts of legal paperwork. That'll keep them busy for a bit."

"And it shouldn't take Carmine long to figure out where the money goes and how it's sliced up," Alban said.

"Chris and the feds will help on that end," I said. "And my crew will give you anything you need. And if your guys find cash none of us know about, that's your business, not ours."

"What my guys take, they take," Alban said. "But for me, not a nickel do I want. They owe me something more."

"What?"

"The man who damaged Sasha," Alban said. "I don't want the feds to touch him. I don't want Carmine and his boys to do him harm. And I don't want you and Pearl to take him down. He belongs to me. And he will die the way I choose."

I looked at Alban and nodded. "He's all yours, Alban," I said. "And God help him."

" There will be no help coming his way," Alban said. "Not from God or anyone else."

We both turned and walked slowly down the platform, heading out of the subway station. We walked in silence. Two old friends facing another battle.

36.

SECOND CEMETERY OF THE SPANISH AND PORTUGUESE SYNAGOGUE

CARMINE SIPPED FROM A LARGE FRENCH-ROAST COFFEE AND gazed down at a weathered tombstone from another century. "This guy died in the 1800s," he said to the three men standing near him. "Probably was nothing here but woods and cabins back then, I would imagine."

"I'm surprised this cemetery's still here after all this time," one of them said. "You figure some developer would have made a move to buy it and put up a condo or an office building by now."

"Maybe even developers know not to mess with the dead," Carmine said.

He turned to face the three men. Tommy Bustalino stood to his left. He was heavyset, in his mid-fifties, with thick dark hair and a trimmed three-day growth. Frank Siminaci was in the middle. He was the oldest of the group, in his seventies, trim and wearing a cotton jacket, tailored slacks, and black loafers. Carlo Ramini was on Carmine's right. He was decked out in new workout clothes, from windbreaker down to white Nike sneakers. Carmine had known them for decades and was partnered with them on several of their numerous legitimate businesses. They were old-school mobsters, smart enough to make loads of money and even smarter about keeping it from prying eyes. They were now senior citizens or close enough to it, allowing them the luxury to sit back and enjoy the benefits of a life devoted to criminal activities. Of the four, only Tommy had done prison time, a three-year stretch for loan-sharking when he was in his early twenties.

"Tell me you didn't drag me away from my bocce game to look at some old headstones," Frank said to Carmine. "I'm going to be planted under one of these soon enough. I don't need a reminder."

"You're like that old pasta pot no one throws out, Frank," Carmine said. "You'll be the last one of us to go."

"Why are we here, Carmine?" Tommy asked.

"I need you to reach out to a few of our friends," Carmine said. "Specifically, the ones you may know have some of their money invested in an accounting outfit name of Curtis, Strassman, and Randolph."

"Why them in particular?" Carlo asked.

"I hear they might be skimming money off the profits," Carmine said. "Taking advantage of some of our friends."

"But you don't know for sure," Tommy said.

Carmine shook his head. "I know they always show a profit for the ones who hand over their money. No denying that. What I don't know is if they show just enough of a profit to keep everybody happy and then tuck the rest in their pockets."

"I know a few guys have their money with that firm," Frank said. "From what I hear, they clear anywhere from six to nine percent profit each year, like clockwork."

"I hear the same," Carmine said. "But what if it turns out that yearly profit is higher—say, ten to fifteen percent a year? Where do you suppose the rest of that cash goes?"

"In their pockets," Carlo said.

"You know anybody's been burned by them?" Tommy asked.

"Not yet," Carmine said. "But the fact that I don't doesn't mean it isn't going on."

"You put cash in with them?" Frank asked.

"I put my toe in the water," Carmine said. "One hundred and fifty thousand. But it's too soon for me to see if they're dealing from the bottom of the deck."

"In other words, you don't trust them," Tommy said.

Carmine smiled. "This one time, a guy took his son out to the playground. The boy was about eight, maybe nine years old. The father puts him up on a ledge, a few feet from the ground. Dad stands there, his feet spread apart on the cement, his arms open wide, and asks his son to jump. The kid looks down and he's scared. He shakes his head. His father says, 'Jump. Don't be afraid. Trust me. I'm your father. I'll catch you.' The kid still hesitates. The father says, 'Don't worry. Just trust me and jump. I'll catch you.' The kid shuts his eyes and jumps. The father moves out of the way. The kid lands hard on the cement. Scrapes his legs, elbows, cuts his chin. He's got tears in his eyes. He looks up at his father. The father bends down and holds his son's face in both hands. Then he tells him, 'In this world, kid, you never trust anybody.' So, to answer your question, no, I don't trust the accountants."

His three friends nodded and sipped their coffee. Carmine, in casual dress—dark button-down shirt, tan slacks, brown loafers, and, as always, no socks—glanced at the street beyond the small cemetery. After a few moments, Tommy asked, "If you feel that way about them, why give them any of your money at all? There's lots of places for you to park cash. Places that wouldn't raise any of the red flags this crew does."

"I'm doing a friend a favor," Carmine said. "In the course of doing that, if you help me find that the firm is ripping off some friends of ours, then we'll be doing them a favor, as well. And, as you all know, that's always a good chit to have in our back pocket."

"So we put a bug in a few people's ears," Carlo said, "and have them go and sniff around. Then, let's say, they find out the firm is skimming from them. What do we do about it?"

"Nothing," Carmine said. "If our friends are being taken advantage of, they'll know how to handle it."

"We're just there to give them a heads-up, nothing more," Frank said.

"That's the long and the short of it," Carmine said. "We're not looking for a cut of the action or any money coming back our way. I'm doing a favor for a friend and, by spreading the word, you'll be doing one for me."

"If these accountants are skimming from our crowd, then they're most likely taking from other accounts, as well," Frank said. "From what little I heard about them, they do business with the cartels and some high-end drug dealers. It's not just Wall Street money these guys are hooked into. It's money from every street they can find."

"Which means they most likely have muscle of their own to back them up in case the shit ever hits the fan," Tommy said.

"And with the kind of dough a firm like this brings in, they can reach out and hire whoever they want to cover their ass," Carlo said.

"All that's true," Carmine said. "They're not your corner H&R Block. But it doesn't matter how many hired hands they have at the ready. If you help find out they're stealing from our friends, the accountants are going to need those dragons from *Game of Thrones* to knock down that crew. Those guys are going to be out not just to get their money back. They'll be looking for a blood payment. Nothing less will do."

"We'll check it out for you, Carmine," Carlo said. "Shouldn't take too long. You tell a mob guy someone might be messing with his cash, he'll run out the door like one of those Kenyan marathon runners to see if there's any truth behind it."

"I had no doubts you would," Carmine said. "If there's anything you need from me, just say the word."

"I wouldn't say no to a nice meal at your restaurant," Frank said. "I haven't been there since my Grace died. Three years this October."

"Door's open, anytime," Carmine said. "Day or night."

"One more thing before we wrap this up," Tommy said.

"Name it," Carmine said.

"These accountants might put it together that you're the one that fingered them on the skimming," Tommy said. "They might decide to throw some of that muscle your way. Look to bring a hurt to you."

"Maybe so," Carmine said.

"If that does indeed happen, just know they'll have to deal with us, too," Tommy said. "We may be a bunch of old rain dogs, but they're the ones that bite the hardest."

37.

WINSTON CHURCHILL SQUARE

CHRIS WALKED NEXT TO PEARL, WHOSE ELECTRIC WHEELCHAIR easily navigated along Downing Street as they eased their way toward Bleecker and Sixth Avenue. They were a few feet from the small park named after the British prime minister who had helped steer the course to victory in World War II. The park was shaded and lined with benches, a comfortable place to read, enjoy a lunch, or settle into a quiet conversation.

They were each eating a large salted pretzel and enjoying the late-afternoon sunshine. "Let me tell you," Pearl said. "Nothing would please me more than to see the Yankees in the World Series. But I just don't see it happening."

"The new guys they brought up are playing out of their minds," Chris said. "They got the pitching, the hitting, the speed."

"It's just not their year," Pearl said. "The Astros are going to be tough, and the Red Sox are always a coin flip."

"You'll see," Chris said. "They'll be there at the end. Raise another flag at the stadium."

"They win a few more championships, they might have to think about adding another pole," Pearl said.

They entered the park and found an empty bench. Pearl lined his wheelchair up across from Chris, who sat and took the last bite of his pretzel. "You start school pretty soon," Pearl said, when both were settled. "You good with that?"

"A little nervous," Chris said. "I've met a couple of the kids who will be in my class. They seem nice enough. But, still, the first couple of weeks will feel weird."

"No doubt," Pearl said. "It's like the first day of anything. I remember my first day as an active cop. I was so nervous, sweating so much it looked like I had malaria. I counted every minute of that first shift. Couldn't wait to get it out of my system."

"Did you make any arrests?"

Pearl shook his head. "It was a quiet day, thank the Lord. If I had run into trouble, I don't think I would have been able to slap the cuffs on an old woman, let alone some hard-ass I needed to chase down."

"How long was it before you felt relaxed?" Chris asked.

"The very next day," Pearl said. "Whatever the reason, when I hit the street that morning, I wasn't nervous, didn't feel any unease wearing the uniform or walking my beat. I felt like I was where I belonged. And, more than that, I felt like a cop."

"Do you still?" Chris asked.

"Yes," Pearl said without any hesitation. "My legs may have left me, but that feeling never has. Working with your uncle has helped keep that alive for me, being around him and now living in his brownstone. And being assigned these cases, tough as they might be to crack, keeps the feeling going. Some days it's like I never left the job."

"You think Tank feels the same way?" Chris asked.

"If I had to bet, I'd say no," Pearl said. "Don't get me wrong. He loved being a cop and he gets revved up working these cases. But if you took those away, he'd still be a happy man. He's got his world and his life together. Being a cop was just one slice of it. You remove that slice, he'd be okay without it. Sure, he would miss it some but not enough to derail his day-to-day."

"I'm sure having me show up on his doorstep threw him off his game," Chris said. "I'm probably the last thing in the world he wanted or expected."

"Maybe at first," Pearl said. "But if you put it to him now, there's no question Tank feels as much at home with you as you seem to be with him. No one likes how it came to happen, but I think it's been good for Tank to have you in his life. And just as good for you to be there."

Pearl's eyes moved from Chris to the street beyond. His upper body tensed, and he eased his wheelchair away from the park bench in order to get a closer look at the street traffic beyond the trees. Chris noticed the shift in posture and the slight movement. "What's wrong?" he asked.

"That's the third time that van has driven past us in the time we've been here," Pearl said. "Might be the driver's lost. Or it could be he's already found what he's looking for."

"What do you want to do?"

"You get up from that bench nice and easy," Pearl said. "Say your goodbyes to me and then head out of the square at the far end, away from that van. Don't make it look like a panic move. Once you get out of their line of sight, call and text Tank, let him know where I am and what I suspect. Once you do that, head straight for the brownstone. No stops for any reason. Let Tank know you're doing that, as well."

"I won't leave you here alone," Chris said. "If you're right, there's bound to be more than one guy in that van. I can call and text Tank right from here. I won't leave you behind."

Pearl glanced from the van to Chris. "Listen to me," he said. "You have one job, and that's to get Tank here as soon as possible. You can't find Tank, get Bruno or Carmine. Meantime, I'll head out there and find out if my hunch is on the money or I'm just being my old paranoid self."

Chris stared at Pearl and noticed how his entire body language had changed. He was focused on his target, one hand resting on the mechanism to move his chair, the other hidden under his long-sleeve T-shirt. Chris had never seen this side of Pearl, who, up until this moment, had always been relaxed and at ease in his presence. But now, sitting here in a historic square, he was on full alert, tense, his instincts in high gear. Despite the wounds he had suffered, despite the disability he lived with day in and day out, Pearl was still all cop.

Pearl didn't look at Chris. "Go," he said. "Cool Hand Luke it until you're out of the square and then motor. I'm counting on you, little partner. You go and bring in the troops while I stay back and hold down the fort."

Chris nodded and stood. He reached out his left hand and clutched it tightly around Pearl's wrist. "Be careful, please," he whispered.

Pearl gave him a casual smile. "I'm too old to be careful," he said. "But I still got enough in me to be dangerous."

Chris headed out of the square, walking along the perimeter back toward Downing Street. Pearl eased away from the park bench and made his way toward the van, closer to Bleecker. It was a working man's van, windows only on the front passenger and driver's sides, both rolled down, letting in blasts of a hot and humid summer breeze. As he turned out of the square, Pearl saw smoke coming out of the exhaust. There were two men sitting in the front, the driver's arm dangling against the side of the van.

Pearl needed to be sure they were on the lookout for him, and he got his answer when he caught the driver staring at him through his side-view mirror. The driver sat up and brought his arm back inside the vehicle. The rear of the van began to shake, telling Pearl he had more than two potential shooters to contend with. He slowed his wheel-chair and scanned the traffic snaking its way up the avenue.

He didn't figure them to come out blasting, not with so many po-tential witnesses and a high probability of collateral damage. None-theless, Pearl kept his hand on his .38, nestled under his T-shirt, and waited for them to make the first move.

Seconds later, the double-panel doors at the back of the van swung open and three men jumped out, two white and one black, all dressed in similar gear—jeans, cutoff sweatshirts, and dark sneakers. They were middle-aged and chunky around the gut, slowed by too many years spent in bars washing down greasy burgers with mugs of tap beer. They stood in a semicircle around Pearl and smiled down at him. "Nice wheels," one of them said. "You own or do you lease?"

Pearl glanced up at the three men and recognized two of the faces. For a number of years, the duo had been members of an elite narcotics unit put together to help bring down the rising number of crack-cocaine gangs riding roughshod in some of the city's poorest neighborhoods. And while they did bring down a few of the gangs, the bulk of their time was spent protecting the dealers and allowing their businesses to flourish. They were handsomely rewarded for their efforts, taking in as much as six figures a month, divided equally among each member of the unit. The two New York tabloids tagged the unit with the nickname "the Dirty Dozen."

"Hey, Jackie," Pearl said to one of the two men gazing down at him. "Last time I saw that ugly mug of yours was about seven, maybe eight years ago. On my flat-screen, in living color on the news. It was right after you were convicted—you and your hangdog lawyer were doing a mea culpa on the courthouse steps. Nice to see you made it through the system in one piece. Tell the truth, isn't early parole a blessing?"

"We're not here to talk about me," Jackie said. He had short hair the color of sand and bloodshot, puffy eyes. His gun was clipped to a hip holster, visible under the right side of his floppy sweatshirt.

"I'd love to go down memory lane with you, Pearl," the one standing in the middle said. "But I only do that with friends. And you and that jack-off partner of yours were never that to me. Not even close."

"That's because me and Tank had little use for cops who took their marching orders from dealers," Pearl said. "So, to us, Paul, you were nothing more than shit under our shoes."

Paul, the oldest of the three, in his mid-forties, fit the stereotype of the corrupt cop—multiple marriages, a handful of kids spread throughout the five boroughs, and a gambling itch no amount of money could satisfy. "And while you and Rizzo were doing your good deeds, we set ourselves up for life. Where did that badass bullshit you two pulled on the job get you? A soft, cushy seat in a wheelchair. You'd have been better off working with us. Less stress and a thicker bank account."

"If you're as set for life as you claim," Pearl said, "then why are you here? Riding in the back of a beat-up van, looking to roust a poor old cripple like me. That kind of work pays chump change, which means your pockets are nowhere as deep as you like to pretend."

Paul stepped forward, reared back, and slapped Pearl hard across the face. The blow was swift and fast and stung Pearl, causing his right eye to tear. "Enough bullshit," Paul said. "We're going to put your sorry ass in the van. Resume the rest of our conversation in a quieter spot, a place where we can enjoy a little privacy."

He turned to Jackie and the third man, who stood with his back to the van, his eye on the passing pedestrians. "Help me lift him up," he ordered. "Let's get him in the back and then get the fuck out of here."

Jackie bent down and gripped one side of Pearl's wheelchair, one hand around a wheel, the other holding on to the back end. He froze when he felt the muzzle of Pearl's .38 against his temple. "I'm a heavy lift to begin with," Pearl said. "It's going to be a whole lot harder to do with a bullet hole in your head."

Paul reached for his holstered weapon but then stopped. The third man stared at Pearl, not sure what to do. The two men in the front of the van stepped out and made their way toward the rear, anxious to see what was causing the holdup.

"Anyone pulls a gun and you can say goodbye to Jackie," Pearl said. "Now, I'm not sure if you give a shit or not. But, dollars to donuts, I bet Jackie here does."

"You can't take five of us down," the silent man said. "From what I hear, you were damn good with a gun. But that was a long time ago, when you were younger and not locked in a chair. So maybe you do take down Jackie. Maybe even get off a second shot at one of us. That's all you'll get. And you still end up in the back of the van. Only this time with a bullet in you. Which, from the looks of you, is the last thing you need."

"Better to be found dead in this chair," Pearl said, "because, sure as God rested on a Sunday, there is no damn way I'm gonna let you shove me in the back of that van. At least not while I'm still alive."

"Breathing or not," Paul said. "Makes no difference to us."

Pearl looked down at Jackie. "How are those legs of yours holding up?" he asked. "Must be pretty numb by now, crouched down like they been all this time."

"Fuck you, Pearl," Jackie said.

Pearl turned away from Jackie and smiled, his eyes looking beyond the men surrounding him. "I know you're a betting man, Paul," Pearl said. "I'll put my hundred against your ten that this day is not going to end the way you thought it would."

"I'll take that bet," Paul said, moving a step closer to Pearl's wheelchair. "Your money will look a whole lot better in my pockets than it does in yours."

"Count me in, too," Tank said. He stepped out from behind a tree, holding his gun against his left leg.

"Don't leave me out," Carmine said, coming at them from the traffic side of the van. "After all, I'm the only legit bookie in the crowd."

"I don't usually bet," Bruno said as he stepped in behind the driver of the van. "But in this case, I'll take some of Pearl's action."

"Well, gentlemen," Pearl said, "looks like we got ourselves a game."

38.

SIXTH AVENUE AND BLEECKER STREET

MOMENTS LATER

I MOVED CLOSE ENOUGH TO PAUL TO SMELL HIS FOUL BREATH. He glared at me, but I could tell he'd been caught off guard by our sudden arrival. Going up against Pearl, armed as Paul was with four gunmen by his side, should have been an easy takedown. But now, with me, Bruno, and Carmine on the scene, along with Pearl, the situation was not quite so neat. "Where were you told to take Pearl?" I asked. "And who was it that told you?"

"He looked like he could use some fresh air," Paul said, one hand resting on his still-holstered gun. "He probably doesn't get out much. Given his condition and all."

I took a step back and then lifted my right knee into Paul's groin. He jolted over, gasping for air. In two swift moves, I leaned in and pulled his gun from his holster, then smashed my left knee against his exposed throat. The second blow sent him sprawling to the ground. He gagged, unable to speak and desperate to take in air. I turned to my left and jammed Paul's gun against the chest of the third man. He had been standing there motionless.

"I don't think we've met," I said to him. "I know the other clowns in your little posse from when me and Pearl were on the job. But you're an unknown."

"Victor," he said, his eyes as much on the gun jammed in the center of his chest as they were on me. "The name's Victor."

"You off the job like the rest?" I asked.

He nodded. "About two years now," he said. "Worked out of the Bronx and Queens, mostly."

"I was looking for a yes or no," I said. "Not a résumé."

"So, what happens now?" It was Jackie, still holding on to Pearl's wheelchair, my partner's gun only a few inches from his face.

I answered without turning away from Victor. "Glad you asked, Jackie," I said. "We can play this any number of ways. I can have Carmine reach out to some old friends and have you and your buddies dropped off in a landfill on Randall's Island before sunup. I'm sure Carmine's bunch would love the chance to flex their muscles again."

"Be a pleasure, no doubt about it," Carmine said. He had both hands by his sides and was staring at the van's driver, a nervous young man whose white T-shirt was stained with sweat.

"Or I can let Bruno here loose and see how many of you he can pound the shit out of before a punch gets tossed his way," I said. "I've never seen him go one against five before, but he has a better-than-even chance of taking on the entire bunch and coming out whole."

"Bet your pension on it," Bruno said. He never went looking for a brawl but didn't shy from one, either.

I took a quick glance at the street and sidewalk around us. A small crowd had gathered, curious to see what was about to happen. There are few cities in this world where a street fight can occur, even one with as many as nine brawlers, and not only would bystanders gather and watch but a handful would cheer us on. New York is one such city.

"You made your point, Tank," Paul said. "We'll get out of your hair. At least for now."

I nodded. "You do that," I said. "And while you're at it, do one other thing."

"What would that be?" Paul asked.

"Pass a message to your gatekeeper Kenwood," I said. "He reached out and tried to touch someone close to me. That doesn't sit well. Not one bit."

"That it?"

"No, that's not it," I said. "Add this to the memo: I'm going to nail his ass for sending an innocent kid to jail. We're going to find Rachel's killer. Then I'm going to turn him over, make him pay for the other innocent kids he put away. By the time I'm done, he'll be begging me to kill him just to keep his sorry ass out of a prison cell."

"Tough talk, Tank," Paul said. "I'll be sure to pass it along. Just remember one thing, though. There's more of us than there are of you."

I turned to Pearl and smiled. "You hear that, Pearl?" I said. "It never changes, does it? We always seem to be outnumbered and outgunned."

"Just the way we like it, partner," Pearl said.

39.

THE BROWNSTONE

I PACED THE LIVING ROOM, A GLASS OF BRUNELLO DANGLING OFF the fingers of my right hand. Pearl was against a far wall, watching me, a cold can of Bud Light clutched in his hand. Carmine and Connie sat on the couch, one drinking a bottle of Perrier, the other cradling a large bowl of baked ziti. I stopped pacing and turned to face them. "The situation today could have gone south in so many ways," I said. "This wasn't the first time we've had the ones we're chasing make a reach for us. So far, they've mostly focused on Chris and Pearl."

"We're the most vulnerable," Pearl said. "Makes sense for Kenwood to make a move against us. The same holds true for the accountants. You take down your weakest targets. It's the smart play."

"And it's also one that could end up getting one of you killed," I said. "We've already lost one of our team on the last job. I don't want to make a habit of it."

"Pearl can take care of himself," Carmine said. "As he proved today. It's Chris who's the bigger concern. We need to protect him better, that's for damn sure."

"And how do we do that?" I asked. I was angry, frustrated, and felt myself losing control over the two cases I had taken on.

There was one more thing eating at me about the accounting firm, or, to be more precise, my brother's dealings with them. I bought that he was about to turn whistleblower and it was more than likely the reason to want him out of the way. But he had been at that firm for years and was on the fast track to make partner. He wasn't a junior-level accountant who fell upon some files he shouldn't have seen. He was a member of the inner circle, which, to me, meant he might have known about some of the dirty dealings they were involved in.

How deep into it was Jack? What caused his sudden come-to-Jesus moment? Was he an innocent pawn or a guilty associate who decided to come clean before the heat came down on the firm? And if any of those concerns proved true, then how the hell would I explain it to Chris and not make him hate his father as well as me in the process?

It was Connie who broke the silence. "You need to find someone to be by his side night and day," she said. "Someone he trusts beyond any doubt."

I looked at her and shrugged. "You mean a bodyguard?" I asked. "I'm good with that, but he would hate it."

"I don't think she's talking about a Liam Neeson type," Carmine said. "More like something shorter and with four legs."

"A dog?" I said. "You want me to get Chris a dog? You think that will help keep him safe?"

"It will help keep him occupied," Connie said. "And he'll stick closer to home. Between working the computers for you and helping to train a puppy, there won't be much time for him to venture far out of sight. Then you can put eyes and ears on him—not so conspicuous for him to notice, but close enough to come to his aid next time a situation pops up."

"He's told me at least a dozen times already how much he loved walking Alban's dog yesterday," Pearl said. "And a dog can help the boy in more ways than any of us maybe can."

"How do you figure?" I asked.

"He's part of our team, that's true," Pearl said. "And he's adjusted well to living with us, even though we are not the easiest bunch to hang with. But a dog would belong to him, be his friend and companion, give him a better sense of belonging. It would help fill the void he must still be feeling."

"Let's not lose sight of it," Carmine said. "As smart as he is, as much help as he's been, he's still a kid and he's still hurting over his loss. His parents. Then Joey. A dog could go a long way toward helping heal those wounds."

"I don't know anything about taking care of a dog," I said. "Neither do any of you."

"What's to know?" Carmine said. "Feed him, walk him, love him. The dog does the rest."

I took a long sip of my wine and shook my head. Then I smiled. "You already got the dog, didn't you?"

"Technically, no," Carmine said. "But I did put a cash deposit down with a breeder I know upstate. Guy's been around forever. He moves a dog, you can count on it being top-shelf."

"Does Chris know?"

"Not yet," Connie said. "We thought it would be best if that came from you. Be your gift to him."

"What kind of dog are we talking about?"

"Olde English Bulldogge," Carmine said. "Stubborn, loyal, loving, and very protective. Anybody goes near Chris will have to get through Gus first."

"Gus?" I said. "How'd you come up with that name?"

"That was me," Pearl said. "First, it's a great name for a bulldog. Second, I named him after Gus Zelden. Remember him?"

I nodded. "One of our instructors at the police academy. We were in his class when we first met."

"That's the one," Pearl said. "Figured he helped put you and me together in a way, be a nice tip of the hat to him."

"Before I sign off, who takes care of Gus when Chris starts school?" I asked.

"There's plenty of us to go around," Carmine said. "He can hang with me in my garden when the weather is nice, and me and Bruno can take him for long walks. Bruno already said he'd take the dog down to the gym, have the kids there spend some time with him."

"Food, vet bills, shots, sleeping arrangements?" I asked.

"All bases covered," Connie said. "He'll sleep in Chris's room. I already ordered him two of the cutest beds. They have his name stenciled on them. And he'll have his name and phone number on his collar, too."

"Whose number?" I asked.

"Your cell," Pearl said, smiling. "Figured you'd want to participate in some small way."

"How soon will he be here?"

"I can drive up tomorrow to pick him up," Carmine said. "With luck, be back just after lunch. Give you plenty of time to plant the surprise on Chris. That is, if you're good with the move."

"Do I have a choice?" I asked.

Connie stood and walked over to me and put her arms around me. She leaned in and kissed me on the cheek. "The dog's not just for Chris," she said to me in a low voice. "He's for you. For all of us."

I held Connie close to me and looked at Carmine and Pearl and nodded. "Looks to me like we got ourselves a dog."

40.

INWOOD HILL PARK

TWO DAYS LATER

I WALKED PAST A LARGE BOULDER, THE WOODS AROUND ME DENSE, shielded by tall cliffs and massive tulip poplar trees. I could hear the cars on the West Side Highway sweeping past me below and could see the lights of the George Washington Bridge above. I walked along a small path, making my way slowly up the trail, finding solace in the darkness that engulfed me in what was most likely the last park of its kind in New York City.

I have always loved this park. Its history dates as far back as 1626, when it was a prosperous Reckgawawanc Indian village, with streams filled with fish of all stripes, fresh game living in the tidal marshes, and low fields filled with rows of planted corn and squash. It was a special place, steeped in history and, during the daylight hours, surrounded by stunning views of the New Jersey Palisades and the Hudson River. I had come here many times during my years as a cop, to escape the grime and grind of the job, just to walk in the shadow of generations past and let the beauty of the land and the sounds of the flowing streams set my body clock back to normal.

But not on this night.

This night I was here to meet Eddie Kenwood.

He had reached out to me through Zeke Jeffries. Kenwood wanted to talk things out, see if we could reach a resolution to our situation before it escalated beyond our control. He asked to meet with me alone, told Zeke he had information to pass my way that only I needed to hear. I chose Inwood Hill Park. Kenwood chose the late hour. I stopped next to a massive tree and looked around. Except for the occasional light that sliced its way through the thick foliage, it was as dark as a cave. If Kenwood wanted to do me in, I had walked into the perfect setup.

I saw the light from a lit cigarette and a trail of smoke making its way toward me. I turned and there was Eddie Kenwood, standing a few feet to my right, the end of a filter-tip clutched in his teeth. "Leave it to you to pick such a romantic spot," he said. "This where you would bring one of your girlfriends back in the old days? I know I did, many a time. Or are you one of those guys that likes the place only for the view?"

"We're not here to go over old times, Kenwood," I said. "You asked for the meet and you got one. It's late, so whatever it is you got to tell me, might as well get to it now."

"Fair enough," Kenwood said. "First, you need to walk away from this Randy Jenkins bullshit. The girl is dead, the guy confessed, he got convicted, and he's in prison. End of story."

"He didn't kill Rachel Nieves," I said. "We both know that, don't we?"

Kenwood took a deep drag on his cigarette. "Just for argument's sake, Tank, let's say he didn't," he said. "Let's say someone else killed her. What difference does it make? Sooner or later, the rate Randy's criminal career was going, he was going to kill somebody and go down for that. And the guy that maybe did kill Rachel, he's probably in the slammer for another murder he committed or he's long since dead from some overdose. You see my point?"

"So it doesn't matter if you busted the right guy or not," I said. "Since they're all going to be guilty of something. That how you look at it?"

Kenwood stubbed out the cigarette with the tip of his right shoe and then smiled. "We're *all* guilty of something, Tank," he said. "Nobody knows that better than you."

"That's probably true," I said. "But what I'm looking to do now is free the one who's not guilty. Do the right thing, Kenwood. Just this one time. If Randy Jenkins is innocent, he deserves to be a free man. You're the one standing between him and a get-out-of-jail free card."

Kenwood stepped closer to me. As he did, I heard sounds of leaves rustling and twigs snapping around the two of us and knew he had not come alone. "I'll tell you what, Tank," Kenwood said. "You and me make a deal right here and now. I tell you what you need to know about Rachel and Randy, then you tell me about someone I want to know about."

"Who?"

"We'll get to that," he said. "To help put your mind at ease, I'll go first. That okay by you?"

"I'm all ears," I said.

"Here's what you know," Kenwood said. "Randy and Rachel were seeing each other, on and off. He was really into her, she less so. He wanted her to be his one and only. She was young enough not to want to get bogged down with just one guy. She was seeing a few of the neighborhood turks. Randy was just one can in a six-pack."

"Goes without saying," I said. "She was a beautiful girl. Probably lots of eyes looking her way. I'm surprised you weren't one of them."

"Who says I wasn't?" Kenwood said. "Me and her, we had some good times together. We had an understanding. I fed her needs and she fed mine. As long as that held firm, she had no worries from me."

"Why would she have any worries from you?" I asked.

"If she was going to be my side dish, she needed to stay away from the guys she had been seeing," Kenwood said. "You know me well enough by now, Tank. I'm not the kind of guy that likes to share."

"So, you get wind that Rachel is still keeping Randy close by," I said. "And that hot temper of yours moves from slow boil right into the red zone."

"You nailed it," Kenwood said. "Her coming to me for drugs and some cash in return for a little sheet time, while she was double-dipping with a rotating convict like Jenkins, didn't sit right with me. So I went and had a little chat with my girl. I was looking to make her see things the way they ought to be, not the way they were."

And that's when I knew. I was standing a few feet away from the man who murdered Rachel Nieves.

"You were getting played," I said. "And a guy like you, with your street rep, you can't let anything like that happen. The street has to fear you. That fear is your strength. And you cannot let anyone mess with that. Not even someone you may have been in love with. It's too big a risk."

"Save that love shit for the Hallmark Channel," Kenwood said. "Rachel meant nothing more to me than a warm body and a good time. She wasn't somebody I was dying to bring home to meet the family. When it came to that end, I grow my own. I don't buy second-hand."

"So you went to see her," I said. "Had your face-to-face with her and figured you'd made your position clear. But she didn't listen. She kept seeing Jenkins. He was the one she wanted. Not you. And that burned your ass even more, didn't it?"

Kenwood put his hands in his pants pockets and smiled. "It doesn't matter now, does it?" he said. "She's long dead and Jenkins is closing in on twenty years inside a cage. And I'm out here talking to you."

"You're right, Kenwood," I said. "It doesn't matter. I walked right into your little trap. There's no way you're letting me out of this park tonight. From the sounds around us, I'm guessing you brought along four, maybe five, of your crew to make sure I don't live to see another sunrise."

"You heard them, did you?" Kenwood asked.

"It's not like you have Seal Team Six working for you," I said. "A pack of school kids would be making less noise. So, knowing that, why not let me die by having me hear the truth? There won't be much I can do about it once I'm dead."

Kenwood stared at me for a few moments and then nodded. "You know, we're a lot alike, you and me. I know you don't think so. But I know so. We have one very big thing in common."

"And what would that be?"

"What I came here to tell you," Kenwood said. "We both got away with murder. Me with that pass-around bitch Rachel. And you, back in a cabin on a summer day a long time ago. Or did you forget all about Frank Muncie?"

Kenwood caught the look on my face, the shock of hearing a name I had tried so hard to erase from my memory. The sudden realization that my once-buried past was known by a man I considered a blood enemy.

"How the hell do you know about that?" I asked. My shirt was streaked with sweat, and my hands had begun to tremble.

"You and your folks didn't cover your tracks as well as you thought you did," Kenwood said. "But you don't need to worry, Tank. I'm not going to rat you out any more than you're going to rat me out. Your secret and mine stay here in this park."

I leaned against a tree and closed my eyes, visions of that day from so long ago filling my mind. I was dizzy and nauseous. I wiped the sweat from my face and looked around. Five of Kenwood's men were circling me. Kenwood walked up and stood inches from my face. "You should have known better than to go against a guy like me," he said. "There was no win in it. I'll let the boys here finish up. I'm heading out. Park gets dangerous this time of night."

41.

INWOOD HILL PARK

MOMENTS LATER

THE FIVE MEN DREW THEIR WEAPONS AND SPREAD OUT, ANTICI-
pating that I'd use the darkness to shield me from their bullets and
make a run for it. I still had my back to the tree, my body drenched in
a cold sweat, attempting to get my mind to focus on the situation
around me.

"You can shout for help if you care to," one of the men said. "This
time of night, this deep into the woods, ain't nobody going to hear a
sound."

"It's going to take them a while to find your body, I would guess," a
second one said. "We'll toss it in the thick bushes. Let the rats and
whatever the hell else is out there chew away at you for a few days."

I took a deep breath and stepped away from the tree. "Is that how
you would like your bodies to be found?" I asked.

"Our bodies?" he said with a laugh. "Look around, clown. There's
five of us and one of you. Our guns are already out. You'll probably go
down before you can even reach for yours."

"I'm not going to reach for my gun," I said. "I won't be needing it."

The five men glanced at one another and smiled. "What are you
planning to do?" one of them asked. "Bum-rush us?"

I shook my head and sat down on the wet grass. "I'm going to rest here for a few minutes," I said to them. "It's been a long night and it didn't go exactly as I planned."

"No shit on that," one of them said.

"Are you all off the job?" I asked. "None of you are currently active?"

"We're all on pension," one said. "Not cop lotto like you, just a regular twenty and out. That's why we need to do these odds jobs. Pick up some extra walking-around money."

"There are better ways," I said.

I looked above the heads of the five surrounding me—two men hung upside down from a pair of trees over two of the ex-cops. They had long blades in their hands and with a swift motion sliced the throats of the unsuspecting duo. Before the other three could react, they were jumped from behind by three men coming out from the thick foliage and one of the massive trees. Their knives moved silently and went deep into flesh. In less than thirty seconds, the five ex-cops were spread out on the moist grounds of the park, dead.

I looked at the five assassins and nodded. I then glanced up and saw Alban. He leaned over and reached out a massive hand. I took it and he yanked me to my feet. "You heard?" I asked him.

"I heard Kenwood tell you he killed the girl," Alban said.

"And the rest of it?"

Alban shrugged. "He killed for no reason other than he could," he said. "I've known you long enough to know that what you did was done for cause. Just like what happened here tonight."

I glanced over Alban's shoulders and watched as his men emptied the pockets of the dead, taking their money, wallets, watches, and rings. "They used to be cops," I said to Alban.

"They used to be alive, too," Alban said. "And they weren't good cops. If they were, they wouldn't be here tonight."

"What happens next?"

"You need to find a place to clear your head," Alban said. "We'll deal with the damage here."

"I need to give a heads-up to the chief," I said. "About what went down."

"That's your end," Alban said. "Mine is to help strip these bodies and get them hidden in the brush. I doubt you want to stick around to see that."

I shook my head. "No, thanks," I said. "I've seen and heard more than enough for one night."

42.

MID-MANHATTAN LIBRARY

THE NEXT DAY

I WAS ON THE THIRD FLOOR OF THE LIBRARY, WHERE OVER FIVE million images from a variety of sources are kept and cataloged. The reference archives culled from old postcards, books, newspapers, magazines, and pamphlets comprise a visual journey into our past and, over the years, had afforded me a pleasant escape from the burdens I often bore in my years as a cop. I also came here during my time recuperating from the wounds my work had inflicted on my body. It was a place where I could forget about the present by focusing on the faces and images of the past.

But not today. My past was now, thanks to Eddie Kenwood, chainlinked to my present. I had come here to seek a few moments of calm as I attempted to sort my way through the time bomb Kenwood had set off. But not even the sight of serene photos and images from the city's past could soothe or calm me.

I had walked away from the park and the bloodshed that occurred there and managed to make my way back to the brownstone. I was reeling and numb, my emotions a mixture of anger, confusion, frustration, and fear. I had always believed, no matter how often I tried to convince myself otherwise, that my long-held secret would eventually rise to the surface and force me to confront it. I just never imagined that my secret was shared by Eddie Kenwood.

How did he know what had occurred so many years ago? How did that single, horrible event find its way to his attention? And what did he intend to do with that potentially devastating information now that I had survived his attempt on my life?

What I did know as I aimlessly scanned an assortment of photos taken decades, sometimes centuries, earlier was that I had to bring my secret out of the darkness and into the light. I would have to face the people I loved and cared about more than any others and have them hear the words from my lips: I had killed a man. And my brother, Jack, had seen me do it. And that was the reason my brother and I had not spoken for far too many years. The secret we shared was the wall that separated us. Our silence allowed the two of us to learn to live with what had been done, our secret known to only a select few. Four people knew about the murder. My parents, me, and Jack. Connie knew only that Jack had seen me kill a man. But she could never imagine the circumstances under which that murder had occurred.

I thought the accounting firm might have known. They did intense background checks on prospective employees and constantly monitored their activities, both past and present. And they were very good at it. There was the possibility, slim as it might be, that they had uncovered the event while looking into Jack's history and, rather than reveal it, kept it quiet to be used as a potential weapon against him should the need arise. Instead, they chose a deadlier direction when it came to Jack.

I set aside the photos and looked around the quiet room. I glanced at the faces of the assorted men and women, each lost in their quest for a postcard or a photo to take back as a memento, and wondered what secrets they each held close to their heart. What horrible act was in their past that could suddenly rise from the ashes and bring them shame? We all have secrets, some deadlier than others, and we all do our best to keep them hidden from public view. Now I had no choice but to reveal to the ones who mattered most what I had kept from them for so long.

And they would need to hear it from me. Not from Eddie Kenwood, that was for damn sure. And once my secret was revealed to them, it would cost Kenwood the only card he had to play. If I was the one who exposed what I had long ago buried, it would leave him nothing to hold against me.

I had no clue as to how any of them would react. Would Pearl feel betrayed? Would Connie cringe at the brutality of the murder she knew so little about? What about my team? And how would Chris deal with yet another fresh blow coming his way mere months after the tragic loss of his parents? Carmine would be more forgiving, but he might have second thoughts about my trustworthiness, and his unease could be passed on to Connie. Not all of them would casually shrug it off as easily as Alban had done. But Alban lived in a world soaked with the blood of others. For him, taking a life, so long as it was justified, was the price of doing business.

I closed my eyes and leaned back against a cool wall. I would tell each one the truth and take it from there. I had no other choice. They needed to know, and they needed to hear it from me.

And then I would deal with Eddie Kenwood.

We had worked each other into a corner and had both come away holding an ace. Kenwood let me know he knew about a murder I had committed. In turn, he had admitted to killing Rachel Nieves and pinning the murder on Randy Jenkins. We could agree to leave it at a standoff. He would hold on to my secret and I would hold on to his. But that's not how it would play out. That's not in his DNA, and it sure as hell isn't in mine. I'll admit to my crime and let the revelation take its charted course.

And I planned to nail Eddie Kenwood for the murder of Rachel Nieves. I would allow no win for him. No matter what happened to me once I revealed my past sin, Kenwood would not be allowed to walk free. The one benefit that came out of knowing that my secret would soon be exposed was that it allowed me to see, perhaps for the first time, the full picture of the man I was. I am as much a danger to Kenwood as he is to me.

I will leave him two options. The only options a man like him deserves—a prison sentence or a grave.

43.

HUDSON YARDS

LATER THAT DAY

BOBBY WAS WAITING FOR ME ON THE CORNER OF THIRTY-FOURTH and Tenth Avenue. He was holding two cups of bodega coffee and handed me one. We were surrounded by massive cranes and dozens of construction trucks as the newest section of Manhattan was in the process of being raised. "Just what the city needs," Bobby said, glancing at the giant glass-encased structures that had already been built. "A few hundred more seven-figure condos."

I shrugged. "This area was pretty much abandoned for a long time," I said. "What they're putting up is not to my taste, but, then, nobody bothered to ask me."

"Not a dream come true for me, either," Bobby said.

"What does suit you?" I asked.

"A nice house in the woods, maybe by a lake," Bobby said. "A couple of dogs, a fireplace, tons of books, a case of Pappy Van Winkle. I get that and I will die a happy old federal agent."

"I didn't hear mention of a wife," I said.

"All those other things I can go get on my own," Bobby said. "All you need is money. Finding someone to fall in love with, that needs some luck and timing. I haven't been good with either one."

I glanced over at him. "Ever come close?" I asked.

Bobby looked at me and smiled. "Just once," he said. "But I let her get away."

I nodded and turned back to glance at the heavy street traffic. "Tell me about this guy we're meeting," I said. "Is he solid?"

"He's been my inside guy at the firm," Bobby said. "Started feeding me info a few weeks after I started looking into their operation. He's given me enough to work off of. Trouble is, he's not high up enough to get me to the partners. He's junior level. Your brother was about three rungs above him."

"So, he gives you what he might overhear along with office rumors and gossip," I said.

"Along those lines," Bobby said. "Everything he's come back to me with has proven out."

"Is this how you usually meet with him?"

Bobby shook his head. "He calls me using a burner," he said. "About once, sometimes twice a week. We never do face-to-face meetings. He called me the other day, said he had something hot to pass on. But he needed to do it in person."

"Any idea what he's coming to you with?" I asked.

"Not sure," Bobby said. "But he sounded nervous on the phone. His voice cracked a few times. He must think it's important or he wouldn't expose himself like this. Out in the open. He's taking a big chance."

"You think the firm got wise to what he was doing?" I asked.

"I hope to hell the answer to that is no," Bobby said. "He's a good guy, just took a job with the wrong firm."

A dark-blue sedan pulled up to the corner, doing a hard skid between a hot-dog vendor and a cement truck. Bobby and I tossed our coffee containers and pulled our weapons from their holsters. He yanked his federal shield and chain from under his shirt and let it dangle across his chest.

Two well-dressed young men stepped out of the car and walked toward us, stopping several feet away. "I guess we're not who you were expecting," the one on my left said. He had long brown hair and a dark goatee, his eyes hidden by wraparound shades.

"No, you're not," Bobby said. "But I'm always open to making new friends."

"Your boy is no longer with the firm," the man in the shades said. "He wasn't a good fit."

"Took two of you to come tell us that," I said. "A text would have worked just as well."

"He no longer had access to a phone," the man said. "Of any kind. And the firm didn't just send two of us. They sent three. We drove. Mark, the guy behind you, he's a mass transit kind of guy."

I kept my eyes on the two in front of me. Bobby was to my right and standing sideways. "Can you make out the third guy?" I asked him.

"Hard to miss him," Bobby said. "He's got a gun braced against his right knee and his back to the wall."

"He's yours," I said. "I'll deal with these two."

I walked away from Bobby and started toward the two men. Each put a hand inside his jacket pocket, fingers gripped around a weapon. A group of four construction workers crossed between us and I made my move. I slid past one of the workers and rushed the man with the shades. I caught him at chest level and sent him sprawling to the ground. I was bent over and aimed my gun at the man left standing. "Before that piece leaves the holster," I said to him, "you'll be bleeding from two bullet wounds."

I glanced down at the man with the shades. He had both hands on the cracked pavement. "I figure you're in charge," I said to him. "So I'll make it your call."

The man took a deep breath. "We got a job to do," he said. "And being arrested by a fed and a broken-down ex-cop wasn't part of the plan."

"Guys like you never take the easy out," I said. "You'd rather die for some guy who doesn't give a shit whether you live or not."

I couldn't see his eyes, because of the shades, so I focused my attention on his right hand, slowly inching its way from the pavement toward his holster. The guy standing to my right held his position, waiting to make his move. "Take him, Dale," the guy with the shades said to his partner.

Dale reached for his weapon, and as he pulled it, I shot two bullets in his direction. One hit him in the shoulder, the other shattered his gun hand. The pain sent him to his knees. The man with the shades pulled his weapon, lifted himself up, and fired one round. I felt the heat as it whizzed past, praying it didn't hit a bystander. I moved to my left, took aim at the man in the shades, and fired one clean shot into his stomach. His gun fell from his hands and he clutched at his gut.

I moved quickly and kicked both guns away from the wounded men. I glanced around and was surrounded by construction workers and a handful of pedestrians. "Stay back," I said. "It's a police situation."

I pulled my cell phone and speed-dialed the chief's line. A woman answered on the second ring. "This is Tank Rizzo," I said. "Tell the chief we've got a ten-thirteen on Thirty-fourth and Tenth Avenue. Send backup and a truck. There's two down, both wounded. A federal agent is on the scene with a third gunman."

I slid the phone off, holstered my gun, reached down and picked up the gunmen's two weapons, and went to check on Bobby.

44.

HUDSON YARDS

MOMENTS LATER

BOBBY AND MARK WERE SQUARED OFF AGAINST EACH OTHER. Their weapons were on the ground and they were both in crouched fighting position. Mark was bleeding from his lip and had a cut above his right eye. Bobby's nose was bleeding and he was spitting blood. Bobby ducked under a right cross and landed two strong blows to Mark's midsection, forcing him to bend at the waist. Bobby then lifted his left knee and landed it hard against the man's face. Even from several feet away, I could hear the sound of bone splintering and see the geyser of blood flow down the man's face and stream onto Bobby's previously crisp white shirt. Bobby then reared back and landed one final blow to the left side of Mark's head. He stood watching as the bigger man swayed and then fell to the pavement, his head landing with a hard thud on the cracked cement.

Behind us, sirens came from all directions, and I knew that the situation was under control.

I walked over to Bobby and checked on his facial wounds. "I heard shots fired," he said. "Glad you weren't the one taking the bullets."

"Cops will be here soon," I said. "The two on the ground are going to the hospital. Looks like their pal Mark will be joining them."

"They can take the collar," Bobby said. "As long as they don't cut them loose on a bond once their wounds heal and before I get a chance to talk to them."

"Chief Connors will handle it," I said. "These three aren't going anywhere. Not for a while at least."

"You should have let me go up against the two," Bobby said. "You could have handled Mark as easy as I did."

I glanced at the blood covering Bobby's face. "It doesn't look like he was that easy to me," I said. "You look like you went fifteen rounds with Smokin' Joe."

"He sucker-punched me," Bobby said. "I thought he was going to pull his gun and he almost decked me instead. I haven't been in one of these kinds of brawls since my first year on the job."

Three RMPs and an ambulance pulled to a stop. At the corner, a uniform officer began to redirect traffic. "You need to go to the hospital, too," I said. "You might need some stitches. At the very least something to stop the blood from coming out of your nose."

A uniform patrolman came up behind us and we pointed him toward the fallen Mark, still lying on his side, bleeding and moaning.

I started to walk with Bobby toward a second ambulance pulling up to the scene. "They might keep you for a few hours," I said. "I'll let Connie know. She'll have the kitchen cook up a meal for you and bring it over."

"I'd like that," Bobby said with a smile. "I can't think of a faster way to heal than to have a great meal with Connie sitting by my side."

"You'll get the meal," I said. "Only Connie won't be the one bringing it to you."

"What?" Bobby said. "You don't trust me with her?"

"Not for a minute," I said with a smile of my own.

45.

ONE POLICE PLAZA

THE NEXT DAY

I SAT ACROSS FROM CHIEF CONNORS, WAITING AS HE READ THROUGH several pages of police reports and memos. The chief dropped the pages on his desk, sat back in his thick leather chair, and flipped off his reading glasses. "Looks like you've kept yourself busy the past couple of days," he said. "Five dead ex-cops up in Inwood Park. That seems to be the main course. The three you put in the hospital—one critical, by the way—were the dessert."

"It sounds grim," I said. "And you can pass on all the heat you're taking back to me."

"I can handle the heat, Tank," the chief said. "That stays on me. But what I won't tolerate is you going out there out of control. And five dead—ex-cops, to boot—and three in the hospital reads to me like you're out of control."

"Those five ex-cops were part of Eddie Kenwood's crew," I said. "And, if it means anything, they had come there to kill me."

"Maybe so," the chief said. "But, meanwhile, you're sitting across from me alive and well and they're getting powdered and dressed in their best suits by a Long Island mortician."

"I wasn't the one who took them out," I said.

"I don't need a connect-the-dots puzzle to reach that conclusion," the chief said. "They went down with knife wounds put to them by people who know how to handle a blade. In all the years I've known you, the only time I've seen a knife in your hand is when you're cutting into a steak."

"As for the three yesterday," I said, "the two I shot were both in self-defense. They were armed, as the report there no doubt states. The weapons were handed over at the crime scene. The third guy in the hospital was put there by one of Dee Dee's guys. Not by me. And if he hadn't put him there, the guy would have taken out a federal agent for sure."

"Look, Tank," the chief said, "I'm not trying to throw a pity party for any one of these bastards. If the Kenwood bunch had their way, they would have taken you down and it would have been weeks before we found your body. So I'm not losing a second of sleep over them."

"The three from yesterday were hired hands from the accounting firm we've been looking into," I said. "We were there to meet with a confidential informant. The CI never made it to the meeting. The three that did came looking to do some serious damage. We were lucky. They weren't."

"Is the CI dead?"

"Most likely," I said. "These guys don't play games—they've got too much to lose. The same holds true for Kenwood and his bunch. What's happened so far might well be just the beginning. I have a feeling it's going to get a lot worse before both cases are wrapped up."

The chief took a deep breath and stayed quiet for a moment. "With Kenwood you need to prove that someone else killed Rachel Nieves. And with the firm, as dirty as they may well be, you need to prove they orchestrated the death of your brother and his wife. How close are you to either one?"

"Kenwood killed Rachel Nieves," I said.

The chief stared at me, then he slammed a closed fist against the top of his desk. "Kenwood? Are you sure? Are you locked-down god-damn sure?"

"I got a confession," I said. "From Kenwood himself. He was at the meeting in Inwood Park. I guess he figured with five of his surround-ing me, I didn't stand a chance of walking out of there alive, so he might as well come out with it. And he did."

"Still leaves it your word against his," the chief said, slowly regain-ing his composure. "You're going to need at least one more witness to pin it on him."

"There was another witness," I said. "He's been working with me, helping out on both cases. The U.S. Attorney has agreed to give him blanket immunity. If you can get the higher-ups here to do the same, then we might be able to work out a deal."

"I'll see what I can do," the chief said.

"You'll need his name," I said.

The chief smiled. "I have his name," he said. "There's only one guy with a crew as good and as lethal as his. And, to top it off, they cleared out the pockets and took all the possessions of the dead ex-cops. That's not something your regular gangbanger has a habit of doing."

"Alban doesn't work for free," I said. "Not for me. Not for anyone."

"And we might need one—if not more than one—of Kenwood's ex-cop crew to flip on him on the Nieves murder in return for a re-duced sentence," the chief said. "Providing any of them are still alive by the time you're done."

"I think we're getting close on the firm, too," I said. "They wouldn't be sending three heavy hitters after me if they didn't feel our heat. Plus, Carmine is working his end."

"How so?"

"He put a bug into the right ears," I said. "The mob guys who are invested with the firm have their own accountants looking deep into their numbers. If they find out they've been screwed out of even one nickel, they will be less than pleased, and when that happens, blood usually flows."

The chief nodded. "I'll clean up the mess you left behind," he said. "The Inwood situation can be written off as a turf war with some bad badges caught in the middle. And Dee Dee is already at work on yesterday's incident. Her guy gets jumped by some bad guys, a heroic ex-cop comes to his rescue. Something along those lines."

"There's one more thing you need to know," I said. "Kenwood has something on me. Something big."

The chief rested his reading glasses on his desk. "What?"

"It's something everyone close to me needs to know," I said. "I plan on telling them in a few days. I'd like you to be there. I'll let you know when. Would do it sooner, but we have a surprise lined up for my nephew, and I don't want to do or say anything to spoil that for him. Kid's been through enough shit as it is."

"Is it back from when you were a cop?"

"No," I said. I stood and turned to leave the office. "It happened long before I joined the force."

"Whatever it is, you do seem shaken by it," the chief said. "If I didn't know you better, I'd even say you look scared. And that's a look I've never seen on Tank Rizzo."

I met his eyes and nodded. "You're right about that, Chief," I said. "I am scared. Scared to death."

46.

THE BROWNSTONE

CARMINE AND CONNIE CAME IN CARRYING LARGE PLATTERS PILED high with food from the restaurant. Chris walked in behind them, two large baskets of bread curled in his arms. "There's plenty more food coming our way," Carmine said.

Connie rested the platter on the dining room table. She then walked over toward me and wrapped one arm around my waist. "He has no idea," she whispered. "Dad made everyone in the restaurant take an oath not to say anything."

"Where's the crate?" I asked.

"I put it in your office and closed the door," Connie said. "In case the puppy made any noise. I left him water and a little bit of food."

"Kibble or veal cutlet?" Pearl asked, smiling.

"I can't wait to see the look on his face," Connie said.

"Who's going to give it to him?" I asked.

"I think this falls under your command, partner," Pearl said. "Your house, your nephew, and now your dog."

"Thanks, roomie," I said. "But remember, he's Chris's dog and he's the team's responsibility. We all agreed, at least that's how I remember it."

"Go get the puppy, honey," Connie said. "We'll worry about the logistics later."

I walked out of the room and headed toward my office. As I passed Chris, I smiled and gave him a warm pat on the shoulder. The truth was, despite my initial negativity, I'd warmed to the idea of Chris having a puppy. I began to realize the good it would do for him, as well as for me and for Pearl. For all of us.

The past few years had been difficult ones for many of the members of my team—me and Pearl being shot off the job and then having to make the adjustment to civilian life and maneuvering our way toward a new career path. And Pearl had the additional burden of coping with the physical and mental anguish of life in a wheelchair.

Working our previous case earlier in the year, we'd had to bear the loss of Joey, a man too talented and young to be felled by a bullet that was meant for me. His death is another that can never be erased from my mind. He died in my arms, the blood from his wound seeping through my fingers and drenching my clothes, his body spread across a cracked and stained New York City sidewalk. He died because of me. There is no one else to blame.

Chris lost both his parents—a brother I had once loved, and his wife, who was a stranger to me. I took Chris in to live with me and watched him adapt to a much different life, a fifteen-year-old boy forced to grow up faster than he should have. His anger at their deaths and his resentment toward me had dissipated somewhat these past few months, but traces of it lingered.

Carmine had suffered a brutal beating at the hands of a drug lord I butted heads with in the spring. It took him a few weeks to recover and he more than got a taste of revenge, helping in the fight to take down the dealer. But it had slowed him down and made him more aware of his age and limitations. Even though a fresh battle against a hard-to-take-down opponent is like rocket fuel to a former crime boss like Carmine.

Alexandra had had to deal with two thugs, one who was more than ready to slice off a chunk of her face. She used her wiles and a loaded gun to ease her way out of that traffic jam, but, still, the very thought of the damage she could have suffered troubled me.

Carl had come out of the previous case more determined than ever to prove his value to the team. The combination of the loss of Joey and the arrival of Chris had matured him in some ways, and he realized he needed to step up and be as much of a role model for my nephew as his friend had been. And through it all, Bruno had helped me keep the crew united and focused. His was the steady hand, always there when needed, fearless, willing to step into any situation, regardless of the danger.

Things between me and Connie had also changed, but for the better. Chris had drawn us closer and, rather than becoming a wedge between us, had fortified the bond that already existed. And while the addition to the team of her old college boyfriend didn't exactly give me cause to jump for joy, I didn't think of Bobby as a threat to our relationship.

And now we were ready to add a dog to our menagerie of misfits. An olde English bulldogge, meant as a gift for Chris. My hope was that, in time, he would prove to be a gift to us all.

I opened the door to my office and flipped on the light. The gate to the small crate was open and empty. I looked around the office and found the puppy snuggled under my chair, tiny head curled against his two folded front legs, one eye open and glancing up at me.

I bent down and sat on the wood floor and lifted him gently into my arms. I held him close to my chest and rubbed the back of his soft neck. "You picked the lock on the crate," I whispered to him. "Considering you've only been up here less than an hour, that's impressive. I have a feeling you're going to fit right in."

47.

THE BROWNSTONE

MOMENTS LATER

WE ALL STARED AT CHRIS, OUR FACES HARD AS STONE, DOING our best to contain our enthusiasm and hide our smiles. "What's going on?" Chris asked.

"We've added a new member to our crew," I said. "He's young, inexperienced, and is going to need quite a bit of looking after. That's going to fall on you, at least the bulk of it."

"Who is it?" Chris asked.

"His name's Gus," I said. "He's going to be rooming with you. The space is big enough to hold the two of you."

"How young is he?"

I shook my head. "To tell you the truth, I'm not that clear on those details," I said. "I wasn't the one who picked him out."

Behind me, Gus let out two yelps that passed for barks and eased his way past my legs and moved toward Chris. "He's on the short side," Carmine said, "but trust me, that's gonna change."

We all spread out and watched my nephew reach down and grab the puppy and hold him in his arms. His eyes were filled with tears and he had the widest smile I'd yet seen on his face. I looked at my entire team and saw the same reaction.

"You got us a dog?" Chris said. "I can't believe it! You got us a dog!"

"No, honey," Connie said. "We got *you* a dog. We're his family, but he belongs to you."

"His papers are all in order," Pearl said. "And we signed him up with the vet around the corner. They'll take care of him in case he gets sick, give him shots."

"We even got him health insurance," Carl said. "I can't believe he's got medical coverage."

"Something you should consider," Bruno said to him. "Might come in handy one day."

"I ordered a bunch of food for him," I said. "The vet gave us a list of what he should and shouldn't eat. He's got enough in the pantry for a few weeks."

"And he can't play with other dogs until he gets all his shots," Carmine said. "Don't want him catching anything he don't need to catch."

"Does he have a leash?" Chris asked.

"He's got a couple," I said. "And a few collars with his name and my cell-phone number stenciled on them. And when he's older, we'll have a chip put in him. In case he decides to pull a Papillon and make a break for it. Makes it easier to track him down."

"I don't know what to say," Chris said. His emotions were getting the better of him, and he squeezed Gus closer to his chest.

Chris scanned the room and stared at the faces that, in short order, had grown to become his family. We would never replace what he had lost, nor would we attempt to do so. But we could all, collectively, make him at home in what had to still feel like an unfamiliar environment so he'd gradually accept his new surroundings as his own.

"The little guy might be hungry," Carmine said to Chris. "You'll find a couple of bowls in the kitchen, on the island there, hard to miss. They have the pup's name written on them."

"And don't give him tap water to drink," Bruno said.

"Why not?" Carl asked.

"None of us drink it—why should Gus?" Carmine said. "Give him the Acqua Panna, that's the best. If you're in a pinch, Poland Spring is a good substitute."

"I'm glad to see we're not going to spoil him," I said. "Maybe I should have ordered his food from Tramonti's instead of the vet's office."

"That would have been a better way to go, you ask me," Carmine said. "But he's a baby still. We got time before we break him in on eggplant parm with a side of baked clams."

Chris walked over toward me and held Gus out for me to hold. "Can you take him for a minute?" he said. "There's something I need to show you."

I lifted Gus and cradled him in my right arm. Chris reached into the rear pocket of his jeans and pulled out a folded batch of papers. He flipped them open and handed them to me. I grabbed them with my free hand and scanned the first page. There were fifteen names typed down the left side of the page, with dollar amounts next to each one.

"What is this?" I asked.

"There are forty-five names on those pages," Chris said. "The figures are how much money each has invested in the accounting firm. The money is kept in offshore accounts and, as far as we can tell, none of it has been reported as income to the IRS."

"Who is 'we'?" I asked.

"Bobby helped me follow the money trail," Chris said. "He had a working list of one hundred and sixty-five names, which we narrowed down to the ones on the list."

"Is the firm funneling money without their knowledge?" Pearl asked.

"We don't know yet," Chris said.

I rested Gus on the wood floor and flipped through the pages, scanning both the names and the large sums of money attached to them. "Some Russian mob, some Italian," I said. "A couple of cartel guys, and the rest are high-end business types not eager to share their wealth with Uncle Sam."

"Which means nobody on that list is going to run and spill their guts to the cops," Carmine said.

I got to the last page and froze when I saw the name on the bottom.

I looked at Chris, who stared back and then lowered his head. "One of them was thinking of doing just that," I said. "And, as we know, all it takes is one."

"Who?" Pearl asked.

I reached for Chris and brought him to my side and held him close to me. "You want to tell them?" I asked.

Chris nodded. "My dad's name is on the list," he said in a low but strong voice. "And next to his name is the amount the firm invested for him."

The room stayed silent for several moments.

"How much?" Pearl finally asked.

"One and a half million dollars," Chris said.

"You think he knew about it?" Carmine asked.

"No, I don't," I said. "Not at first, anyway. But he was good at what he did. Maybe he started sniffing around, found the same list Chris and Bobby dug up and saw his name on it, right next to the mob guys and the cartel bosses. And that might be when he started thinking of making a move against the firm."

"So it's dark money," Pearl said. "Not to be seen until the heat is on. Then they open the books and point to guys like Jack. Make it look like they were the ones skimming money. Gives them a chance to skate away clean."

"Unless they decided Jack could no longer be trusted," I said. "Carmine's right. The names on the list are not going to go running to the cops. It's not in their interest. But Jack's a whole different story. He could go to the cops and lay it all out for them."

"And that makes him a threat," Pearl said. "And that's not something these guys can risk. Especially from one of their own."

"So, to keep that list buried . . ." Carmine said.

"They needed to bury Jack," I said.

48.

BRYANT PARK

THE NEXT DAY

I GOT THE CALL AS I WAS HEADING OUT FOR AN EARLY-MORNING run. Ray Connors was on the other end. The chief didn't waste time or words. "Get up to Bryant Park soon as you can," he said. "Pearl, too."

"What's there?" I asked.

"A crime scene," the chief said, and then he ended the call.

Less than thirty minutes later, me and Pearl were gazing down at the battered and bruised body of Zeke Jeffries. He was facedown under a park bench. The upper half of his body was resting on the cracked pavement, his legs stretched out under the slabs of the bench, his sneakered feet at rest on the edges of a small pile of mulch. His body was rigid and thick; dark patches of blood had formed under his head, chest, and stomach. A paperback copy of *Pimp* by Iceberg Slim rested a few inches from his right hand.

There was yellow police tape closing off the area around Zeke's body and a full boat of cops, CSU technicians, and detectives scanning the area. Chief Connors stood next to me and Pearl, a cold container of coffee clutched in his right hand.

"He was beaten to death," I said, my eyes still on Zeke. "It had to have happened at night, when he was alone. Zeke had too many friends in these parks for anybody to come at him in daylight hours."

"That's my guess, too," the chief said. "The medical examiner will make the final call, but it has all the markings of a beatdown."

"And it had to be more than one primary," Pearl said. "Zeke might have slowed up some, but one-on-one he could be a handful. Bad knees and all."

"He always had a cane with him," I said. "Had a switchblade hidden at the base. All Zeke had to do was tap on a button near the handle to flip it out. That turn up anywhere?"

The chief nodded. "One of the techs found it in the brush, past that tree to your right. The blade was out and there was blood on the knife and the lower portion of the cane. We had it bagged and sent to the lab."

"This doesn't have the feel of a mugging gone south," I said. "Go up a few blocks and you have your pick of the tourists heading to a Broadway show. Go down and you got a sold-out concert going on at the Garden. The pickings in this park, especially at night, are pretty slim. Even for a street junkie looking for a quick score."

"Zeke was targeted," Pearl said. "And they didn't come looking to warn him. They came to kill."

"And who would 'they' be, if you don't mind my asking?" the chief said.

I glanced at Pearl and he nodded. "Eddie Kenwood and his crew," I said.

"You got anything to back that up?" the chief asked.

"We talked to Zeke a few days back," I said. "Asked him to keep an ear out for anything worth a listen. You know how plugged in he was to what was going down on the street. It's not a stretch for Kenwood or one of his bunch to get wind of that."

"You're going to need more than that for me to send two cops knocking on his door," the chief said.

I gazed out at the crime scene. "You're not likely to find any of Kenwood's prints around here. Even the blood results won't come back pointing in his direction. But Zeke's murder has his mark on it. I'd bet my life on it."

Pearl nodded his head toward the paperback. "He wouldn't touch Zeke," he said. "Kenwood's too smart for something that stupid. But he might have grabbed that book. Be a good idea to have the techs bag it and check it for prints."

The chief flagged down one of the CSU technicians and pointed at the book. The young man pulled a clear bag from his gear and picked up the book with gloved hands. He placed it in the bag and zipped it shut.

"I need those prints soon as you can get them," the chief said to him.

Pearl looked at me and then back down to Zeke. "Seeing that book brings back many memories," he said. "It was old Zeke here that turned me and Tank on to it in the first place."

"How so?" the chief asked.

"There was a brief time, in between our stints in narcotics and homicide, that me and Tank got assigned to the vice squad," Pearl said.

"It was known as the 'pussy posse' back then," I said. "And me and Pearl had no idea how to tackle the job. We weren't looking to bust hookers. They have it tough enough as is. We were eager to take down some of the higher-volume pimps. But those guys had their own lingo, you know? And it was one we didn't know."

"We were talking to Zeke about it one night, and he thought the best way to learn the language was to read Iceberg Slim," Pearl said. "Slim was a pimp himself. And the book not only had the terminology down, it had the street lingo me and Tank needed to make us sound like we knew what the hell was what."

"How did he get the name Iceberg Slim?" the chief asked.

"That's a story in itself," Pearl said. "Seems Iceberg was sitting in a bar late one night, knocking back a few, when a guy stepped up to him and held a pistol to his head and put a bullet right through his skull."

"And Iceberg didn't even flinch," I said. "Instead, he sat on that barstool and he finished his drink."

"Of such tales, legends are made," Pearl said. "Iceberg was one. Zeke was another."

"Did Zeke give you anything about Kenwood?" the chief asked.

"He gave us a name," I said. "A muscle head working as a bouncer at a club in the Meatpacking District. We talked to him already. He's got ties to Kenwood and has agreed to snitch for us. He hears anything worthwhile, he's to bring it our way."

"You figure him for this?"

I shrugged. "He might have been called in on it," I said. "But it's not something he would have done on his own. He'd only be here if Kenwood told him to."

"What's his name?" the chief said.

"J. J. Livingstone," I said.

The chief looked at me and then at Pearl. "I know you would love for me to bring in Kenwood for questioning," he said. "But I don't have an inch of proof he was involved in this, and, let's not forget, he's a decorated ex-cop."

"Nothing would make me happier than to see that bastard sweating under the lights of an interrogation room," I said. "But I know it's a tough call. I got him to cop to one murder. And if his prints pop on Zeke's book, then we got him on a second. That would be reason enough to slap cuffs on him and haul his ass downtown. *If* he's still alive by then, that is."

The chief stayed silent as he stared at both me and Pearl. "I hate the prick as much as you do," he said. "But death isn't what a guy like Kenwood fears the most. In fact, if given the choice, hard time or a coffin, the easy money puts him under the ground."

"I'm not looking to end him, Chief," I said. "If it comes down to him or me, then that's a choice I'll have to make. But I agree, behind bars is where he belongs and where I'd like to put his sorry ass."

"He won't be lacking for company on any of those prison tiers, that's for damn sure," Pearl said. "All those young guys he put away long ago are now hardcore convicts. They'll welcome him with wide smiles and open arms."

"Not to mention a few of those hand-carved wooden knives and knuckle-wrap bed springs," I said.

"Nothing would please me more," the chief said.

I bent down and rested one hand on top of Zeke's bloody head. I reached for his left hand with mine and held it tight. I stayed that way for several moments. The chief and Pearl circled closer to Zeke's body, the three of us mourning the loss of an old and trusted friend. "The ones who did this will pay, Zeke," I said, my face streaked with tears. "That's not a promise. It's a blood oath. They will pay."

49.

THE BROWNSTONE

THE NEXT DAY

THEY WERE ALL THERE. PEARL. MY ENTIRE TEAM. CARMINE. CONNIE. Chris. Chief Connors. Bobby. I didn't leave anyone out. The time had come for me to confront them with my past, expose my deepest-held secret. The moment had arrived for them to see me for who I truly was.

A murderer.

I poured myself a glass of Brunello and took a long sip. I gazed at the faces gathered around me and took a deep breath and a second sip of wine. "I have something I need to tell all of you," I said. "Something I should have told you long before today. I don't know what you'll think of me after I've said my piece. Whatever way you may end up feeling, I want you to know this: Everyone I love and respect is in this room. Nothing that happens today will ever change that. Nothing."

"The same goes for me, partner," Pearl said. "No matter what you have to tell us. The way it was between us yesterday will be the way it is tomorrow."

I smiled at Pearl and faced the room. "When me and Jack were kids, my parents would rent a cabin in Maine every August. To get us out of the city, breathe some fresh air, go sailing, ride canoes, hiking, mountain climbing, all the things we didn't have much chance to do here. It was in a great little town called Rockport, near Camden. My dad loved it for the fishing, my mom loved the fresh lobster and the relaxed way of life. Me and Jack loved the nearby pools we could swim in and the lakes we could take boats on. It was a week we always looked forward to. A great time for the four of us to get away."

"I remember you guys taking those vacations," Carmine said. "Your pop would come back and talk about all the sailing he did, the fish he caught, the mountain trails you all hiked. Every August it was like I was talking to Jack London instead of your old man."

"It was a great place," I said. "For each of us. Until that last summer we went up. I was fifteen, Jack was twelve. We always rented the same cabin. But it didn't really matter. They all looked alike and were all bunched together. Small two-bedroom places with outdoor grills and front porches. You could sleep with the windows open, that's how cool it would get at night. And how safe the area was. For a few years, the same couple came up with their kids from someplace down South and we would spend some time with them. All of us driving to Miss Plum's for ice cream or down to the lobster pound for the Friday night special."

I reached for my glass and took another sip of wine. I looked around the room as I did. They all sat or stood in place, eager to hear the heart of the tale, knowing as well as I did that what they had just heard was merely the setup. I held the glass cupped in my hands and noticed the slight tremble of my wrists and fingers. The vision of what I was about to relay now coming into sharp focus in my mind.

"That last summer, that other family didn't make the trip up for whatever reason," I continued. "Their cabin, just down from ours, was rented instead by a single man in his late thirties, maybe a little older. He was brawny, sullen, and stayed to himself. Whenever we crossed paths with him, he would barely acknowledge my parents, but he made a point to smile or wink at me or at Jack. I noticed he left the cabin early in the morning, usually about sunup, and returned in the mid-afternoon. He drank a lot and there were bottles of bourbon or scotch, usually empty, tossed around the porch. There were no TVs in the cabins, but he brought along a cassette recorder and played heavy-metal rock all hours of the day and night. My father wanted to go over and ask him to turn it down a couple of times, but my mom always talked him out of it."

I put my glass on the coffee table and felt the sweat running down the back of my button-down shirt. I took a deep breath and continued. "This one day, Jack wasn't feeling well, coming down with a cold," I said. "My folks headed into Camden to pick up food and supplies and asked us to stay close to the cabin. I was specifically asked to keep an eye on Jack. We were between the two cabins, ours and our neighbor's, playing catch, when the neighbor showed up earlier than usual and seemed to be drunk and angry. He stared at us for a few moments and then went into his cabin. After a bit, me and Jack took a break from the game. He wanted to go down to the lake, cool off. I went to the cabin to change while Jack waited outside, bouncing a ball against the wall."

The crowded living room was still and silent, as if they were sitting through a horror movie, waiting for the killer to emerge. No one ate, no one drank, no one moved. I watched as Connie refilled my wine-glass, her right hand trembling slightly.

"I was back out in ten minutes," I said. "Maybe less. I spotted Jack's glove in a thick patch of grass, the ball resting against it. His Little League bat, the one that had his name stenciled on the barrel, was up against a tree that stood between our cabin and the next one, where the neighbor was staying. I looked to my left and to my right and didn't see him. I called out his name a few times, each one louder than the last, and got no reply. I knew he wouldn't have gone down to the lake without me. Jack wouldn't have gone anywhere without me. I glanced over at the next cabin and noticed the screen door flapping. I grabbed Jack's bat from the tree and held it in my right hand. To this very moment, I have no idea what made me reach for the bat. Instinct. Luck. Nerves. But grab it I did, and I held it against the side of my leg and walked toward the neighbor's cabin."

I looked at Connie and saw tears running down her face, as if she knew what I was about to say and couldn't bear to hear it. All the others in the room sat and listened, each one hanging on to my every word.

"I was about five feet or so from the screen door when I heard Jack's voice," I said. My throat was dry and my voice was cracking. I closed my eyes for a moment, the scene from long ago now as vivid as if I were there once again. "Then I heard something fall to the cabin floor and shatter, a lamp or a bottle. I stepped up to the screen door and looked in. Jack was lying facedown on the filthy floor, the man's left hand gripping the back of his neck, holding him in place, ignoring the kicking and writhing. The man's breaths were coming in spurts as he attempted to undo his pants with his free hand. I stood there, drowning in sweat, my heart racing, my hands clutched around the bat, gripping it as tightly as I could."

Connie reached out a hand for mine and I took it, holding it as tight as I had held the bat. "The sight of the man unbuckling his belt and lowering his jeans around his thighs, his white bare skin visible in the sharp sunlight, snapped me out of my frightened pose. I swung the screen door open and stepped into the room. 'Get the fuck off my brother' were the only words I said to him. He turned the minute he heard me and caught the first swing of the bat hard across his face. He toppled onto his back, falling off Jack, the pants bunched around his upper legs. Jack turned and looked at me. I will never get that look out of my head, no matter how many years pass by. It was a look of fear and terror, and seeing it shook awake something in me I had no idea was even there. 'Let's go, Tank,' Jack said to me. 'Let's get out of here.'

"I heard the words, but they were lost on me. I moved past Jack and stood over the fallen man. He had a glazed look in his eyes and blood streaming down the front of his face and neck. I raised the bat and hit him on the side of his head. I could feel the weight of the bat crack through bone and slice flesh. I lifted the bat and swung it down again. And again. And again. And again. I swung the bat until I could no longer lift it."

I took several deep breaths, my body coated with sweat, my hands shaking, my legs weak. I leaned against one side of the couch and wiped my forehead with the back of my right hand.

"I fell to my knees and gazed down at the damage I had done," I said. "Even though I had never seen a dead man before, I was sure the beaten and bloody mess that lay before me was no longer breathing. I turned away from the man and looked at Jack. He was on his feet, crying quietly, both hands clutched against his mouth, as if he were swallowing a scream. His eyes were wide open, and his tanned skin now seemed to me to be ghost white. I stared at Jack and he stared back at me, the dead man on the ground a bloodied barrier that lay between us."

"You had no choice, Tank," Carmine said, breaking the silence in the room. "He was hurting your brother. If it were me in that room, on that day, I would have done the same thing. Probably even worse."

"I could have stopped after the first blow," I said. "But I didn't. It unleashed a rage inside me that I didn't know was there. That scared me as much as killing the man. From that day to this, I knew that hidden rage would always be a part of me."

"That's something I'm afraid we all have," Pearl said. "We're born with it, I suppose. Don't really know why it's there, inside of us, but it does rise to the surface now and again. And, on that day, it was a damn good thing it did. For you and for Jack. God only knows what that sick bastard could have done."

I looked at Pearl and nodded. The voices around me sounded like echoes in a cave, and my eyes could barely focus on their faces. Instead, all I could see, no matter how often I tried to blink it away, was me, Jack, and the dead man, all in that tiny, disheveled room in a cabin reeking of booze and smoke.

"Time stood still for us in that room," I said, "so I don't know how long it was before our mom and dad showed up. By the time they did, Jack had made his way out of the cabin, walking backward, hands still clutched across his mouth, his face still covered with tears, his nose running. My father came into the cabin, gazed down at the bloodied body, and gently took the bat from my hand. 'Let's get out of here, Tank,' he said in a calm voice. 'Get you out of this shithole and away from all this.'

"I turned to my father and took one final look at the man I had beaten to death. 'I killed him, Dad,' I said. 'I killed that man.' My father didn't respond. He just walked me out of the cabin, his arm around my shoulders."

"Did you go to the cops about it?" Chief Connors asked.

I shook my head. "We didn't tell the cops," I said. "We didn't tell anybody. My dad left me and Jack with my mom while he emptied our gear from the cabin into our car. He cleaned the place, left it spotless. We waited until it was dark, and then the four of us got in the car and drove away. We never bothered looking back. The next day was set to be our last day at the cabin, so no one would find it odd that we pulled out the night before. We drove most of the way in silence and turned our backs on Rockport forever."

"Is that why you and my dad never spoke to each other?" Chris asked.

"Yes," I said. "Jack wanted to forget what did happen and what could have happened in that room. Not talking about it helped him come to terms with that. Plus, I imagine he saw a side of me that scared him almost as much as what that man had planned to do to him. And, to be honest, I wasn't eager to revisit it, either. So we never talked about it. Not me, not Jack, and not my parents. It made it easier for us to live with it. There were no winners that day. A man died, deserving or not. I lost my brother and he lost me."

"So, as far as Rockport PD is concerned, it's still down as a cold case," the chief said.

I nodded. "The dead man's name was Frank Muncie. He was a predicate felon with a long rap sheet, including two convictions for rape of a minor."

"Never for the life of me will I understand why they let scum like that out of prison," Carmine said. "You do harm to a child just once, you lose the right to call yourself a human. Toss him in, lock the cell, and lose the key."

"It's a cold case but not one anyone was all that eager to solve," I said. "Seems the cops up there had the same attitude Carmine has. One less child rapist for them to worry themselves about. There wasn't much activity on it back then, even less as the years passed."

"Did the local cops reach out to your folks?" the chief asked.

"They got our home number from the guy we rented the cabin from," I said. "Called the house and asked my dad a few questions. He told them what he knew about Muncie, which wasn't all that much. Dad answered all their questions, they seemed satisfied with his answers, and they never called again."

"So no one knows it happened?" Bruno asked.

"Somebody knows," I said.

"Who?" Chief Connors asked.

"Eddie Kenwood," I said.

I took one final sip of wine, rested my glass on the coffee table, and walked slowly past my crew and friends and out of the room. I needed to grab some fresh air, take a long, slow walk, and let them digest what I had told them.

As I began my walk through the tree-lined streets of my neighborhood, I wondered how it would affect Chris and if it would alter the relationship the two of us had managed to forge. And what about Connie? Would her love for me change now that she knew the full details about the man Jack saw me murder? Yes, she had been raised knowing what her father did for a living and she knew being a cop came with the risk of taking a life. But this was out-and-out murder, in the most cold-blooded of ways. A murder committed by a man she loved.

I wasn't sure if it would affect how my crew perceived me. If they would now view me under a different scope. And the same was true for Chief Connors and Pearl. The two of them, along with Carmine, had known me for decades and seen me in action. They knew what I was capable of and that I had a temper that would erupt if provoked. I never went looking to cause trouble or bring harm to anyone. But if trouble came my way or if someone close to me was in danger, then I would react, often in a deadly way.

As concerned as I was about the reactions of my friends, one question kept returning to the front of my mind: How did Eddie Kenwood know my secret?

I stopped at a corner and sat on the middle step of a brownstone stoop. I raised my face to the warm sun and closed my eyes. As I sat there, soaking up the sun and looking to erase the image of a much younger me swinging a bat at a defenseless man, I hoped I would not need to wait long for the answers to my questions or the resolution of the two cases that lay before me.

All it would take was for more blood to be spilled and more bodies laid to waste.

What had been true back in Rockport, Maine, would prove to be even truer in New York City.

50.

TRAMONTI'S

TWO DAYS LATER

CONNIE SAT ALONE AT THE BAR, WORKING ON THE DAY'S MENU, her second cup of decaf resting near her right elbow. This was her favorite time to be in the restaurant, early in the morning, the streets outside dark and silent, the mad rush of the day still a few hours away. She glanced at the legal pad, put her pen down, and lifted the warm cup of coffee to her lips. Her early-morning ritual was also a good time for Connie to clear her head and give some thought to any concerns she needed to confront.

Her life with Tank was in a warm comfort zone; not even his admission of what she believed was a justified murder committed by a frightened teenager would be strong enough to damage the love they shared. She worried about the effect the two cases he was working were having on him, but she also knew he was strong enough to take them on. She knew how important it was for him to resolve both, how much it mattered to the entire team, and knew there was little for her to do but be by his side and help in any way she could.

The transition of having Chris move in with him was getting better by the day, helped no doubt by Pearl joining them and now the addition of a puppy. Still, Connie couldn't help but wonder if Tank and Pearl had bitten off too big a piece. They were often outnumbered, but in this instance, the opposition seemed more ruthless and dangerous than the last case they had taken—a drug boss doing all he could to hang on to the mini-empire he had built. But the drug lord had limited resources when compared to those of Eddie Kenwood and the accounting firm. The combination of the two lethal forces was enough to keep her up at night.

A noise came from the back of the restaurant, over by the kitchen. It was too early for any of the workers to be starting their shifts and too late for the cleaning crew to still be working. Connie put down her cup, slid off her seat, and walked toward the rear of the restaurant. She had turned off the alarm when she came in less than an hour earlier and all had seemed to be in order. But she hadn't gone to the kitchen area. Instead, she went behind the bar, brewed herself a pot of coffee, and began work on the day's schedule.

She entered the kitchen and looked from left to right. Everything was where it should be—pots and pans hanging off hooks, cleaned and polished; stove tops scrubbed free of grease and oil; the floor mopped and shiny. Connie nodded and smiled. A clean kitchen was a point of pride with her, as it had been with her mother, and she was unrelenting in her quest to keep it as spotless as possible. "She's the police commissioner of the kitchen," Carmine liked to say, teasing her in an approving way. "Just like her mother was. If you can't see your reflection in any of the pots, pans, countertops, floors, there will be hell to pay."

She felt the harsh breath of the man the second before he wrapped an arm around her neck. He had been hiding in a corner of the kitchen, behind one of the swinging doors, and came at her with silent footsteps. "Do what I say," he whispered in her right ear, "when I say it."

He turned her around and led her out of the kitchen and back into the main area of the restaurant. "The register's empty," she managed to say, the man's forearm wedged tight against her throat. "We take the money out every night at closing time."

"That's good to know," the man said, pushing her deeper into the restaurant. "Especially since I'm not here for any of your money."

They stood in front of a booth and the man released her and shoved her against the side of a table. He kept both hands on his waist, revealing a holstered gun on his hip. "Sit down," he said. "Now."

Connie caught her breath and sat in a corner of the leather booth. "Well, you must have come here for a reason," she said. "If not money, then what?"

"To teach you a lesson," a second man said from over her shoulder. She turned and gazed up at a thin man in a brown leather jacket and tailored white slacks. He was holding a pair of brown leather gloves in his right hand. He turned to the first man, who wasn't as well dressed, was much more muscular, and had an angry look on a ragged face that made him appear much older than he probably was. "Get me a chair, Jerry," the second man said to him. "I want to sit as close as possible to the lady. Make sure she hears every word I'm going to tell her."

Connie and the second man stared at each other, waiting as Jerry pulled a chair from one of the empty tables and brought it over to the booth. The second man sat down and took a deep breath. He rested the brown leather gloves on the table and folded one leg over the other, careful not to put too much of a wrinkle in the crease.

"What do you want?" Connie asked.

"I'm here to deliver some news," he said. His voice was soft and low, with a slight hint of a foreign accent. "None of it good, I'm afraid."

"Let's hear it, then," Connie said. "And make it fast. The sooner you're out of here, the better it will be for you. The staff should start arriving soon."

The man smiled and shrugged. "I'm well aware," he said. "And I don't wish to keep you from your business, so I promise to be brief."

"I see your lips moving, but I haven't heard one word I need to hear," Connie said. She was angry and doing her best to keep her temper at a low boil.

"You are indeed your father's daughter," he said. He turned to look at Jerry, hovering on the other side of the booth. "Don't you think so?"

"She's better looking, I'll give her that, Mike," Jerry said. "But the flash temper sure as shit was passed down."

"You bet your ass I'm his daughter," Connie said. "Even more my mother's. She always kept a sharp—very sharp—kitchen knife in her apron, all day, every day. Came in with it in the morning, left with it at night. If only I had held up that family tradition. I'd be sitting here drinking coffee, watching you spitting up blood."

"Well, you didn't and we're not," Mike said.

"What's your news?"

"Someone close to you is going to die," Mike said. "Your father, perhaps. Your boyfriend. Maybe even the boy living with him or his friend in the wheelchair. The target has been chosen, but that particular piece of information has not been given to me."

"And who is going to kill that someone?" Connie asked. "You? Or your steroid-chugging pal?"

"You don't need to know that," Mike said.

"So far you don't seem to know shit," Connie said, practically spitting out the words.

Mike took the brown leather gloves from the tabletop, raised them, and slapped Connie hard across the face. He landed three forceful slaps, causing her face to redden and her eyes to tear. "You need to learn to be polite," he said. "Allow me to finish what I came here to tell you. Have I made myself clear?"

Connie nodded.

"The target will die within the next forty-eight hours," Mike said. "Now, I'm in no position to prevent that from happening. But you are."

Connie didn't say a word. She stared at Mike, her moist eyes filled with anger, pain, and concern. She never raised a hand to her face, ignoring the burning caused by the fierce blows.

"Have your boyfriend back away from his investigation of a legitimate and very successful business, and perhaps no further bloodshed will be necessary," Mike said. "But he needs to do so today. If he insists on continuing, then I'm afraid someone you hold dear will die. Can I count on you to relay that message to him?"

Connie shook her head and for the first time that morning smiled.

"I think it would be better if you told him yourself," she said. "It would mean so much more to him to have it come from you."

Mike looked at his watch and then back at Connie. "Tell him, don't tell him, it's all the same to me," he said.

I SPOTTED THE TWO men as I walked past Tramonti's on my way from the brownstone. Through the glass windows I could see one sitting and the other standing, both too occupied with Connie to take any notice of me. I opened the front door as quietly as possible, crouched down, and rested my morning papers on the floor. I moved on hands and knees until I reached the back of the first booth. I leaned with my back against the soft leather and listened to what they were saying. I then got back to my knees and poked my head out, long enough for me to catch Connie's eye. I stood and moved toward the two men.

I came up behind Jerry and landed two hard kidney punches to his right side, then crashed my left elbow against the side of his head. The blows sent Jerry to his knees and happened so quickly that Mike had little time to react. I reached over and yanked him, sprawling, to the ground. I glanced up and saw Bruno running in from the front door toward the booth. "Keep an eye on the guy on his knees," I said to him. "I'll deal with the tough guy with the leather gloves."

I grabbed the brown leather gloves off the tabletop. I picked Mike up by his shirt collar and rained several blows down on his face with the gloves, and I didn't stop until his face was beet red and blood oozed out of his nose and down his lips.

I tossed the gloves back on the table and turned to Connie. I took one look at her face, welts forming across her left cheek, and once again I snapped. I picked up a chair and smashed it down on Mike. One of the legs splintered off, and the back end caught Mike flush on the top of his head. I kicked him in the chest and then jumped on him, my legs straddling his upper body, and punched him with both hands, each blow harder than the previous one.

From the corner of my eye, I saw Jerry reach a hand inside his jacket, and in the same moment I heard Connie shout, "He's got a gun, Bruno!"

Bruno punched Jerry in the center of his gun hand, cracking bone with one blow. He then grabbed the man's hand and snapped it back, the crunching sound loud enough to be heard by the five of us. "He's got a broken wrist, too," Bruno said.

I got off Mike and stood above him. I stomped my feet against his hands, looking to break as many bones as I could. I kicked at his chest and stomach, hearing him moan and watching him cough up thin lines of blood after every blow. Mike turned on his side and I landed hard kicks against his spine and upper back. My fury was unleashed, doing damage to a man who had dared to hit Connie. I was lost in a dense fog of violence. It was a place I had been before and had found solace in.

Connie got up from the booth and I looked at her, my right leg lifted to lay down another blow on the crumpled and bleeding man. She was scared and trembling. "Stop, Tank," she said, her words barely above a whisper. "Please stop."

I stared back at her and nodded. I lowered my leg and reached out for her. It was then I noticed both my hands were coated in blood and the skin on my knuckles had been flayed off. I put my hands back by my sides. "You okay?" was all I could manage to say.

"I'm fine," she said. "You and Bruno need to get these two out of here. My father could walk in the front door any minute."

"I'm sorry, Connie," I said. "I hate that you just saw that."

"But I did, Tank," she said. "And it scared me. Scared me more than these two did."

"We'll get them to a hospital," I said to her.

Connie started to walk toward the back of the bar, making her way to the kitchen. "I'll clean up the blood," she said. "And the less my dad knows about this, the better." When she reached the bar, she stopped and turned around. "Would you have killed him, Tank?" she asked me. "If I hadn't stopped you, would you have beaten him until he was dead?"

I gazed down at Mike. His body was curled in a tight ball, one of his hands resting limply by his side. His face was a red mask and he was having trouble breathing. I looked back up at Connie and shook my head. "I don't know," I said. "And not knowing that scares me as much as I know it scares you."

Connie nodded, not bothering to hide the tears in her eyes or the sadness etched across her face. She stared at me for a few moments and then disappeared silently into the kitchen.

51.

ONE POLICE PLAZA

LATER THAT DAY

I STOOD FACING CHIEF CONNORS AND DEE DEE JACOBS, THE U.S. Attorney. Dee Dee was to my left and the chief was sitting behind his desk. They were both drinking coffee and staring at my bandaged hands. "You going to fill us in?" the chief asked. "Or make us guess?"

"The firm sent two guys to rattle Connie early this morning," I said. "They went there to warn her, not to do damage. But one of them did hit her."

"Are they still among the living?" Dee Dee asked.

"They're at Beekman Downtown. Me and Bruno got them there. They're a little banged up, one more than the other, but they should be good to go in a week or so."

"I put in a few calls up to the Rockport police department," the chief said. "Asking about the Frank Muncie case. See what they had to say about it, if anything. And I filled Dee Dee in on what happened up there between you and Muncie."

I shifted my feet and my mouth went dry. "What did they say?" I managed to ask.

"Well, first I had to ease their curiosity as to why the NYPD Chief of Detectives was calling about a case I have no business in," he said. "I danced around it as best I could. Told them Muncie's name had come up during a routine interrogation one of my homicide detectives was working on."

"Not exactly a lie," Dee Dee said. "Not the truth, either. But still."

"They buy it?" I asked.

"Seemed to," the chief said. "They called back after about an hour. They needed time to dig up whatever file they had on the case."

"And?" I asked.

"Muncie was someone they had their eyes on since he moved to the area," the chief said. "He was a known pedophile and liked to hang around playgrounds and schools. Cops ran him off whenever they spotted him. He was close to normal when he was sober, but once he started on the bottle, that's when the demons shook loose."

"They have any suspects from back then?" I asked.

"More than one," Dee Dee said. She had an open folder in her hands and was reading from the chief's notes. "He had a few threats against him from fathers demanding that he stay away from their kids."

"The Rockport cops figure he got too close to one kid and was done in by a father, a brother, a relative," the chief said.

"That's more on the money than they know," I said.

"In short, they didn't look into his murder too hard back then," Dee Dee said. "And they're even less interested in it now. Just another dead pedophile who got what he deserved."

We all stayed quiet for a few moments. "So how did Eddie Kenwood come to find out what happened?"

"You were seen, Tank," the chief said.

His words caused me to take a step back. I lowered my head and tried to piece together all the images from that day. "We got out of there as fast as we could," I said. "We didn't have much to pack and the cabins were usually empty at that hour, most people either hiking or hitting the tourist sites."

"All you need is one pair of eyes," Dee Dee said. "A guy named Jason Chatwood was sitting in a garden chair under a shady tree. Just down the road from your cabin. He saw you come out of Muncie's cabin and then saw you and your family hustle up, pack, and pull out."

"But he didn't go to the cops, right?" I asked.

The chief shook his head. "He talked to them, but he didn't tell them everything he saw," he said. "Not sure why—maybe he was one of those mind-your-own-business guys. But he never forgot what he saw. So it became a story for him to tell, sitting around the dining room table or at the local bar. Something to share with close friends."

"How'd you find him so quick?" I asked.

"He was an assistant to the landlord who rented out to your folks," the chief said. "I imagine he thought a random murder wouldn't do too much damage to the business. But a pedophile living in one of the cabins might cut into his family-vacation trade big time and cost him a job."

"Which still leaves Kenwood," I said. "When does he come into it?"

"That's where the words 'It's a small world' enter the picture," Dee Dee said. "Kenwood's mother was named Edie Chatwood. Jason was her uncle on her father's side. Jason would often come down to New York during the holidays, spend time with the family. Might not have mentioned the story for a few years. If at all."

"But you and Pearl started getting lots of tabloid attention from all your busts," the chief said. "As was Eddie Kenwood from his. If it was just the name Rizzo, old Jason might not have made the connection. But not many kids are named Tank. And not many cops are, either."

"So you figure he put two and two together and passed on what he knew or thought he knew to Eddie?" I said.

"That's as good an answer as we can come up with," the chief said. "At least for now."

"If what we dug up is right, and I'm pretty sure it is," Dee Dee said, "then you caught some luck. Again, I might add."

"How do you figure that?" I asked.

"Jason Chatwood died two years ago," the chief said. "The cabins are still there but have been refurbished and modernized and go for a lot more money than your parents paid."

"The original detective assigned to the case is dead, too, as is his boss," Dee Dee said. "Kenwood's parents are long buried, as well. And that leaves Eddie Kenwood with a story he heard from an old family relative. He might still be able to prove you were up there when the murder happened. A big maybe, the way I imagine cabin rental books were kept. But that's all he can prove."

"And that's not going to take him very far," the chief said.

"And where do I stand with you?" I asked, looking from the chief to Dee Dee.

"I have no jurisdiction in Maine," the chief said. "And the very last thing I'm eager to do is look to solve a pedophile's murder."

"I don't work the local news," Dee Dee said. "You got no worries from my end."

"How did you connect Jason Chatwood to Kenwood?" I asked.

"Chatwood didn't have any family, other than his sister and his grandnephew," the chief said. "He didn't have much in the way of money, either. But he did have a small piece of land in Portland, Maine. He left that land to Eddie Kenwood."

"And we got our hands on Chatwood's phone logs going back five years," Dee Dee said. "We matched his number with the one we have on file for Kenwood and they talked at least three, sometimes five times a month. From there, we put two and two together until we crossed the goal line."

I nodded. "Thank you," I said. "And I'm sorry I didn't come to you sooner with this. I honestly didn't know how. Frank Muncie deserved what he got. I can't stand here and tell you different. But his murder cost me my brother. And Muncie sure as hell wasn't worth that."

"No," the chief said. "He wasn't worth that."

"But finding your brother's killer is worth something," Dee Dee said. "Peace of mind, if nothing else."

"For you," the chief said. "And for his son."

"You've both earned that," Dee Dee said.

I looked at them, turned, and walked quietly out of the office.

52.

THE BROWNSTONE

IT DIDN'T TAKE LONG FOR WORD TO SPREAD ABOUT WHAT HAD occurred at Tramonti's. My crew rushed to my place as fast as they could, joining Pearl and Chris in my living room. Chris stood next to Connie and held her hand, Gus between them, eagerly chewing on one of Chris's sneaker laces. Carmine sat in a lounge chair in a corner of the room. His demeanor was calm, but I knew that below the surface a hurricane was brewing. In the world where Carmine spent the greater part of his life, there was one rule that was absolute and sacrosanct: Never touch family. I looked at him and we exchanged a glance and I nodded. If we were going to take down the accounting firm for the murder of my brother and his wife and an assortment of other crimes, I would need Carmine at his best. And nothing stoked an old gangster's engine more than attacking someone who'd dared threaten a member of his family.

Along with my usual crew, Alban and Bobby Gregson had been invited to the meeting. I glanced around the room, waited as Carl found a seat next to Bruno and while Alexandra passed a cup of hot coffee to Alban, and then walked next to Pearl and picked up the two thick folders he had resting on his legs.

"Bobby and Chris have done great work digging into the financials of the accountants," I said. "The money trail begins in New York and stretches down into Mexico and South America, across the country into Los Angeles and Hawaii, and across the Atlantic into a number of banks I hope no one in this room has any money in."

"They cover their trail well," Pearl said. "Everyone who invests with them turns a sizable profit, anywhere from twelve to eighteen percent a year."

"But the actual profit numbers are higher," Bobby said, stepping away from the wall he was leaning against and moving deeper into the room. "Which means they skim as little as three and as much as six percent from each of their deep-pocketed clients."

"Just to be clear," Alban said, "you're the fed?"

"That's beginning to sound like my middle name," Bobby said. "But, to answer your question, yes, I'm the fed."

"How much does that kind of skim earn them?" Carmine asked. "Ballpark it if you don't know for sure."

"Judging from the numbers from the last calendar year, I would put it at anywhere from three to five million per client," Bobby said. "All nontaxable, clean, and laundered in offshore accounts."

"How can they hide so much and the clients not get a whiff of what's going down?" Carl asked.

"The clients have nothing to complain about," Chris said. "They're making lots of money themselves. It would be different if the firm were making profits and they weren't. But these guys know how to keep their investors happy."

"How hard was it for you two to dig up all this information?" Bruno asked.

"My office has been looking into it for a while," Bobby said. "We were able to string a few threads together, navigate our way through the dozens of LLCs these guys set up. You need a tour guide to help you through these financial waters."

"Is what you have enough to get you a search warrant?" I asked.

"More than enough," Bobby said. "Once the papers are drawn, we'll hit the firm and take everything they have, from hard drives to printouts to investment folders. And we'll also bring in the partners and charge them."

"So now we know they steal," Alban said. "We also know they rape and beat young women. We know they have people willing to kill for them. We know they have millions they can use to keep their secrets safe. What we don't seem to know is what are we going to do about it."

"We're going to rat them out," I said.

I caught Carmine's smile and watched him stand as he addressed the room. "Turn them over," he said. "Take those numbers Chris and the fed dug up and put them in the right hands. Then let the mob take care of the rest. They'll know what to do, and they won't be shy about doing it."

"I will do all that is asked of me," Alban said. "Alexandra will, as well. But I will not stop there. The man who did damage to Sasha must be turned over to me. And what happens to that man is no one's business but mine. Agreed?"

"No issues there, Alban," I said. "And the same holds for the one who ordered the job on my brother and his wife."

"Somehow, little of this sounds anywhere close to being legal," Bobby said. "Just thought I'd throw that fact out there."

"Tough shit," Carmine said. "Nothing these guys do is legal. They're no different than any other outfit racking in large scores. They need to go down, plain and simple. Anybody that helps us get that done is on our side."

"If being in on this gets you jammed, we'll help clear you of it any way we can," I said to Bobby. "We're here to take down some bad people, not jam up a good cop."

"I appreciate that," Bobby said. "But I want these bastards as much, if not more, than anyone in this room."

"Not more than me," Chris said.

Bobby glanced over at Chris and nodded. "I'm sorry," he said. "I'm here to help you see them get taken down."

"Carmine is dealing with the mob crews with money tied to the firm," I said.

"I'll do the same with the hedge-fund guys," Bobby said.

"I have contacts with the cartels," Alban said. "I'll start feeding it into their pipeline. In time, no one in that firm will be safe from their hands."

"We need to pull the U.S. Attorney's money out of their cash flow," I said.

"Leave that to me," Carmine said. "Me and Randolph owe each other a chat. I handed the dough over in cash, expect it back the same way. It shouldn't take long. Next to what he's hauling in, the hundred and fifty large I gave him is small-time."

"He likes to keep contact with his clients to a minimum," Pearl said. "And, if he has to meet, he likes to do it in a place nobody will notice."

"No worries," Carmine said. "I got a place for us to do our business. Quiet and out of the way."

"Let's move on to Eddie Kenwood," I said. "We're looking to pin a murder rap on him, which means he will come at us hard. And we need to be ready for when that happens."

"We keep Chris, Carl, Alexandra out of the line of fire," Pearl said. "We lost one team member last time out. I don't want to see that happen again."

"They stay in the backup vans," I said. "And only come out when we give the all-clear."

"You can count on my help," Alban said. "You'll have my men by your side."

"And who better to help take down a gang of dirty cops than a bunch of past-their-prime mob guys?" Carmine said.

"I want Kenwood taken alive," I said. "He deserves to spend time behind prison bars. That will kill him faster than any bullet we can put in him."

"The chief backing you up on this?" Bobby asked.

"He'll have his men in place," I said. "Kenwood and his crew are a stain on the department. And he wants to be rid of the whole bunch."

"So, if I got a clear picture of all this, which I think I do," Bobby said, "I'm helping close out two cases working alongside Carmine's mob buddies and Alban's Seven Samurai crew?"

"Now, you tell me," Carmine said. "What fed could ask for better company?"

53.

HUBBA'S, PORT CHESTER, WESTCHESTER COUNTY

CARMINE SMILED WHEN HE OPENED THE WHITE DOOR LEAD-ing into the tiny restaurant hidden in the middle of a nondescript suburban street. Carmine had broken all protocol. He called David Randolph directly and told him there was something crucial they needed to discuss and it would best be done free of any prying eyes.

For such a meeting, Hubba's, on a late Sunday morning, was the perfect place.

It had been a hangout for decades for nearby public and private high school students, who flocked to it after a concert, movie, or club-hopping excursion. It was the size of a subway car, with swivel stools at a counter instead of tables and chairs; paper plates had been tacked to the wall in place of a menu. The specialty of the house was a small hot dog on a toasted bun topped with chili, onions, and melted cheese. The drink of choice was "Hubba water"—red Kool-Aid. The lines were around the block on any weekend night, and on most school days students were lined three-deep along the narrow strip. Once inside, they would order everything from a burger with the works—which meant the same toppings you got with a hot dog—to bowls of the spiciest chili in the county. Late Sunday mornings were the only time the place could be counted on to be deserted.

"Ain't this great?" Carmine said with a wide smile, slapping Randolph hard across the shoulders. He waved to a burly man working behind a hot grill in a corner and smiled at a young waitress who stood ready to take their order.

"You better have a damn good reason for forcing me to meet you in this swamp," Randolph said, not bothering to hide either his anger or his frustration. "It barely registered on my GPS."

"Watch your tongue," Carmine said. "These people have worked hard to make this an in-demand place. Once you get a bite of their food, you'll have a change of heart, guaranteed."

"I didn't come here to eat," Randolph said. "I came to hear you tell me what it is that you claimed was so important I was the only one you could share it with."

Carmine ignored Randolph and asked the waitress to bring him two dogs with the works and a glass of Hubba water. She looked to the man behind the grill, who nodded. "I got you covered," he said. "Be there in a few."

"You sure you don't want anything?" Carmine asked Randolph. "You'll be missing out on a treat."

"Positive," Randolph said. "Now, please, get on with what you need to tell me. If not, I'll be out of here before you take a bite out of whatever it is you ordered."

"All right, then," Carmine said. "Let's get down to it."

Carmine reached out a left hand and gripped the back of Randolph's neck. He then slammed the thinner, well-dressed man's face down hard against the Formica counter, causing blood to spurt from Randolph's nose. Carmine pulled a handful of napkins from the small container sitting between the ketchup and hot sauce, lifted Randolph's head, and dropped them on the counter, helping to soak up the blood.

"You made a move on my kid," Carmine said. "Nobody's ever done that before, and I've done business with some pretty hard-ass types in my time. But you didn't have the cubes to do it yourself, did you? So you sent some goons to do her harm."

Randolph clutched a wad of clean napkins and held them to his nose. His eyes were glassy, and the front of his monogrammed white shirt was spotted with blood. "I don't know what you're talking about," he managed to say. His hands were trembling, and his eyes betrayed both his fear and his lie.

"Don't bullshit me," Carmine said. "Otherwise, the next shot won't be against the counter. It will be against the grill."

"Your daughter wasn't hurt," Randolph said. "It was just to send a message to her boyfriend, the cop. Which, by the way, you neglected to mention when you first approached me about investing with my firm."

"My daughter is free to date anybody she wants," Carmine said. "It's none of my business, and it sure as shit ain't any of yours."

"It is when that boyfriend is the brother of the man who worked at my firm," Randolph said.

Carmine shrugged. "Save the fake anger, Randolph," he said. "You knew the minute I walked into your office that Tank Rizzo was keeping company with my daughter."

Randolph dabbed the wad of napkins against his damaged nose. "Get to your main point," he said.

Carmine nodded. "You got one hundred fifty thousand dollars of my money stashed," he said. "I expect to have that back in my hand before dark. Me and you are done doing business. And you can forget about me bringing anybody else I know into your firm. Not going to happen. As a matter of fact, I reached out to a few people I know that have their money invested with your firm. You're going to meet a couple of them soon enough. Before me and them had our little chat, they were happy with you and your partners. After I was done, not so much."

Randolph's face turned a shade whiter, and sweat began to form on his upper lip. He eased himself off the stool and stood with his back to a wall decorated with signed one-dollar bills. "What are you talking about?"

Carmine smiled. "You know, the profits that should have gone to my pals, which made their way to you and your partners instead. Yeah, you were slick enough to show them some gains to keep them happy. Only not the kind of gains their money was really taking in. That found its way into your pockets."

Carmine got up from the stool and stood inches from Randolph's face. "You had it down pretty smooth, I admit," he said. "Had it all figured out. One of your partners beats up a girl, leaves her ruined for the rest of her life, no big deal. You ship the guy out of the country for a spell and that's the end of that. But you went even further. You crossed the line into murder."

"You're talking nonsense," Randolph said. "And I don't need to hear another word of it."

Randolph attempted to ease past Carmine and make his way out of Hubba's. Carmine took two steps back to give him even more room. "I'm not going to stop you if that's your thinking," he said. "You walk out that door and there's a nightmare waiting for you."

Randolph turned to Carmine. "What is that supposed to mean?"

"You got a boatload of problems, is what I'm trying to tell you," Carmine said. "And I don't mean just my friends alone. Or the feds, for that matter. They're going to be coming after you like a dog on a T-bone. But do you for a minute think that young lady your partner ruined came into this world alone? She's got blood family, and they'll be looking to peel the skin off your partner's body."

Randolph glanced from Carmine to the closed door, then back to Carmine. "What is it you really want?" he finally asked, after a few moments that seemed to tick away like hours.

"Jack and Susan Rizzo," Carmine said. "Who ordered the hit and who carried it out? That, and my money, is all I need and want. The rest of it—the investors you've been ripping off, the schemes your firm is wrapped up in, the attack on Sasha—you're going to have to work out with others. Not me."

Randolph licked his lips and lowered his head. He was shaking as if he were in the middle of a winter storm. "Jack was going to ruin the firm," he said, the words coming out in spurts. "We couldn't let that happen."

"That answers the first part," Carmine said. "You were the one that laid down the order. You carried it out?"

"He'll kill me if I tell you," Randolph said.

"Don't let that stop you," Carmine said. "I might kill you for the scare you put into my kid. The cop might kill you for ordering his brother's murder. The mob boys might kill you for skimming their money. Looks to me like your dance card is pretty packed when it comes to your possible demise."

Randolph closed his eyes, the weight of what stood before him slowly beginning to sink in. He looked up at Carmine. "I can pay you, if you help me," he said. "I can pay you a lot of money. More than you've ever seen in your life."

"One hundred and fifty thousand dollars is all I want," Carmine said. "Not a nickel more or less. Now, the next words I want coming out of your mouth, and the *only* words I want coming out, is the name of the guy you gave the contract to."

"Samuel Butler," Randolph said. "I gave it to Samuel Butler."

Carmine glared at Randolph for a moment and then sat back down on the stool and nodded to the man behind the grill. The man walked over to Carmine, holding two paper plates in his hands, each one with a Hubba's hot dog with the works on it. He dropped them in front of Carmine. "Enjoy," he said.

"I always have," Carmine said to him.

Carmine poured some hot sauce on his food and then turned to look at Randolph standing a few feet away. "You sure you don't want to try any?" he asked him. "As last meals go, you could do a lot worse."

54.

OUTSIDE HUBBA'S

MOMENTS LATER

DAVID RANDOLPH STOOD IN FRONT OF HUBBA'S, STARING AT the two men in front of a black four-door limo, engine still running. "We need to talk, you and me," the bigger of the two men said. "Inside the car might be better. Got the AC on high."

Randolph hesitated for a moment and then said, "Mr. Massamilio. Mr. Conte. How nice to see you both, even in this rather barren place. Now, if it's business you wish to discuss, it would be better if we met at my office. This would allow me to have your investment portfolios in front of me to better answer any questions you may have."

"No worries there," Mario Conte said. "We brought all the paperwork you need. It's in the car."

Nick Massamilio opened the rear door, stepped aside, and glanced over at Randolph. "It's hot out here," he said. "And I hate the heat. So get in the fuckin' car."

Randolph froze briefly, then slowly made his way to the car and got in. Masamilio gazed inside. "Not in the back—that's where we sit. Across from there, next to the guy in the suit."

Massamilio and Conte got into the car and slammed the door shut.

Inside, there were two other men—one behind the wheel and one sitting next to Randolph. The accountant looked over at the man. He was in his mid-thirties, easily twenty years younger than either Massamilio or Conte, with a strong upper body hidden under the folds of his well-tailored gray jacket and slacks. "I don't believe I've had the pleasure," Randolph said, putting out a hand to shake. "I'm David Randolph."

The man looked at Randolph and ignored the outstretched hand. "I don't give a fuck who you are," he said.

"Don't worry about Lou," Massamilio said. "He's cranky in the early part of the day. It's us you need to worry about."

"What makes you say that?" Randolph asked.

"Show him, Mario," Massamilio said.

Conte lifted a briefcase onto his legs, snapped it open, and pulled out a thick pile of ledgers.

"Now, pay attention, Randolph," Massamilio said. "Hang on every word Mario's going to say. And when he's done, you better have the right answers to all his issues."

Mario flipped through the ledgers for a few moments and then rested them between him and Nick. "It comes down to this," Mario said. "The numbers on these ledgers tell us you've been fuckin' us out of our money since we started our business with you."

"I don't know where you got those numbers, Mr. Conte," Randolph said. "But clearly they are incorrect. You've made a profit, a substantial profit, every year you've invested in my firm."

Massamilio nodded at Lou. Lou turned and punched David Randolph, the blow landing at his neckline and causing him to bang his head against a door panel. "I told you to listen," Massamilio said, "not to talk. You interrupt again and Lou is going to get very angry."

"You're right, bookkeeper," Mario said. "We have turned a profit every year with you. But we didn't see all of it, did we? You sent a fair share to us and the rest went into your fuckin' pockets. These numbers don't lie. But I have a strong feeling you do."

"It's been true all our lives," Massamilio said. "Guy like you, fancy schools, diplomas on the wall, looks at guys like me and Mario and sees two street wops he can shine on. Throw us a bone and we walk away happy. What the fuck do we know about investments and numbers and the rest of that bullshit, am I right, Mario?"

"A hundred percent," Mario said. "Except what guys like you don't figure is that me and Nick here, we've been dealing with numbers all our lives. And we don't write them down, we remember them. We know when we're ahead, we know when we're behind, and we know when we're being fucked."

The inside of the car was AC cool, but David Randolph was still sweating, his mouth desert dry, and he was short of breath. "If there are any errors at all, they will be corrected," he said in a voice no longer coated with its usual arrogance. "And if you are owed any additional monies, they will be paid to you."

"We don't give a fuck about that," Massamilio said. "You screwed us out of some dough. So you tossing us some extra cash that should have been ours to begin with won't make what you did right. Won't make us even. If that's what you're thinking."

"If anything, they're simple accounting errors," Randolph said. "Happens all the time. And not just at my firm. At any firm."

"Maybe so," Mario said. "But, number one, we're not at any firm. We're at your firm. And number two, I don't give a shit if it happens all the time. It *never* happens to us."

"Mario, you remember that guy—forget his name now—tried to take us for four hundred dollars?" Massamilio asked. "It was back when we were just starting out. Even younger than Lou there. Remember him? Remember what happened to him?"

"I do," Mario said. "Joey Dalli. They called him 'Joe Doll' on the street. He was a shark working around Midtown, restaurants and bars mostly."

"That's right, Joe Doll," Massamilio said. "We put some money out with him, at his request, and were told we'd get back fifteen percent profit on our initial investment. Back then, me and Mario were hustling for every dime we could get, so you can imagine how good a fifteen percent return sounded to us. Instead, Joe Doll took our cash and forgot about our profit. So tell him what happened then, Mario."

"I should prepare you," Mario said to Randolph. "This story does not have a happy ending. At least not for Joe Doll. It seems he had an accident. Somehow—and please don't ask me how—he ended up locked inside a dryer in one of those twenty-four-hour laundromats. It had been on high heat for quite a while. He had all his clothes on, but his pockets had no cash in them. Which is strange, since he always made a point of packing thick wads of money in each pocket. They found the body. They just never found the money."

Massamilio nodded and smiled. "Memories," he said. "Me and Mario, we're getting older, you know? Memories are one of the things we hold on to. One of the other things we like to hold on to is our fuckin' money." He looked at Lou. "See if Tony up there is awake," he said to him. "Time to get back on the road."

Tony perked up, put the car into gear, and eased out of the parking space in front of Hubba's.

"Where are we going?" Randolph asked in a low voice.

"Me and Mario are going home," Massamilio said. "But we'll make sure to drop you off first. No worries. We're full-service. Just like your outfit."

"I don't wish to be a bother," Randolph said. "Besides, I drove here. My car is parked at the next corner."

"It's no bother," Massamilio said. "Believe me."

"And don't worry too much about your car," Mario said. "It's not going anywhere. For now, at least."

"Does the driver know where I live?" Randolph said.

Massamilio shook his head. "No," he said. "He only knows where we're dropping you off."

Randolph slumped into his thick leather seat and closed his eyes. "I can make it right, Mr. Massamilio," he pleaded. "Just give me a chance. I will make it right."

Massamilio leaned closer to Randolph and spoke in a near whisper. "This is making it right, Randolph," he said.

55.

TRAMONTI'S

THE RESTAURANT WAS EMPTY. I SAT IN A BACK BOOTH ACROSS from Connie and Chris, Gus curled up on the floor, his head resting against the soft side of the booth, sound asleep.

Connie and I were drinking hot cups of coffee; Chris had a large glass of Diet Coke, which he had barely touched. Both looked tired and seemed to be battling mixed emotions over my revelation a few days earlier. "I'm sorry I dropped it on you the way I did," I said. "I just didn't want to have to go over it more than once. Figured it was best to get everyone who needed to hear it in one place."

Connie reached out and gripped both my hands, holding them tightly in hers, fingers wrapped around mine. "I know it wasn't easy for you, Tank," she said.

"Did hearing it scare you?" I asked. "All the details, I mean."

Connie took a deep breath before answering. "You were just a boy when it happened," she said. "And you reacted out of fear and concern for Jack. So hearing that didn't scare me."

"What did?" I asked.

"Watching you beat that man who came into the restaurant," she said. "That was a part of you I've never seen before. And that's what scared me."

"It's a part of me, Connie," I said. "It was there in Maine and it was there the other day. And if you or Chris or Pearl or anyone I truly love and care about is put at risk, that part of me will surface again. There's nothing I can do to change it."

"I know," Connie said. "I'm not asking you to change it, Tank. Because I know you can't. I just need time to have it sink in. I'm sure my father has that same dark side. But knowing it and seeing it are two very different things."

I squeezed her hand. "Take all the time you need," I said.

"Did you and my dad ever talk about it?" Chris asked. "I mean after that day?"

"It wasn't easy. Not for me and not for him. Our parents thought it best if we didn't discuss it until we were back home. But, even on the drive back, me and Jack knew things between us would never be the same. I had seen Jack at his most vulnerable. He had seen my rage at full throttle. Both those images would be welded in our minds forever."

"But it wasn't my dad's fault," Chris said, his voice breaking slightly. "And all you did was come to his defense. It would have been much worse for him if you didn't show up and do what you did."

"I didn't have to kill the man, Chris," I said.

"I understand why my dad didn't want to talk about what happened," Chris said. "And I understand why you didn't want to talk about it, either. But why did you decide not to talk to each other at all?"

"It seemed the best way to put it behind us," I said. "I know it's hard for you to understand. I didn't want Jack to look at me and flash on what could have happened to him that day. And I didn't want to look at Jack and see the fear and horror in his eyes."

"Did your parents send you to see someone?" Connie asked. "Someone to talk to, maybe somebody who could help you come to terms with what had happened?"

"Like a therapist, you mean?"

Connie shook her head. "I know how people from here feel about therapists," she said. "My dad would rather eat his own leg than open up to a stranger sitting across the room from him."

"Especially a stranger charging him a hundred dollars every forty-five minutes," I said. "Besides, me and Jack didn't want to think about it, let alone talk about it."

"What about your parents?" Chris asked.

"They figured it out on their own," I said. "Once we got in the car for the drive back to the city, we left it all behind."

We stayed quiet for a few moments, each of us grappling with what to say next. "Did talking about it help in any way?" Connie finally asked.

"I felt relieved," I said. "Never figured I would have to face up to it. And I never counted on somebody like Kenwood being the one to bring it to the open. That one knocked the wind out of me."

I looked at Connie and Chris and then slid out of the booth. I stood in front of them, my left hand resting on the table. "I'm sorry," I said. "I should have told you. Should have trusted you, the team, Carmine, Pearl. I was scared about . . . well, about a lot of things. Most of all, I didn't want to lose anyone I loved. And I was afraid knowing about what I did and how I did it would lead to that. It had already cost me a brother. I didn't want to lose anyone else."

I gazed down at the puppy, still curled and asleep, his limbs occasionally twitching. "It was wrong," I said. "And I should have known better."

"Go do what you need to do, Tank," Connie said in a soft voice, her eyes misty with tears. "And know that no matter what, we will always be here. Always."

I smiled at both of them and turned to leave the restaurant. As I did, I was aware that my past was entangled in the two cases that needed to be closed. Jack's murder, and the death of a young girl I had never met.

The past never leaves us. It hovers over us, hidden by the passage of time, waiting to strike when we least expect it. It can do damage or ease suffering, its path never truly known until it confronts us.

56.

PRINCE STREET

THE NEXT DAY

I WAS WHEELING PEARL OUT OF VESUVIO BAKERY, BETWEEN Thompson Street and West Broadway, when I saw the two familiar faces step out of their double-parked Chevy sedan and walk toward us. We had both seen them before. They were part of Kenwood's crew, flunky cops who dishonored the badge while still on the job. They walked across the street from us, looking for an opening to make their move. The pedestrian traffic on both ends of the sidewalks was light this early in the afternoon, but it wouldn't prevent Kenwood's guys from risking collateral damage to get to their intended targets—me and Pearl.

"I hope to hell those tarallis you wolfed down were enough to satisfy your craving," I said to Pearl. "We got ourselves serious company."

"I see them," Pearl said. "They've been down these roads before, I imagine. Makes them stupid but not crazy. They won't try to take us on the sidewalk. Most likely wait until we get to a light."

"If they come at us blasting, we have no choice but to do the same," I said. "You bring your piece with you?"

"No worries on that front," Pearl said. "Since you signed on to two cases, I've been taking my drop gun with me, as well. I'm packed and loaded."

"You got a drop gun, too?" I asked. "I know where you keep one gun. But how the hell can you hide two?"

Pearl smiled up at me. "I'm not handicapped, partner. I'm handicapable."

"Good to know," I said. I kept my eyes on the men across from us, the corner only a few feet away. "I figure they'll both cross toward us soon as we get to the light."

"They come at us blasting, innocent folks are going to take hits," Pearl said. "And if we fire back, good as we are, we're going to take some of them down, too."

The two men reached their corner before we reached ours. They turned and began to cross the street, heading in our direction. They had their guns out, held low against their legs. They were halfway across the street when a black Impala came careening toward them and then braked with a squeal to a sudden stop, inches from hitting them.

"What the fuck, you blind?" one of the men yelled at the driver.

The driver jumped out, a gun aimed at the two men. "No," Bobby said. "I saw you. I screwed up. I hit the brakes too soon. I was looking to hit you both. I ended up with a gutter ball, not a strike."

"How about we go and see what's going down?" I said, wheeling Pearl toward the idle car and Bobby.

"Make it fast, partner," Pearl said. "Can't let the fed have all the fun."

I crossed into the middle of the street and stopped in front of the two men. "I forget which one of you is Arthur and which one is Pete," I said. "All you corrupt cops look alike to me."

"The tall, ugly one is Arthur," Pearl said. "The short, dumb one is Pete."

"Fuck you both," Pete said. "And your new friend here, too. We could haul the three of you in, if we wanted. Charges won't matter. We'll make them up on the ride to the precinct."

"But you won't," Pearl said. "Arresting us is not what Kenwood sent you here to do."

I looked over at Bobby and then at Pete and Arthur. "We going to Wild West this situation?" I said. "Or are we going to be smart about it?"

"You and your pal behind the car door can both drop your guns," Arthur said, "and we all take a ride far away from here. We go that way, then the only blood gets spilled is yours. None of these nice people out here minding their business get hurt."

The traffic light had changed to green, but any angry drivers tempted to honk their horns or yell out their car windows stayed quiet, silenced by the presence of men armed with guns. I locked eyes with Pete and Arthur, their guns against the side of their legs, looking from me to Bobby. They were ignoring Pearl, clearly having decided he wasn't a threat.

I knew it was only a matter of minutes before an RMP would pull up to check on us. So, if we were going to make a move, now was the time.

I looked down at Pearl and noticed he had both hands wedged behind his back. Bobby had his arms over the open flap of his car door, gun held tight with both hands.

"You don't have to die," I said to Pete and Arthur. "Not here. Not today and not this way. Especially not for a piece of trash like Kenwood."

"Neither do you or your crippled partner," Pete said. "And whoever the fuck this guy is by the car. You can drop your weapons as easily as we could."

I glanced at Arthur and caught the twitch in his eye and the clenching of his jaw, and I knew that on this day, at least, we would not be spared bloodshed.

Arthur lifted his weapon and aimed it toward me and Pearl. I shoved Pearl's wheelchair closer to the front of Bobby's car and pulled my weapon from its hip holster. I fired at the same time as Arthur did. His slug landed to my left, chipping away a piece of the pavement. Mine caught him in the right shoulder, just above his vest, and sent him sprawling to the ground, the weapon slipping from his hand and sliding under the front of Bobby's car.

Pete seemed caught off guard. He lifted his weapon and hesitated, looking to hit me but conscious of Bobby. He let off two rounds, firing first at Bobby, who dodged the bullet by jumping into the front seat of his car. The second round came my way and missed by several inches, hitting a mailbox on the street behind me. I lifted my weapon but didn't need to get off a second shot: Pearl swung his wheelchair to the left, a gun in each hand, and fired twice, both bullets finding their mark. One hit Pete in his right leg and the second grazed his gun hand, sending him down on his knees. He dropped his weapon and clutched at his bleeding leg with both hands.

Bobby stepped out of the car, his shield hanging on a chain around his neck, and walked toward the wounded men, his gun aimed down at them. I'm sure sirens were raining down at us from all directions and people were screaming and running for cover. But when you're in the middle of a gunfight, even one that took as little time as this one had, every sound is drowned out. You are so focused that you can't feel the wind on your face or the heat of the sun on your back.

I walked up next to Bobby, Pearl right behind me. His guns were now back in their safe place and he had both hands on the wheels of his chair. "Shooting at me and Pearl is bad enough," I said to Pete and Arthur. "That might get you a spin in the can. But Bobby here, he's a federal agent, and pegging a shot at him carries some serious weight."

"We didn't come for him," Pete said, still on his knees, trying to stem the blood oozing out of his right leg.

"Go with that," Pearl said. "Might play well in court."

"He's not going to stop, you know?" Arthur said. "Kenwood. He's not going to stop until he puts you down."

I shrugged. "You're free of that worry," I said. "The both of you. What happens next is between me and Kenwood."

Two RMPs pulled to a stop and four uniformed officers got out. They had their guns drawn and spotted Bobby and the shield hanging off his neck. "Cuff them and bring them to NYU Medical," he told them. "They're on the job still, but that gets them shit. I want them under twenty-four-hour surveillance. Nobody sees them but a doctor. I'll file the charges soon as I get statements from these two witnesses here."

Pete and Arthur were cuffed and hauled into the backseats of the two RMPs. Bobby holstered his weapon and looked at Pearl. "Where did you dump your two guns?" he asked.

Pearl smiled. "What two guns?"

57.

TRAMONTI'S

I SAT ACROSS FROM CARMINE, PLATTERS FILLED WITH FOOD SPREAD out across the table for four. I was halfway through a bowl of linguini with white clam sauce and a side order of broccoli rabe. Carmine was chowing down on a mixed platter of zucchini with eggs and eggplant rollatini. We were sharing a tomato, basil, and red onion salad and a loaf of semolina bread. We kept the drinking light—ginger ale with crushed ice for Carmine, an Arnold Palmer for me.

"Word got out to Massamilio pretty fast," I said.

"When it comes to money, that guy's got ears like sonar," Carmine said. "He treats his money like family, and, if nothing else, Massamilio is very close to his family. Mario, too."

"And I have to hand it to you," I said. "Smooth move sending Dee Dee a platter of ziti and some wine."

"Everybody's gotta eat, am I wrong?" Carmine said. "Besides, she did us a solid and helped get our foot in the door. It was the least I could do."

"Still, it's nice to see you getting all chummy-like with the feds," I said, smiling.

"More the exception than the rule," Carmine said. "Anyway, this time they're on the hunt for real thieves—bad accountants and dirty cops. It was a pleasure to lend a hand. Not that I'm saying I did, mind you. In case anyone should ask."

"Back when I was first on the job, there was a story about Massamilio and coffins," I said. "A few of the older cops mentioned it. Any of that true?"

Carmine rested his fork against the side of his platter and smiled. "The double-deckers," he said. "You have to hand it to the guy. It was a brilliant idea—in my book, right up there with the guy who came up with Uber."

I shook my head. "How did it work exactly?"

"Like all great ideas, it was as simple as it was beautiful," Carmine said. "Your old Aunt Nunzia dies, God rest her soul. Before the wake, they slip in a second body under hers. The two bodies are sealed in together. Come the day of the funeral, they're carried out together and buried in the same plot. No fuss, no muss, and, key to the whole endeavor, no body."

"That explains why every pallbearer working a double-decker looks like an offensive lineman," I said. "The body in the top bunk weighs less than a hundred pounds."

"But not the one on the bottom," Carmine said. "Most of the ones who bite the bullet hover around two hundred, if not more. Last thing you need in a crowded church is to have the bottom drop out. That would be a real crime."

"The accounting firm's not long for this world," I said. "Bobby and his crew are ready to make their move. And I'm ready to make mine."

"I can't wait for that," Carmine said. "It's been a long time coming."

"None of this would have happened without Chris," I said. "Without him, we wouldn't have been looking anywhere near this firm. He did the legwork, broke down the police reports, checked out the car, connected the dots. They would have gotten away with it and would still be riding high and raking in millions."

"That part's more than true," Carmine said. "But he's still a kid, let's not lose sight of that."

"This will help give him closure," I said. "He's come a long way since we first met him. I didn't think the two of us would last a week, but he's found his place with us. And in a way I can't explain, he's made me feel as if I got my brother back, too."

Carmine looked and me and nodded. "That's nice to hear," he said. "And that dog has helped Chris in a lot of ways, as well."

"I heard you fed Gus lasagna yesterday for dinner," I said. "Didn't know that was anywhere close to what a dog should have in his diet."

"He might be an olde English bulldogge by birth," Carmine said, smiling, "but he's living with the Italians now."

"Great," I said. "I can see platters of cannoli in Gus's future already."

"Good move on bringing Alban and his crew in with you," Carmine said. "Those guys can make bodies disappear faster than fog in sunlight. By the time they're done, Dee Dee may be sitting in a courtroom by herself with nobody left to charge."

"I doubt it would keep her up at night," I said. "She gets credit for bringing down a dirty firm. The rest of it she can write off as the price for stealing money from the mob."

We sat back and waited as a waiter cleared away the remains of our meal and then brought over two double espressos and a small plate of biscotti. Carmine stirred his coffee and seemed momentarily lost in thought.

"Go ahead and ask," I said to him.

"When you get your hands on the guy who rigged the car," Carmine said, "what then? You hand him over to the chief?"

I stared into my coffee for a few moments before I answered. "I was there once when my brother was in danger and I killed a man to protect him, to save him from harm. I wasn't there the second time he needed me. And that man got away with what he did. But not for much longer."

"For a lot of people, twenty years in a cell is worse than dying," Carmine said. "You walk him in and pin the murder rap on his sheet. He'd be just as good as dead."

"Is that what you would do if it had been Connie?" I asked.

"No," Carmine said, shaking his head. "But I was never a cop, which means my rule book has a whole different set of instructions."

"I'm not a cop anymore," I said. "Besides, there's one rule that can never be broken, no matter whose book it's written in."

"Which is?"

"You touch family and you die," I said.

58.

161 MADISON AVENUE

THE NEXT DAY

BOBBY LEANED ON A WALL AND GAZED DOWN THE CROWDED hall. He was standing next to the door of the accounting firm of Curtis, Strassman, and Randolph. The hall was filled with federal agents wearing FBI windbreakers, all poised to enter the offices and execute the warrants Bobby held in his right hand.

He looked at the two young agents holding a small battering ram and glanced at his watch. "It's time," he said to them. "Smash that door open."

"It's not locked," a young agent said. "We can just walk in."

"Where's the fun in that?" Bobby asked. "Now, ram the damn door."

It took two hits to pop the door off its hinges. Bobby rushed in, a swarm of agents in his wake. "FBI!" he shouted. "We have warrants to confiscate hard drives, laptops, printouts, folders, memos, and ledgers. We also have arrest warrants for the three partners of the firm. If you all cooperate, we'll be out of here in about an hour, maybe less."

A young secretary stood in front of Bobby, her hands shaking and on the verge of tears. "I didn't do anything wrong," she stammered. "I only file what they tell me to file. I don't want to go to jail."

Bobby placed a hand on her arm. "You got nothing to worry about," he said. "But you can be a big help to us."

"What do you need me to do?" she asked.

"Show my men where all your files are," Bobby said. "And get your-self a fresh cup of coffee."

The agents flooded into the room and began to take computers off desks and toss files and paperwork into empty cardboard boxes. Bobby waited, then signaled to a tall man in a windbreaker to follow him Alban eased past several agents and made his way to Bobby.

"Is he here?" Alban asked.

"His office is in the back," Bobby said.

They turned at a set of cubicles. The offices were plush and well furnished, with expensive art on the walls and light fixtures that cost more than Bobby earned in a year. "I should have brought some of my men with me," Alban said. "They would have cleaned this place out without making as much noise as your crew. The art alone is worth in the seven figures."

"Maybe next time," Bobby said.

A middle-aged man in a Brooks Brothers suit came up to them, his face flushed red with anger. "What the hell is all this?" he demanded. "Who authorized this charade? And what the hell do you expect to find?"

Bobby opened the warrants and placed them in front of the man's face. "It's all there for you to see. Legal and signed by a judge and everything. I'm taking a guess here. You must be Peter Strassman."

"You bet your ass I'm Peter Strassman," he said, looking from Bobby to Alban. "This is my firm, and I will not allow it to be treated like some backdoor brothel."

Bobby turned and gazed at the chaos around him—agents clearing out desks and carting off computers, searching through desks for any-thing that could be carried away. "I've never executed a warrant on a brothel, Mr. Strassman. But if I ever do, I doubt I'll need as many agents on the team."

"I'm calling my attorney," Strassman said. His thick gray hair was razor cut, and a thin beard covered his jawline. He had a pair of glasses hanging off a chain and was wearing a shirt with his initials embroidered on the pocket.

Bobby reached out a hand and held him in place. "You can do that later," he said to Strassman. "This agent will take you where you need to go. You can make your call from there." Bobby glanced up at Alban and said, "He's all yours."

Alban nodded and wrapped a large hand around Strassman's right arm. "Thank you," he said to Bobby.

"Make sure he doesn't get away," Bobby said to Alban.

"You have my word," Alban said.

Alban walked Strassman down the long corridor, passing agents sorting through files and desks, and out the door for the last time.

Alban turned toward an exit door, swung it open, and started down the stairwell with Strassman in tow. "Where are you taking me?" Strassman asked. "I demand to know where you are taking me!"

Alban stopped and glared at Strassman. "We're making two stops," he said to the accountant. "The first is to visit a young lady who you may not remember. A young lady you ruined for life. I want her to see your face, and I want her to know that what you did to her, you will never do to anyone again."

Strassman's legs buckled and his upper body shook. Alban held him up and squeezed his arm harder. "I don't know what you're talking about," was all Strassman managed to say.

"Lying about what happened won't get you out of it," Alban said. "And then the stop we make after our visit will be the final stop. Your final stop. The time has come, Strassman, for you to say farewell to the world."

"You're no damn FBI agent," Strassman said, regaining some of his bluster. "Who the hell are you?"

"That's correct," Alban said. "I'm not an FBI agent. But by the end of this day, you'll wish with all your heart I were."

They walked down the remaining stairs in silence and exited a side door of the building. A white van was parked by the curb, and two men stepped out and took Strassman from Alban. They dragged him into the back of the vehicle, got in, and closed the doors behind them. Alban got in the passenger side and nodded to the driver.

"That FBI windbreaker looks good on you," the driver said to Alban as he shifted the van into gear and out into street traffic.

Alban smiled, "I think I'll keep it," he said "It might come in handy one day."

59.

CHELSEA PIERS PARKING GARAGE

LATER THAT DAY

I WAITED IN THE DARKNESS OF THE PARKING LOT, MY BACK TO the Hudson River. I could see the car—a new Mercedes four-door sedan, black exterior, tinted windows all around. Dim lighting filtered in from the pier. It was a hot, humid night, and the mild breeze coming off the river offered the only relief. I turned to my left when I heard the footsteps and saw the man walking slowly, one hand reaching into his jacket pocket for his car keys. He pressed down on a button and the doors unlocked, the engine kicked over, and the lights turned on.

I waited until the man was a few feet away from his car, and then I stepped out of the shadows and crossed in front of him. I was finally face-to-face with the firm's fixer, Samuel Butler.

"I thought it was time me and you had a talk," I said.

"I make it a point not to talk to cops," Butler said. "Retired or not."

"I figure you to be a guy in the know," I said. "So, you probably already heard, the firm's been shuttered by the feds. They've been hit with so many charges I've lost count. James Curtis has been arrested, waiting to post bond. The other two partners? Hard to say. But somehow I don't think they'll have a chance to post bond."

"I was just a consultant," Butler said. "Nothing more than that. One firm goes down, a dozen others will be in need of a guy like me."

"Don't go modest on me now, Butler," I said. "You handled the firm's problems and made them go away. In some cases, cash did the trick. Maybe even a free trip to somewhere nice. But when none of those options were on the table, you moved on to murder."

"You know, I told Randolph it was a mistake to meet with you," Butler said. "And an even bigger mistake to take money from that old mob guy friend of yours. It was too many people with connections to your brother. And that wasn't a smart way to go. But Randolph didn't listen to me. Truth is, he seldom did."

"I don't know which of the two of you decided to kill my brother and his wife," I said. "The smart money tells me Randolph asked you to take care of it and you did. You messed with his car, sliced some of the brake lining, and fiddled with the electronics. Now, on my own, I wouldn't have known any of that. But my brother left behind a very smart young man. And it was his son, my nephew, who figured it out. So you have him to thank. He fingered you for murder. Not me. I'm just the messenger."

"That sounds awfully hard to prove in a court of law," Butler said. "Besides which, you can't arrest me. You can pretend to be a cop all day, every day. But you're not. Not anymore."

"I'm not here to arrest you, Butler," I said. "I came here to kill you."

Butler looked at me for a moment and then he lunged, both arms spread wide, catching me at chest level and sending us both sprawling to the ground. He scrambled to his knees and landed two solid blows against my rib cage. I swung an elbow across his face, the jab landing just below his jawline, and he fell off me. We got to our feet and circled each other, swinging and missing with punches. He swung another right hand toward me; I ducked it, grabbed his arm, and tossed him against his car. Then I landed several hard blows against his chest and arms. I grabbed his head and rammed it against the trunk. I kept at it until I saw blood coming out of his nose and mouth. I pulled him off the car and threw him violently to the ground.

Butler had his hands flat on the grimy cement, attempting to catch his breath as I reached over and kicked him in the legs and ribs. I stepped back and waited as he slowly got to his feet, bent over, bleeding, desperate to breathe.

"That all you got?" I said. "It's easy to take a man down when he's not standing across from you. When he can't see what's coming. It gets a little harder the closer you get."

"You can beat me all you want and then get me tossed into a cell," Butler said between gasps of breath. "None of that is going to bring back your brother and that pretty wife of his. They'll still be dead."

I left my feet and landed on top of Butler's chest. The force caused his head to hit the ground hard, with a loud thud. I threw several dozen punches at him, as many as I could, hitting him in the face, neck, chest, and arms. My anger was once again released at full volume, and I didn't stop until I could barely lift my arms. I looked down at Butler and saw glazed eyes and a bloody face. I got up off him slowly and rested my hands against my knees. I had my head down, my eyes closed, when I heard Butler's voice. "You've been off the job too long, Tank," he snarled. "You didn't search me when you had the chance. You should always search a suspect, remember?"

I opened my eyes and saw Butler, a small-caliber gun in his right hand, easing himself off the ground. He spit out a thick patch of blood and looked at me. "Don't bother going for your gun," he said. "Mine's out. Yours is holstered."

"I'll take my chances," I said.

Samuel Butler shrugged. "It's your death wish," he said.

He lifted the gun and aimed it at me. I reached for my holstered weapon. Three shots rang out from the other side of the garage, two catching Butler in the chest and one in the stomach. The force of the bullets sent him off his feet, and I watched him hit the ground with one final, fatal fall.

I didn't need to go and check on him. I knew.

Samuel Butler, the man who killed my brother and his wife, the man who made my nephew an orphan, was now dead.

I turned to my right and saw Carmine standing there, a warm gun in his right hand. "What the hell are you doing here?" I said.

Carmine walked closer to me. "I forgot where I parked my car," he said.

"Why did you take him out?" I asked.

"You said it yourself, Tank," Carmine said. "You touch family and you die. You're family. So is Chris. And your brother was, too. Butler touched all of you. He had to go down. That's how I've lived my life. Too late to make changes to it now."

"I could have taken him," I said.

Carmine took a handkerchief from his pants pocket and wiped the prints off the gun and handed it to me. "And, as far as anyone is concerned, you did just that."

Carmine reached out and we gave each other a warm embrace. "You take care of your business here," he said, letting me go and walking into the darkness of the parking area. "I'll see you back at the ranch. There'll be a nice bottle of Brunello waiting for you. We can raise a glass to family."

60.

DE WITT CLINTON PARK

I HAD PASSED THE WORD TO OUR CI, LIVINGSTONE, THAT I WANTED a meeting with Eddie Kenwood. The ex-cop was as eager as I was to settle our differences and jumped at the offer. I chose De Witt Clinton because it was large—stretching from Fifty-second Street to Fifty-fourth Street, between Eleventh and Twelfth Avenues—and it was not heavily trafficked late at night.

I stood near the entrance to the park, my back leaning against the thick base of the World War I memorial that greeted anyone who entered, a statue of a soldier from that epic confrontation standing proud above me. Behind me, the park was an array of gardens, sprinkler pools, playgrounds, dog runs, and an immense ball field where semi-pro baseball games were played throughout the summer. I always thought it to be one of the prettiest parks in the city and one of the least well known.

"No sign of Kenwood yet," Carl said into my earpiece. "But we counted at least a dozen of his guys in different parts of the park."

"I didn't think he would come alone," I said. "How far away did you park?"

"My van's on Fifty-fifth Street," Carl said. "Me and Alexandra. Second van is on Fifty-fourth, on Eleventh."

"That's the one with me and Bruno, partner," Pearl said. "We're not far away, and we'll be there soon as you need us."

"What about Alban's crew?" Carl asked. "Any idea where they are?"

"Don't worry," I said. "They're here somewhere. They do their best work in the dark."

"And don't forget about me," Chief Connors said. "I'm in the command car. We have the neighborhood cordoned off but not in any way Kenwood should notice. We'll have cabs and vehicles rotating up and down the avenues. Even have a few couples walking past, holding hands and eating ice cream cones. Just like any other normal summer night."

I took a deep breath and looked up at the darkened sky for stars. Eddie Kenwood came up next to me, a wide smile on his face. "You picked a nice spot," he said. "I used to play ball in a summer league on that field back there. I was pretty good, too. We won more than our share."

"I didn't ask you to meet with me to talk about your baseball career," I said. "We got more important things to go over."

"Let me take a stab at it," Kenwood said. "You're going to offer me a deal. I don't tell anybody about your murder, and you don't tell anybody about mine. Did I nail it?"

"Not even close," I said. "I don't really care what you say about me and who you say it to. Your words have no weight."

"So why are we here, Tank?"

"Your time is up, Kenwood," I said. "You played your game for far too long and got away with far too much. You and the rest of your dirty crew—the ones lying in wait for me right now. You're all going down. I don't care much about the rest of them. But I do care about you."

"You're not taking me in," Kenwood said. "So what if I killed Rachel Nieves? She's long dead, and the confessed killer is spending another sleepless night in a prison cell. And me? I got away with it. Just like you did. Considering what we both got in common, the two of us should be friends instead of blood enemies."

"We were never meant to be friends, Kenwood," I said. "Not when we were on the job and for sure not off it."

Kenwood shrugged and sighed. "Then I suppose it's not going to be the happy ending I was hoping for."

"You got two coming up behind you," Pearl said into my earpiece. "From the corner side."

"I see you brought along some friends," I said.

"I don't like to travel alone," Kenwood said. "Especially at night. The city's never as safe as they say it is."

I turned and faced two of Kenwood's crew; both were holding iron bars in their hands and looking to their boss for the signal. "I'll let you three get acquainted," he said. "And in the event you make it past these two, there's a bunch more waiting for you all across the park."

"You were never one to fight your own battles, Kenwood," I said, turning back to him. "Unless you went up against a defenseless young woman or an old man like Zeke Jeffries."

"Why take a chance, right, Tank?" Kenwood said, smiling. "I forgot you and that crippled partner of yours were tight with Zeke back in the day. You should have let him be. He was happy and content sitting on park benches, watching basketball games, and talking about his glory days. Didn't need you nosing around."

"You took him out for talking to me and Pearl," I said. "I should kill you just for that."

"But you won't, Tank, will you?" Kenwood said. "Because deep down, you know as well as I do, I'll beat that rap, too. You can't touch me and you never could. Not once in all these years."

"That's because I never came looking for you," I said. "Until now."

Kenwood nodded over my shoulder at his two men. "Take good care of my old friend here," he said to them.

I didn't turn to face the men again. I kept my eyes on Eddie Kenwood.

"You should forget about me and deal with what's behind you, Tank," he said.

"There's nothing behind me I need to be concerned about," I said.

Two of Alban's men jumped out from behind a thick row of hedges and ran their knives into Kenwood's two men, who, seconds earlier, were going to beat me to death with their iron pipes. I glanced behind me—Alban's duo had disappeared as fast as they had appeared.

"You're right," I said to Kenwood. "This city is a lot more dangerous than they say it is."

Kenwood looked at his two fallen men and then at me. "I figured you'd come with company," he said.

"I must admit, it's nice to have friends," I said. "Especially around guys like you."

Kenwood turned and ran. He passed the benches and made a left toward the bathrooms. I followed him as fast as I could run. "He's making his way to the baseball field," I said into my earpiece.

"He won't be alone once he gets there," Pearl said. "His crew is moving in that direction, too. Might as well make a game of it. Me and Bruno will catch up with you there."

"Carl, you and Alexandra stay in the van," I said as I ran past the bathrooms, heading toward the gate leading to the ball field. "Understand?"

"We hear you," Carl said. "We don't like it, but we hear you."

"Did you pick up everything Kenwood said off my body mic?" I asked.

"Every word," Carl said. "He admitted to killing Rachel and Zeke. Picked it up clean and clear."

"You got him on two murder raps, Chief," I said.

"I heard," the chief said. "We'll move in and sweep up the whole bunch of them."

"Not just yet, Chief," I said. "Please. As a favor to me. Let me and Pearl be the ones who hand him over to you."

"You got Alban's crew out there," the chief said. "They can turn this whole thing bloodier than the Red Wedding in no time flat."

"I'll make sure it doesn't get to that," I said.

"If I see it turning bloody, I'm sending everybody in and bringing it to a stop," the chief said. "Until then, Eddie Kenwood's all yours."

61.

DE WITT CLINTON PARK

THE LIGHTS IN THE BALL FIELD HAD BEEN TURNED ON. I WAS in the center of the large area, Pearl to my right and Bruno to my left. Kenwood stood in front of a pack of six of his crew members. Alban and a half dozen of his men were stationed around the perimeter of the park.

I walked closer to Kenwood, stopping when I was less than five feet away. I looked past him at the men surrounding him. "I'm only here for your boss," I said to them. "Take a look around. The two behind me won't get into the fight unless they have to. The ones around the park just need a nod from their leader and they will kill each and every one of you and strip you of everything you have on you. If that happens, it will be because you made the call. This fight is between me and Kenwood, and if you let it play out that way, you'll walk away alive."

Kenwood glanced back at his men and saw the hesitation and heard the quiet mumblings. "But you're not going to walk away free," he said to them. "He's got this place surrounded by cops. If you don't believe that, then you're just kidding yourselves. You'll be busted before you can get to the gate leading out of here."

"He's not lying to you," I said. "There are cops with eyes on every single inch of this park. But so far, from what I can see, you've done nothing to give the cops reason to arrest you. You lift a hand or a weapon to me or to the two behind me, though, then you've crossed a line, and that, as you all well know, leads to handcuffs. And if you should be foolish enough to lift a hand to the ones standing around the perimeter, you'll be pulling back a stump."

Kenwood stepped toward me and smiled. "Have it your way, Tank," he said. "If I can't take a washout like you, then maybe I deserve to die."

"I was thinking the very same thing," I said to Kenwood.

He landed the first blow, a hard right to my jaw. The booze and cigarettes may have slowed him down over the years, but he was still strong and his punches still packed heat. I ducked under a left and then took a glancing swing off my right arm. Kenwood bobbed and weaved as he inched closer to me. I moved from left to right and snapped two quick jabs to his face. I ducked under a right cross and landed with a sharp uppercut to his stomach, then followed that up with two more blows to his rib cage. I had spent a good deal of time working out in Bruno's gym in my time off the job and had learned a lot from the ex–heavyweight contender. Bruno always preached the old boxing maxim of "If you take the body, the head will follow," and that was what I wanted to do. Kenwood was more brawler than boxer, and he was trying to close in, jump me, and pin me to the ground. Once he had me there, it would be to his advantage. His weight would hold me down and I would be helpless to stop the barrage coming my way.

Kenwood lunged for me, one hand open, looking to grab me by the hair and yank me down. I landed three quick and hard jabs to his stomach and heard him gasp for air. He pulled away and kicked my right leg, just below the kneecap. My leg buckled, and I waited for him to get closer. He leaned toward me and punched the left side of my neck. The blow stunned me for a second as I scrambled back up to my feet.

Kenwood rushed me, his body bent at the waist, and I spun around and wrapped my hands around his head and slammed us both to the ground. He crashed face-first on the hard dirt, while I let my ass take the brunt of the fall. I lifted his head and smashed it against the ground several times, rubbing his face in the brown soil, raining punches on his neck and back. I held him down and got to my knees and straddled him. I lifted his head one more time, his dirty face now up enough for his red eyes to glare at me. I wrapped my hands around his throat and began to ease it back. I braced one of my knees in the center of his back.

I could feel his neck muscles tighten and knew, from this position, I could snap his neck and end his life. I pulled his head farther back and dug my knee deep between his shoulder blades.

I looked down into Kenwood's eyes, my body poised and ready to take away the life of a man who had brought pain and ruin to so many.

"Tank," Pearl shouted. "Don't do it. Don't do that piece of shit any favors. It's not time for him to be lowered into the ground. He needs to go to prison. That's where his coffin is waiting. Not on this ball field."

I looked away from Kenwood and at my partner and closest friend. Pearl wheeled himself nearer to me. "He needs to pay," Pearl said. "For Rachel. For Zeke. And for all the ones he sent to prison for no reason. He needs to pay."

I took a deep breath and let go of Kenwood's neck. I lifted myself off him and started to walk away. Then I stopped, turned, and delivered one final hard kick to the side of his head. "That's for Zeke," I said. "He would have done it himself if you came at him one-on-one."

Pearl grabbed my arm and squeezed it. "Proud of you, partner," he said.

I looked at Pearl and nodded.

Within minutes we were surrounded by Chief Connors and a small platoon of uniform and plainclothes officers. I looked past the cops and watched Alban and his men disappear into the darkness of the park. Chief Connors came up to me and held out a set of handcuffs. "You want to cuff him?" he asked.

I smiled. "I'm not a cop anymore, Chief, remember?" I said.

The chief returned the smile. "You'll always be a cop," he said.

I took the cuffs from the chief, walked back over to Eddie Kenwood, and placed both his hands behind his back. I slapped the cuffs on his wrists and locked them in. "You're under arrest, you son of a bitch," I said.

I got back to my feet and shook the chief's hand.

"Case closed," he said.

"Case closed," I said, and began a slow walk off the baseball field

62.

ATTICA, NEW YORK

TWO WEEKS LATER

IT RAINED THE ENTIRE WAY UP FROM THE CITY, HARD AND HEAVY drops blasting at us from all sides. Pearl sat in the passenger seat, a Frankie Valli and the Four Seasons CD playing on low volume.

"You've always loved listening to these guys," Pearl said. "Ever since I've known you."

"They were my Beatles," I said. "Their songs fit me and the neighborhood. Just like you feel about the Temptations. Those songs stay with us, reminders of who we were and who we still are."

Pearl nodded. "I'll never forget what you did," he said. "Getting this kid out of jail is not something I could have managed to do on my own. I don't know how I can ever thank you, Tank."

I glanced over at him and smiled. "Just stay my friend, that's all," I said.

"No worries there," Pearl said. "We're in this together for the long haul."

"You could also take the dog for a walk now and then," I said. "And maybe you and me could go to a movie or a show. Grab a bite. Make a night of it."

Pearl laughed. "You need me as a friend," he said. "Who the hell else would put up with you?"

"Looks like we're here," I said.

I eased the car to a stop under a canopy of trees. I got out and pulled Pearl's wheelchair from the back and opened it. I slid open his door and helped him into his seat. The rain was coming down as if off a waterfall. "I don't think I have an umbrella, Pearl," I said. "Although with this wind, it wouldn't be of much help anyway."

"I don't need one," Pearl said.

We both stared through the rain and haze at the gates leading to the Attica Correctional Facility. "Randy should be by the front door," I said. "I called the warden earlier and told him what time to have him ready for release."

"You coming with me, right?" Pearl asked.

"No," I said. "This one's all you, partner. I may have helped free the kid, but it was you that brought the case to me. If he needs to see and thank somebody, that somebody is you."

Pearl looked at me, nodded, and made his way to the gate.

I leaned against the front of my car, the rain pouring down on me like an early-morning cold shower. I heard a door creak open, and then the gates began to rattle and slide. And then there he was, walking slowly toward Pearl.

When Randy Jenkins got to the wheelchair, he fell to his knees and hugged Pearl, both of them as wet as if they were in the middle of the ocean. They stayed that way for the longest time. It was a grand moment to see.

I took a deep breath of the cool air and watched my friend hold on tight to Randy, no longer a prisoner for a crime he did not commit. He was out of a system he should never have been put in.

Randy lifted his head to the sky, his arms still wrapped around Pearl, and he let out a loud and happy cry.

It was the cry of freedom.

And Randy Jenkins had waited a very long time to let out that cry.

63.

GATE OF HEAVEN CEMETERY, WESTCHESTER COUNTY

THREE DAYS LATER

I STOOD IN FRONT OF THE HEADSTONES FOR MY BROTHER, JACK, and his wife, Susan. Chris was by my side, his puppy, Gus, nearby, spread out and happily chewing on blades of grass. It was the first time either of us had visited the grave site, and I felt a twinge of sadness for not thinking of bringing Chris up here earlier.

Gate of Heaven is a massive cemetery, with hundreds of headstones and mausoleums covering the manicured paths. Many of my friends, family, and some enemies are buried on the grounds.

"Should we tell them?" Chris asked.

"Tell them what?" I asked. "That you're living with me?"

"That's one of the things," Chris said.

"What's another?"

"That you caught the people who killed them."

"First of all, *we* nailed those bastards," I said. "Together. You leading the way, me and the crew following. With help from Bobby and Dee Dee."

"I'm glad we came," Chris said. "I miss them so much, but I try my best not to think about it all the time. It hurts, you know?"

"Yeah," I said. "I know. And it will for a long time. I miss Jack, too. And I'm sorry I didn't get to know your mom."

"They both would want me to be happy," Chris said.

"I do, too," I said. "I'll never take your dad's place, and I don't expect to. But I am glad that we're together, you and me."

"And Gus and Pearl," Chris said.

I smiled and nodded. "You know, it forced me to dredge up memories of what happened so long ago, something I was so afraid of doing."

"Are you sorry you did?"

"No, not at all," I said. "I think it helped me get straight with Jack. I always loved him and missed having him in my life. I'm sorry he had to die for me to get him back. But I feel connected to him again, through you. And it's a good feeling to have."

"Can we come back and see them again?" Chris asked.

"As often as you like," I said. "It's a good thing for us to do together."

I leaned over Jack's headstone and placed my right hand on top of the cold marble. "Rest easy, little brother," I whispered. "And don't worry about Chris. I got his back. And he's got mine."

I stepped away and waited as Chris bent and laid a kiss on both headstones and bowed his head, saying a short, silent prayer for the parents taken away from him much too soon.

He turned toward me and wrapped his arms around my waist, his head resting against my chest. Tears flowed down both our faces.

I glanced over at Gus, still chewing on the grass, digging his paws into the soft earth. "We should go," I said. "Before Gus leaves this place a barren field."

Chris let go of me and picked up Gus's leash, and we made our way toward my car. We both turned to take a final look at the two headstones, gleaming in the morning sun.

"Isn't eating grass supposed to be bad for dogs?" I asked. "Can't be good for his stomach."

"Gus thinks it's like having a salad," Chris said.

"Gus is wrong," I said.

AUTHOR'S NOTE

I WANT TO THANK MY PARTNER IN CRIME, MY EDITOR, ANNE Speyer, for the hard work and effort she put into this book. Her edits and suggestions improved the story at every point. Plus, she loves dogs—it's a tough combination to beat.

Suzanne Gluck at WME has always had my back and always will. She's not just an agent. Even better, she's a friend.

To my Random House/Ballantine family—thank you. I have been at this for a lot of years now and we've always been there together. As one.

Thanks to Vincent, Ida, and Anthony of Manducati's, and to the one and only Giuliano of Primola and his top-notch crew for keeping me well-fed all year long. You won't find two better places to eat and drink in any of the five boroughs. They are simply the best.

To my children, Kate and Nick, who are always there for me—with a phone call, a dinner, a drink, and, yes, for our yearly trip to our beloved island of Ischia in Italy. Love you both more than you can ever imagine.

And welcome to the new crew of dogs—Sweet Siena and the lovable duo of George and Henry. Gus and Willow would be honored to have you on the team. No worries, Gus—you will always be top dog.

ABOUT THE AUTHOR

LORENZO CARCATERRA is the #1 *New York Times* bestselling author of *A Safe Place, Sleepers, Apaches, Gangster, Street Boys, Paradise City, Chasers, Midnight Angels, The Wolf,* and *Tin Badges.* He is a former writer/producer for *Law & Order* and has written for *National Geographic Traveler, The New York Times Magazine,* and *Maxim.* He lives in New York City and is at work on his next novel.

lorenzocarcaterra.com

ABOUT THE TYPE

This book was set in Caslon, a typeface first designed in 1722 by William Caslon (1692–1766). Its widespread use by most English printers in the early eighteenth century soon supplanted the Dutch typefaces that had formerly prevailed. The roman is considered a "workhorse" typeface due to its pleasant, open appearance, while the italic is exceedingly decorative.